THE ROSE KEEPER

JENNIFER LAMONT LEO

The Rose Keeper by Jennifer Lamont Leo

Published by Mountain Majesty Media

PO Box 638, Cocolalla, ID 83813

ISBN: 978-1-7337058-7-5

Copyright 2021 by Jennifer Lamont Leo

Edited by Robin Patchen

Cover and interior design by Hannah Linder

Author photo by Cary Burnett

For more information on this book and the author, visit https://www.jenniferlamontleo.com

Library of Congress Cataloging-in-Publication Data

Leo, Jennifer Lamont

The Rose Keeper / Jennifer Lamont Leo 1st ed.

Printed in the United States of America

THE ROSE KEEPER

God places the lonely in families (Psalm 68:6a, NLT)

❧ I ❧

July 1944
Cicero, Illinois

Clara Janacek's knees weren't what they used to be. On a muggy July morning, she eased down the concrete steps in front of her home, one hand on the brick railing and the other wielding gardening shears. When had stairs become so confounded difficult to navigate, especially first thing in the morning? Seemed like yesterday she was springing down those steps with ease. Now, it seemed that her springs had rusted. The long hours she spent walking on hard hospital floors didn't help matters either. Middle age was not for weaklings.

But there'd be no time for dawdling today. Her friend and landlord, Jerry Stevenson, would be down any minute from his own apartment to accompany her into the city, and she hated to keep him waiting. It grated Clara's nerves to be late for anything. Punctuality was a point of pride. Better three hours too early than a minute late, Shakespeare had supposedly said, although he probably said it when he was still a young sprout with good knees.

Focused on her purpose, she hurried past the small flower bed that flanked the front of the brown brick two-flat, observing in passing that the peonies and phlox were in bloom. She paused in front of the rose-bush, her pride and joy, where it stood proudly in the narrow gangway between her building and the identical two-flat next door. The roses glowed a glorious cherry-red in spite of the infernal heat wave that had plagued the Chicago area for weeks.

"Good morning, my beauties. How splendid you're looking," Clara said, as if the blooms could somehow hear her. She was pleased that her hard work of pruning and mulching was paying off. All summer long, three days a week, she lovingly tended her flowers. The remaining days were devoted to the backyard vegetables—the cabbages and carrots, beans and tomatoes, onions and beets that would fill her pantry come winter. A "victory garden," people were calling it these days, though Clara had been growing things since long before doing so was considered a patriotic gesture. But when the war started, with Jerry's permission, she'd dug up more of the yard and made it even bigger.

Quickly she checked over the blooms on the rosebush, then snipped off the one she judged prettiest. A rose for remembrance. After a moment's hesitation, she clipped a second one as well, this one from the back of the bush where it wouldn't show. It might cheer her up later to see it indoors, in a pretty vase, in case she was tempted to wallow.

The morning air hung hot and humid and gray, tinged with the scent of rain. It had rained then, too, that long-ago morning. But unlike this one, that summer day in 1915 had been unseasonably chilly. *So chilly.* Clara shivered. *And then all that terrible cold black water—*

"Watch out you don't prick your fingers on them thorns."

Startled, Clara wheeled around to see Jerry descending the steps, dressed nattily for a day on the town.

"Jerry Stevenson, for the love of Pete," she blurted, heart hammering, suddenly conscious of her faded cotton apron. "How many times have I told you not to sneak up on me like that?"

The man grinned. Still sturdy and square-jawed at fifty-six, his snowy hair combed neatly under a black homburg, he stood dapper and dignified in his Sunday suit in spite of the heat.

"Who's sneaking? Just came out to see if you're ready to go."

She stiffened. "Your being early doesn't make me late."

"Didn't say you were, *miláčku*," he said, and the Czech term of endearment smoothed the rough edges of her indignation. "Though usually you're the first one out, tapping your foot and frowning at the rest of us slowpokes."

"I don't frown," she said, frowning. Why did he have to be so all-fired irritating? "Just checking on my roses is all."

"Sweet-talking them, you mean," he said. "Clara Janacek, I swear, you care more about them flowers than for any human being alive."

"That's not true." Was it her fault that flowers were easier to talk to than people? She brushed past him. "Just give me a minute to collect my things."

"No hurry." He drew a pipe and a matchbook from his breast pocket and squinted up at the sky, where gray clouds hung low. "Better grab an umbrella, too, while you're at it. Looks like rain."

Looks like rain. Clara recalled her sister's fluting voice as she'd stood at the window in her skivvies on that long-ago morning. *Looks like rain, Clara. Rain will ruin everything!* And then her own voice, calm and reassuring. *Don't fret, Aneta. Nothing will spoil your fun. Certainly not a little rain.*

Clara shook her head to clear it. At what point had she become responsible for everyone's happiness? Besides, there'd be time enough later for remembering. Right now she needed to shake a leg, as the young people said.

Inside her flat, she turned on the kitchen tap, soaked a rag, and wrapped it around one rose. The second she placed in a china bud vase, which she set on an end table in the front room. The rag-wrapped flower she slid into her purse. Then she yanked at the ties on her apron and hung it on a hook near the front door. Peering into a small mirror hanging on the wall, she pinned on a straw hat, tucking a few stray wisps of silver-streaked auburn hair under the brim. She grabbed her purse and an umbrella and stepped out through the common entryway, locking the door behind her.

On the sidewalk, Jerry crooked his elbow. She slipped her arm through his.

3

"I was thinking maybe we could go to the Berghoff after," he said as they strolled companionably down the street. "I've got a taste for wiener schnitzel."

"I don't see why not." By then the hardest task of the day would be over, and a hearty lunch might perk them both up. "I wouldn't turn down a slice of apple strudel myself."

"We'll have plenty of time. The new tenant's supposed to move in later today, but not until late afternoon."

Clara cocked her head. "Really? I thought you said she wasn't coming until August."

"Slight change of plans." Jerry shrugged. "Starts her new job on the first. Asked if she could move in a week early. I saw no reason to say no, seeing as how the basement apartment has been sitting empty for a month."

"Where will she be working?" Clara asked.

"At the Western. Some kind of defense work."

"I heard they've been getting some big government contracts. Military equipment, radar and what have you. I suppose they've been staffing up."

The sprawling plant of the Western Electric Company, which during peacetime manufactured telephones, was Cicero's largest employer. Company news spread rapidly through the community grapevine to employees and outsiders alike. Clara's own father had worked at "the Western" until his retirement, assembling switchboards. Clara had considered following in his footsteps before a favorite high school biology teacher steered her toward nursing instead. While she was fascinated by health science and loved learning all about how the human body worked, she found it annoying that human bodies necessarily came along with, well, *humans*. That part she didn't love so much. The people part. People had feelings. Feelings were messy and unpredictable.

"So, another single-lady tenant?" she teased Jerry. "Goodness. People will think you're assembling a harem."

Jerry chuckled. "She's married. Her husband's in the navy, stationed overseas. Somewhere in the Pacific, I think she said."

"I see. Perhaps I'll bake her some *kolacky*." In her mind's eye Clara envisioned herself smartly dressed and coiffed, extending the gracious hand of hospitality to the new neighbor in a time of need—her own pervasive awkwardness around strangers to the contrary.

"That would be nice of you. A plate of your homemade pastries would make anybody feel welcome."

"It's what one does," Clara said simply.

"How's your sugar ration holding out? I got extra, if you need it."

"I have plenty," she said. "Is she friendly, this new tenant?"

Jerry shrugged. "Seems pleasant enough."

Clara wondered what it would be like to have another woman living in the building and hoped she wouldn't be called upon to do much socializing beyond the customary proffer of baked goods. The former tenant of the basement apartment, elderly Mr. Havlicek, had been a quiet sort who kept to himself, as did Clara, and she hoped this new tenant would be equally easy to ignore. Some of the neighborhood women enjoyed gathering in one another's kitchens over coffee and gossip when the morning's chores were done, but between her own housework, her gardens, her reading, and her job at the hospital, Clara didn't have time to waste on the *kaffee klatsch*. With any luck this new tenant, being a factory worker, likely wouldn't have time for that sort of nonsense either. All to the good.

Clara and Jerry ambled down the tree-lined street, past the rows of buildings practically indistinguishable from theirs: dark brick two- and three-flat apartment buildings set close together, each with its own flight of concrete steps and square, tidy patch of lawn. Clara noted with satisfaction that her own patch looked greener than most. Jerry cared for it as faithfully as Clara tended her roses.

They turned the corner onto Cermak Road, Cicero's bustling main commercial thoroughfare. In spite of the early hour, several bakeries attracted an eager clientele lining up for freshly baked bread and pastries. Hand-painted signs in butcher-shop windows bragged of bratwurst, jaternice, and kielbasa. All around them, the musical cadence of the Czech language drifted on the morning air.

The pair climbed aboard a streetcar for the brief ride to downtown Chicago. After they'd found seats and a uniformed conductor collected their fares, Jerry leaned toward Clara.

"A woman got on a trolley car and handed the conductor a ten-dollar bill. 'Sorry,' she said, 'but I don't have a nickel.' 'Don't worry, lady,' said the conductor, 'in a minute you'll have—"

"—a hundred and ninety-nine of them,'" Clara finished for him.

Jerry looked abashed. "You already heard that one?"

"Yes," she said. "From you."

"Oh." He settled back in his seat. Soon the view outside the grime-smeared window changed from squat brick buildings and belching factories to the towering concrete and steel skyscrapers of Chicago's Loop, the central business district where the elevated train tracks rattled in a wide circle high above their heads.

Clara and Jerry transferred to another streetcar that carried them north to the Clark Street Bridge over the Chicago River. There they disembarked and stepped down a wide concrete staircase to the water's edge. They walked along to a certain spot, then paused.

"This is it," Jerry said unnecessarily, gazing over the iron fence into the murky water below.

Clara started to draw a deep breath, then thought better of it. The ripe stench of the filthy river blended with smells of diesel fumes, smoke, and dust from the factories lining the concrete wharves. She stared down at the churning black water. The thought of falling into that disgusting cauldron, being consumed by it, turned her stomach.

Wordlessly she slipped her gloved hand into Jerry's large, callused one. He held it firmly as he bowed his head, and Clara knew he was praying. Not that she minded, but she wasn't the sort of person who prayed. She merely stared down into the dark swirling water and remembered.

Out on the river, a giant barge glided past, carrying grain or some other commodity up the river toward Lake Michigan. Clara wondered where it would end up. Saginaw, perhaps. Or Copper Harbor.

Or Michigan City.

Oh, Aneta. Can you ever forgive me? Mama and Papa never did. Her throat tightened. Almost thirty years. Would the aching never ease?

Jerry stood beside her. She knew he was lost in his own memories of that terrible day, when the much-anticipated company picnic had turned to tragedy in a matter of minutes. After a while he lifted his head, gave her hand a squeeze, and released it. She gazed up at his profile. Such a kind, caring face. He was so good to accompany her on this sorrowful errand, year after year, when he'd just as soon forget. Friends like Jerry didn't come along every day.

She pulled the rose from her purse, freed it from the damp rag, and tossed it into the river. Together they watched in silence as it drifted downstream, a brilliant spot of crimson bobbing against the churning black waves, until they couldn't see it anymore.

"*Odpočivej v pokoji*," she whispered under her breath. *Rest in peace.*

After a few solemn moments, she tore her gaze from the river to her friend. "You'd think more people would come here on the anniversary to remember. We always seem to be the only ones. Over eight hundred dead." Her voice cracked. "Why does nobody come?"

"Because they want to forget the senseless tragedy," Jerry said. "You don't have to keep coming either, Clara, if it upsets you. It makes no difference to Aneta."

"Yes, I do," Clara insisted. "My parents never missed a year, and now I'm the only one left. It's up to me to remember. It's what they'd want."

He shook his head and spoke softly. "Fifty-one years old and still doing what your parents want."

"Fifty," she corrected, ignoring the second half of his remark.

He gazed down at her face. "Are you all right, *miláčku*? Do you need to borrow my handkerchief?"

"No." She wasn't crying. Clara Janacek never cried. She straightened her shoulders. "I suppose we should go and see about that strudel."

They took one last look at the murky river. Then they turned and walked slowly back the way they'd come.

❦   2   ❦

Seated at a table for two at the crowded Berghoff Restaurant, Clara and Jerry maintained a companionable silence over plates of wiener schnitzel and hearty rye bread, letting the rich food comfort and restore them to good spirits after the difficult morning. Conversation would have been difficult anyway over the clatter of dishes and the buzz of voices in the popular German bistro. Clara appreciated this about their longstanding friendship, that they could be quiet around one another without feeling awkward. She and Jerry didn't need to prattle on all the time about nothing just to fill up the air, the way so many people did.

As she savored her meal, Clara admired the restaurant's electric chandeliers and the checkerboard tiled floor. Dark polished wood paneling against white stucco walls gave the place an old-world European feel, like some of the Czech restaurants she loved back in Cicero. The air redolent of roast pork, dumplings, and sauerkraut made her feel at home, comforted and familiar, and the excellent food lifted her mood.

She didn't travel to the Loop often. Even though it wasn't far from Cicero, it felt exotic and strange, like she imagined a foreign capital must feel, having never actually traveled to one. She preferred doing business at the friendly, family-owned shops of Cermak Road to State Street's elegant department stores and boutiques, where she felt frumpy and out of place. Chicago's noise and hustle both invigorated her and made her feel uneasy at the same time. For these reasons she was glad Jerry was still willing to accompany her on her yearly trek to the river. She supposed he had his own reasons for going. Even so, she appreciated his company and the kind gesture of devoting half a day to their private ritual.

Jerry leaned back in his chair, yawned, and released the bottom button on his vest. "That was a fine meal, Clara. The apple strudel was not quite as good as yours, but almost."

"Flatterer." The heat rose in her cheeks, even though she knew what he said to be true. She and Aneta had spent many a girlhood Saturday helping their Czech mother with the weekly baking. "But no one's kitchen skills could hold a candle to your dear wife's. She worked magic with flour and sugar."

"True enough." Jerry glanced at his old pocket watch, a sturdy Elgin passed down from his father. "I guess we should be heading back. I want to take another look at that cranky drain in the basement apartment before the tenant gets here."

Clara folded her white cloth napkin and placed it on the table. "That's fine with me. I hope to get a good, solid rest before work."

"You still working the night shift?" he said, sounding offended on her behalf. "When will that hospital give you a break and put you back on days? You've got seniority there, right? You oughtta be calling the shots by now."

Clara smiled at Jerry's naïve understanding of the way hospital authority worked. "I don't mind," she said. "To tell you the truth, I prefer working nights."

"What are you, a vampire?" Jerry had a fondness for Bram Stoker novels, which Clara found too gloomy for her liking. She preferred clever adventure stories with plucky heroines who used their wits to save the day.

She shrugged. "To be perfectly honest, I always request the night shift when the new schedule is being drawn up."

They scraped back their chairs and stood. "You're a glutton for punishment," he remarked.

"You know I've always been rather a night owl. The pace is slower in the wee hours, and nobody's looking over my shoulder. There's a lot more independence. Plus, many of the patients sleep through the night, and there are no annoying visitors or fussy family members to contend with."

"If you say so."

What she also thought but didn't feel like admitting to Jerry was that working nights was a gesture appreciated by the other nurses, most of whom had sweethearts or husbands and children—busy lives outside the hospital. Therefore they dreaded an assignment to the graveyard shift. Clara, on the other hand, had no one—a truth that she readily accepted but refused to utter out loud lest she sound pathetic. She didn't feel pathetic, just resigned.

"Besides," she added, tugging on her cotton gloves, "putting in plenty of night duty will boost my case."

"What case is that?" Jerry adjusted the brim of his homburg.

"Head Nurse Banning is retiring at the end of the year. I've submitted my name for the head nurse position, and I'm hoping they'll choose her replacement soon. 'They' being the committee in charge of such things."

"And you think you have a pretty good chance of getting the job?"

"Not to toot my own horn, but I've been there longer than any other nurse on the ward, day shift or night shift. Coming up on thirty years now." She rubbed a spot on her glove. "Of course, I'm not the only candidate in the running. But the hospital has a policy of promoting from within, and I have the most seniority. Meanwhile, members of the review committee could be watching us at any minute, so I've got to be on my toes all the time."

"Well, you deserve to be head nurse," Jerry said heartily. "No one works harder than you do."

"I've poured my life into that hospital."

"Yes, you have."

Clara felt a warm glow spread through her chest. He only spoke the truth, after all, and being named head nurse would be the star in her crown, the recognition she'd always craved. She had never married, never had a family of her own. For years her life had been bounded by working at the hospital and caring for her ailing parents in her child-hood home. But now both her parents were gone. There was nothing to hold her back from reaching for the brass ring. As head nurse she'd get the recognition she deserved, along with a boost in pay that would help support her in her retirement. She had a specific plan for retire-ment—a plan she hadn't even shared with Jerry yet. Perhaps it was time. But what if he laughed at her or tried to talk her out of it?

By the time they stepped out of the restaurant onto Adams Street, the sun had broken through the clouds. Jerry grasped her elbow and steered her along the crowded sidewalk.

"Becoming head nurse sounds like an awful lot of responsibility. Are you sure you want to take on all that at this stage of life?"

"I'm not fit for the grave yet," Clara huffed.

"Of course you aren't. But maybe you should be, you know, gearing down a little. Taking it easier. You did have those heart palpitations last year."

"Heartburn. Nothing more." Clara scoffed. "When have you ever known me to slow down?"

"Never," he admitted.

"A few of the younger nurses think I'm too old for the job," she confided. "But I figure I still have several good working years left. I don't want to spend them doing the same things I've been doing for the last thirty."

The streetcar clanged to a stop, and they climbed aboard. In the packed vehicle, Clara found herself wedged on a bench in the middle of a group of gregarious young people bearing picnic baskets while Jerry clung to the leather strap hanging overhead. He'd shucked off his suit jacket and clutched it in his other arm.

"Here, give it to me," she said. She folded the wool garment and placed it on her lap.

"For three decades you've put your job ahead of the rest of your life," he said. "I just think that maybe God is saying to you, 'Clara, you've spent thirty years taking care of other people. It's time to let someone else take care of you for a change.'"

She snorted. "Who's going to take care of an aging spinster, I ask you? Besides, it would mean a respectable raise in salary. I have my future security to think of. With a little extra pay, I can set money aside every week."

"You already set aside money every week. You're not exactly a spendthrift."

"Saving for the future is important."

"So is living in the here and now. Life should be about more than just going to work and coming home."

Clara sensed he was right but didn't see how it applied in her case. She gazed out the smoke-smeared window without answering.

When the picnickers noisily exited the streetcar near a forest preserve, a seat opened up next to Clara. Jerry sank onto it. Gesturing toward the woodsy picnic grove, he said, "That reminds me. The church is holding their annual picnic in a few weeks. Want to go? I'd like your company."

"Every year you ask me, and every year I tell you no."

"Hope springs eternal," he quipped. "Seriously, why won't you come?"

"I don't know." And she didn't, honestly. It wasn't the idea of a picnic, not that she relished sitting on the grass, eating cold food and swatting away bugs. It was the *church* part that always had her refusing. "All those church people. I won't know anybody."

"You'll know me. And strangers are just friends you haven't met yet."

Clara glanced toward the ceiling in wordless exasperation.

"Besides, it's been a long time since we've had a fun outing together."

She cut him a glance. "What have we been doing all day?"

"That's different and you know it. I meant for fun." When she didn't answer he added, "Please come. The fresh air will do you good, put some roses back in your cheeks. You need to come out of your shell once in a while."

"I like my shell."

"I hate to see you spending all your time either at work or at home. Come with me." His dark eyes crinkled at the corners in a way she'd always found endearing. She'd seldom been able to resist his smile when he turned on the charm.

"All right," she said. "I'll think about it."

"That's my girl."

"I said I'd *think* about it. A think is not a yes." But in her heart, she knew the matter was settled.

He sat back and patted her hand. Softly, he whistled a lively rag. She let her mind drift back over the years to a lilac-scented time when the song was young and so was she.

Presently the streetcar passed the black wrought-iron gates of Memorial Hospital, where she would begin her shift that evening after a good long nap. As passengers shuffled off and on the conveyance, she gazed up at the massive brick structure, her second home. Her mind drifted back to her earliest days as a nurse. It seemed it was a morning made for remembering, even those memories one would just as soon forget.

❦ 3 ❦

June 1915
Memorial Hospital
Chicago, Illinois

T he sturdy, red-brick Memorial Hospital towered over the surrounding buildings and cast a shadow over me as I stood, wobble-kneed, on the sidewalk. Future decades would see various wings and additions tacked on until the hospital tripled in size. But as I stood before it on that late-spring morning in 1915, the first day of my nursing career, it had seemed intimidating to me. Even though I had done well in my science classes at J. Sterling Morton High School and had finished close to the top of my class at the Illinois Training School for Nurses, I wondered now if I'd been adequately prepared for this frightful undertaking.

What if I made a mistake? What if someone asked me a question I didn't know the answer to? What if I killed a patient on my very first day?

Important-looking people rushed past me, and I realized I couldn't stand in the doorway forever, blocking the way. A kind volunteer at the information desk directed me to a room with "Superintendent of

Nursing" etched in gold on the glass door. Timidly, I pushed open the door. A middle-aged secretary sat writing something at an oak desk. She glanced up as I entered and looked me up and down.

"First day?"

"Yes." My Sunday-best attire, or perhaps my expression of sheer terror, must have tipped her off.

"Wait here," she said, and disappeared into another room. Moments later she reappeared with a nurse whose posture was as stiff and starched-looking as her uniform, softened only by her reassuring smile.

"Welcome to Memorial Hospital. I'm Nurse Jones. And you are?"

I swallowed back my nervousness. "Clara Marie Janacek." I didn't know why I threw my middle name in there. Maybe trying to give my name some gravitas under the circumstances.

The nurse consulted a paper attached to a clipboard. She made a check mark with a pencil, then said, "Welcome, Nurse Janacek. Follow me to the assembly hall, where you and your fellow nurses will be given an orientation. We'll get you set up afterward with a uniform and locker."

As Nurse Jones led me through a labyrinth of corridors reeking of antiseptic, she pointed out the various departments as we passed them. "Cardiology ... Pediatrics ..." I was sure I'd never remember them all. She also gave me a running history of the hospital.

"Memorial got its start when the founding doctor opened a clinic in his home in 1889," she explained. "Since those humble beginnings, we've grown exponentially. We're quite proud of this modern three-story building. You know we just opened it a year ago."

I liked her use of the term *we*. It made me feel a part of things right away.

The soles of my brand-new black shoes squeaked against the tile floor. I made a mental note to tack on thin rubber soles at the first opportunity, so that I could move as soundlessly as Nurse Jones did.

The tour ended in an auditorium filled with women, some dressed in nurses' uniforms and others in street clothes, looking as new and out-of-place as I felt.

"Here we are," Nurse Jones said cheerfully. "I'll leave you now.

Good luck to you." She excused herself. Watching her walk away, I was seized with a moment of panic, wondering what I should do next.

"Sit here," a smiling redheaded woman said, gesturing to the empty seat next to her. Gratefully I returned the woman's smile and sat. She, too, was wearing street clothes, indicating she was a newcomer like me.

"I'm Marianne Yost." She extended her hand and I gripped it.

"Clara Janacek," I whispered back just as a mature nurse stepped up to the podium. I guessed her age to be around fifty, judging by her steel-gray hair and no-nonsense demeanor.

The speaker introduced herself as Anthea Blair, the Superintendent of Nursing. "Welcome to the new class of nurses at Memorial Hospital," she orated in ringing tones. "Congratulations on having joined a most noble profession. As you are now professional women, your personal behavior must reflect the dignity of your profession."

"Shall we count how many times she says the word *profession?*" Marianne whispered to me. I liked her immediately.

"I guess she's old enough to remember the days when nursing wasn't thought of as a profession. Back when it was considered sort of disreputable," I whispered back. "She probably fought long and hard for that designation."

"And won't ever let us forget it."

"Sssh!" The woman sitting on Marianne's other side gave us an admonishing glare. We turned our attention back to the speaker.

After running through the same brief history of the hospital that Nurse Jones had given me, Nurse Blair returned to the topic of proper nurselike behavior. "The first duty of a nurse is always to her patient. And no matter what, you must check and recheck your work. Never, ever assume anything."

I listened with rapt attention, as though her words held the key to success, even though she pretty much repeated what we'd been hearing for two years at the Illinois Training School for Nurses.

She explained how each of us would be assigned to a ward under the overall supervision of a charge nurse. I hoped for a kind, merciful charge nurse who wouldn't put me on the spot and ask me to do some procedure I didn't know how to do. How horrible would that be, to suffer embarrassment like that in front of my new coworkers?

We'd be overseen more directly, Nurse Blair continued, by a preceptor, or senior nurse, whom we'd accompany all day, every day, until we knew what we were doing.

After the meeting, we probationers without uniforms were taken to a locker room, where we were each issued a blue dress, white apron, and white cap, to be worn over black stockings and shoes. We received instructions regarding jewelry (none), hair (pinned securely underneath our caps), and cosmetics (strictly forbidden, as if any of us would dare). Happily these kinds of regulations were familiar from our training.

After we'd changed, we were taken to our assigned wards. I was assigned to Ward One on the Women's Medical floor. To my disappointment, Marianne—my one and only friend—was assigned elsewhere.

At the ward's main desk I met the charge nurse, who said, "You're with Nurse Prager here." A stout woman, her dark hair slicked back into a bun, looked at me briefly and half nodded. "You can call me Sadie. Except, of course, in the presence of patients. Come on. I'll show you where to put your things. Follow me."

Feeling awkward, I shadowed her on a dizzying round. Sadie was constantly in motion, always doing three or four things at a time, assessing patients, checking under covers, administering medications. And she was so confident. Nothing seemed to rattle her.

Unlike me. Later that morning I nearly panicked when she assigned me to start an IV on an elderly woman.

We'd been taught intravenous infusion therapy in nursing school, even though it was a fairly new procedure. But I felt less than confident about my skills, especially with Sadie looking over my shoulder. Thinking long and hard about all the steps I needed to do, I checked and double-checked the gauze-covered container holding the fluid. I willed my hands not to shake as I pulled on gloves and dabbed rubbing alcohol on the back of the woman's hand. To cover my nervousness, I found myself chattering.

"Did you know that the first successful IV was invented by Christopher Wren in the early 1700s?" I chirped. "It was made from a pig's bladder and a writing quill."

The patient looked at me round-eyed.

"Never mind the history lesson, Nurse Janacek," Sadie warned. "Concentrate on what you're doing,"

Focusing intently, I examined the papery skin on the back of the woman's hand, found the most prominent vein, and inserted the needle. She didn't even flinch. Success.

Sadie examined my work. "Nicely done."

My knees nearly buckled with relief.

Midmorning she was summoned and told that 2-C was coming back from surgery. "A young woman, twenty-four years old, just had her appendix removed," Sadie explained over her shoulder as I trotted to keep up with her. "Let's go."

We both helped pull the patient from the gurney onto the bed, and then Sadie was called away.

The patient looked at me. I looked at her. I cleared my throat and said, "Well, then. I suppose I'm your nurse." I adjusted her covers and pillow.

"Thank you, nurse," she croaked.

Thank you, nurse. Two years of training culminated in that moment. All at once, I felt so helpful, knowledgeable, and competent. A real nurse, taking care of a real patient. Because she was not much older than I was, going through the procedures didn't feel very different from practicing on my fellow classmates at the training school. I checked her dressing, took note of her vital signs, and coiled her drainage tube neatly on the bed, ticking tasks off a mental checklist as I went.

"I'll be back to see you soon," I promised and left to find Sadie.

At lunch time, Sadie told me where to find the cafeteria but didn't accompany me. Marianne, the lively redhead I'd sat next to during orientation, approached me in the line, cheerful as a cricket. "Hi! Want to find a table together?"

Grateful to have someone to eat with, I followed her to a table for two. I toyed with my egg salad sandwich, my stomach too knotted for me to swallow much more than tea, but Marianne's appetite was hearty in spite of the sorry-looking meal. Between bites of her salad, she brought me up to speed on what was happening on her ward, which sounded similar to mine.

"The docs breeze through like cyclones, thunder out some orders, hurl the occasional lightning bolt, and we have to stand there and be polite and agreeable and do whatever they say. How are things on your ward?" Before I could answer, she glanced at a nearby table, then leaned forward and said conspiratorially, "Speaking of docs, that one over there is pretty cute, isn't he?"

I followed her gaze. "Is he? I hadn't noticed." Actually I had noticed, but it didn't matter. All I wanted to do was learn my job and be a good nurse. That was enough. Who had time or energy to put toward flirting?

I didn't contribute much to the conversation, but I didn't need to. Marianne seemed happy to fill the air with her words, and I was happy to have made a friend.

After lunch, I returned to the ward. Sadie was doing paperwork at the large wooden desk but glanced up as I approached.

"Almost done here," she said. "Bed 2-A is ringing the call bell again. Go and see what she wants. And while you're at it, go back and check on 2-C and see how she's doing."

"2-A is Mrs. Merton. And 2-C. You mean Natalie McCambridge?" I'd looked their names up on the patient roster. It seemed heartless to me to refer to people by their bed numbers.

Sadie gave me a stern look. "2-A and 2-C. Go."

I went.

The first patient, Mrs. Merton, only needed her ice water jug refilled, a request I easily took care of. The second patient, the young woman recovering from an appendectomy, appeared to be sleeping soundly, even though a visitor had come to see her. An older man who looked to be around fifty was seated in a chair at her bedside holding a bouquet of flowers. He rose and extended his free hand, and the tense lines around his mouth creased into a smile.

"John McCambridge," he said as he pumped my hand. He nodded toward the patient. "Are you her nurse?"

"Yes, I am."

"She said you were nice."

I felt a glow spread from my chest to my face. My first compliment as a real nurse!

"Here, let me put those in a vase for you." I reached for the flowers, and he handed them over. I took a deep whiff of the bouquet as if he'd brought it for me. "How lovely! Be right back."

Sadie was still seated at the main desk.

"Where can I find a vase?" I asked. She glanced up, looked at the flowers, looked at me.

"You should let the volunteers take care of flowers," she said. "You don't have time for that sort of thing." Nevertheless, she directed me to a supply closet.

After fumbling around, finding a suitable container, and filling it with water, I returned to 2-C and set the arrangement on the bedside table. Then I turned and rechecked the young woman's vital signs.

The worry lines had returned to the older man's face. "How is she?" he asked in a voice laced with concern.

"Not to worry, Mr. McCambridge," I assured him. "Her vital signs are strong, and she's resting comfortably."

"When will the doctor come to see her?"

"I'm sure he'll be here soon," I said, though I had no idea whether my words were true. I gave him what I hoped was a reassuring smile. "Your daughter is in very capable hands, Mr. McCambridge."

The man's expression froze. "She's my wife."

My gut contracted. "Oh! Of course. I mean... Beg your pardon. I thought—"

Mortified, I clamped my mouth shut and busied myself with straightening the patient's blanket. Nurse Blair's warning rang in my head. *Never assume anything.*

Mercifully, my stammering was cut short by Sadie's appearance at the foot of the bed. She looked at Natalie, read over her chart, nodded briefly toward Mr. McCambridge and said "Doctor Graham is on his way." She didn't introduce herself. I hoped she hadn't overheard my gaffe.

She turned to me. "When you're finished here, Nurse Janacek, we're needed in the next ward."

"I'm ready." *More than ready.* "Um ... see you later," I said to Mr. McCambridge, then turned and followed Sadie out of the ward.

"You don't have time to chitchat with the visitors." She made no other comment, to my relief. *Never assume* became my slogan for the rest of the day—indeed, for the rest of my nursing career.

As I continued shadowing Sadie that afternoon, I was run off my feet. Twice she sent me on errands, and twice I got lost in the labyrinth of lookalike corridors. Not only had I skimped on lunch, but I forgot to drink water. By the end of the day, I felt lost, tired, and thirsty as all get out.

But I felt like a nurse.

Things did improve. By the end of my first week at Memorial, I was feeling pretty confident in my abilities to change sheets and bedpans. I was very good at technical things. I could start an IV like nobody's business. So I barely felt a ripple of anxiety when the charge nurse assigned Sadie and me to go on rounds with Dr. Graham, a surgeon famous for chewing up nurses and spitting them out.

Dr. Graham barked out an order in our general direction. "You," he said, pointing at me. "Change D5½ NS to D5W on Bed 2-F."

At least that's what I thought he said.

"And you"—he pointed at Sadie—"come with me."

I stopped in my tracks. Sadie turned to me and said, "What's the matter? Go on now. You'll be fine. You know how to change an IV." She scurried off in the white-flapping wake of Dr. Graham.

I could do this! Eager to be efficient, I obtained the requested solution, zipped over to Bed 2-F, greeted the patient, took down the container that was hanging over the bed, and replaced it with the new one, all without spilling a drop. Impressed with my own competence, I returned to the main desk to await Sadie's—or someone's, anyone's —praise.

Later that day, Nurse Blair called me aside. "I need to see you. In my office. Now." My palms sweated. My stomach churned. I followed her into her office. She seated herself in her chair behind her gleaming oak desk and motioned for me to sit across from her.

Without preamble, she informed me that I had administered the IV fluid to the wrong patient, which constituted two medical errors. According to Dr. Graham's orders, both patients had the wrong IV fluid.

"You should have had the good sense to recognize that," she snapped. "Where was your brain?"

I felt the blood drain from my face.

"In addition, and most important," she informed me, "you failed to double-check the identity of each patient." The word "failed" rang in my ears. I waited for the words "you're fired," or at the very least, "you're suspended" to follow.

But they didn't. Instead she said, "What is the rule, Nurse Janacek?"

"First check the chart," I squeaked.

"What's that? I didn't hear you."

"Check the chart." How could I have forgotten?

"First check the chart. Every time. Even when you're positive you know the patient by sight. Patients get shifted around. Beds get moved. You must check the chart, every time, so this sort of thing never happens."

I sat in silence, mute in my humiliation.

Nurse Blair continued. "Because we're so very short-staffed on nurses, I'm not going to suspend you at this time. You are, however, still on probation and are skating perilously close to the edge." She narrowed her eyes. "Believe me, I'll be closely monitoring your perfor-mance from here on out."

Trembling. I fixed my eyes on her collar button. "Yes, ma'am."

To my horror, my vision blurred, and I felt hot tears stinging the backs of my eyeballs. My throat tightened. *Oh, no, you don't,* I scolded myself. *Do not cry at work. Don't cry. Do not cry!* But I couldn't help it. Tears spilled down my cheeks.

"Pull yourself together, Clara," Nurse Blair said. Her use of my given name made me cry even harder. She opened a desk drawer, pulled out a pristine white handkerchief, and handed it to me across the desk. "You must grow a thicker skin or you'll never succeed in the medical field."

I sniffed deeply and mopped my eyes with the hankie.

She looked at me for a long moment, then softened her posture and gentled her tone. "Rules and procedures are in place for a reason."

I nodded my agreement.

"Now go and wash your face, then get back out on the floor. Your patients need you."

I fled to the locker room to repair my appearance. Then I returned to the ward, wanting to wilt in humiliation. If I'd expected a kind word of comfort, I would have been sorely disappointed. The other nurses backed away from me as if I had a disease.

But I hadn't expected comfort. I'd expected to make no mistakes at all. This was me, after all. Straight-A student in high school. One of the top graduates in my nursing-school class. Not the kind of person who gets threatened with firing or suspension.

I was tempted to quit but stuck it out, mindful of the sacrifices my family had made for me to train as a nurse. Besides, I wasn't a quitter. I was determined not to give up.

But from then on, I made two ironclad resolutions. One, I would be a stickler for following the rules. The stickiest of sticklers. And two, I would forever be resentful at some doctors' callous treatment of nurses, even if I had to accept it as an inescapable fact of hospital life.

4

July 1944

At last the streetcar reached Cicero. Hot and weary, Clara and Jerry trudged home and said their good-byes on the front steps of their building. He headed upstairs to his flat. She thanked her stars that she lived on the ground floor and didn't need to tackle a second flight of stairs with her bad knee. When she'd first moved into the building, she'd rented the upstairs flat, while Jerry and his wife occupied the ground floor. But after Jerry was widowed and Clara's knee started giving her trouble, he'd been very gracious about trading apartments with her.

"I'm not sure this is such a good idea," he'd said at the time. "The upper floor seems safer for a lady living alone. The ground floor might be too easy to break into." That had been back during Prohibition days, when Al Capone established his headquarters in Cicero and introduced shootings, muggings, and all manner of thuggery onto Cicero's formerly peaceful streets.

"Nonsense," Clara had replied. "I'm sure that any landlord would make sure that the building is secure."

Jerry had let the matter drop, but later that week he'd come in and installed new locks on all of Clara's windows. Now, even with Capone in prison and Prohibition long repealed, Cicero's tough, lawless reputation lingered on. Thanks to Jerry, Clara never felt unsafe.

She unpinned and removed her hat, slid into house slippers, and padded into the kitchen to pour herself a glass of iced tea. She stood before the open door of the small white refrigerator, letting the chilled air wash over her, but only for a moment. Even though the refrigerator was a great improvement over the clunky old icebox, electricity didn't come cheap.

She headed for her tidy bedroom, removed her dress, and hung it on a hanger. Clad in her slip and stockings, she switched on the bedside radio. Soft music floated on the breeze that whispered from the electric window fan. Briefly she envisioned a dance band playing on the promenade deck of an excursion boat and thought of how Aneta would have been the belle of the ball, Waltzing with those young factory workers, if she'd been given the chance. *Enough*, she told herself sternly. *Enough of all that.*

She lay down on the white chenille bedspread in the shady dimness and mulled over her conversation with Jerry. Was it true what he'd said about putting her job first, ahead of her life? Maybe it was true. But what choice had she had, under the circumstances? She'd only performed her duty. Did what needed to be done.

She turned on her side and gave the pillow a restless punch. Why had she agreed to go to the church picnic? She had no use for church. Not after the way her life had turned out. If Jerry's God had wanted things to turn out differently, then He should have jolly well made it happen.

She worried that her troubling thoughts would keep her awake, which made sleep even more elusive. She needed to be fresh and rested at work. Dark circles under her eyes wouldn't bolster the impression that she was young and energetic enough to take on the responsibilities of a head nurse. But soon enough, the lulling rhythm of a waltz calmed her anxious mind, and she drifted off to sleep.

Bang!

Clara shot straight up in bed, disoriented, jerked out of a sound sleep by the sharp retort of a pistol.

Bang! Bang!

Land sakes, was the Capone gang back in town, trading gunfire in the middle of Cermak Road?

Ears perked, she heard voices from the street. Hastily she slipped a cardigan over her shoulders and padded out to the wide window in the front room. As she watched, a large van idling along the curb backfired twice.

"Well, I'll be ..." Relief and annoyance flooded through her veins. Just a stupid old truck. Articles of furniture strewn across the front lawn signaled that the new tenant had arrived. Irritated, she turned to go back to bed when she saw an odd creature emerge from the cargo area of the vehicle. She squinted. Without her glasses, the thing looked to be a large rectangular object wobbling up the front sidewalk on two short legs, ending in a small pair of dirty saddle shoes. The apparition continued toward the building until—horrors!—one of the saddle shoes trod right on top of a peony plant that edged the front sidewalk. Without thinking, Clara yanked up the window sash and barked through the screen,

"Hey, you! Watch where you're going! You're trampling all over my peonies!"

The creature froze. The large rectangle wobbled. Within moments a young woman wearing dungarees, her blond curls tied up in a red bandanna, flew out from the narrow gangway at the side of the building and cried out to the thing in a voice tinged with the lilting drawl of the South, "Rosalie, honey, you be careful now. Mind where you're stepping."

The blond woman reached out and hoisted the rectangle—which, on closer inspection, Clara could see was a painting of a windmill—and revealed that the short legs and saddle shoes were attached to a little girl around eight or nine years old.

"But, Mama, I couldn't see where I was going." The girl had the same blond hair as the woman hanging down her back in two Dutch braids.

"I know, sugar," the woman said, "but you need to keep your feet on the sidewalk. Why are you trying to carry such big things, anyway? Leave those to the grown-ups."

Awkwardly, she shifted the painting in her arms and peered over it toward the window where Clara stood. "We're awfully sorry, ma'am. Rosalie here misplaced her eyeglasses on the trip up here, and we haven't had a chance to replace them yet. She didn't mean to step on your pretty flowers. Did you, sugar?"

"No." The little girl solemnly shook her head.

"No, what?" the woman prompted.

"No, ma'am."

Clara grasped her cardigan at the throat, embarrassed at her outburst. She was never at her best when woken from a sound sleep.

"Well. No harm done this time," she called through the screen. "But please be more careful."

"We will." The woman moved a few steps closer. "We're your new downstairs neighbors. I'm Laurie Lucas, and this here is my daughter, Rosalie."

Clara blinked as this new information sank in. Jerry had told her that a woman would be moving in, but he hadn't said anything about a child. Children were noisy. They broke things. They trampled flowers.

When Clara didn't say anything, the woman continued, "You must be Mrs. Janacek. Jerry told me you live on the first floor."

Jerry? She calls him Jerry?

"It's Miss. Miss Janacek. I'm not married." Clara hated how priggish she sounded, but she couldn't seem to help herself. Something about this young woman made her feel awkward and uncertain. It was impossible to feel on top of things when startled out of a deep sleep, not to mention while standing in the front window in one's petticoat.

"Oh, sorry. Well, I'm a missus, obviously," Laurie said cheerfully with a glance toward Rosalie. "My husband's in the Navy. Somewhere in the South Pacific, I think. You know they aren't allowed to say, exactly." She rested the painting against the stoop and shaded her eyes as if trying to get a better look at Clara through the screen.

Clara backed away and closed the cardigan more tightly around her ample frame. "Yes. Well. Welcome to the neighborhood," she said, belatedly.

"I'm very glad to meet you," Laurie said. "Say, would you like to come downstairs in a little while for a glass of sweet tea? I'm afraid the place is a shambles, but I think I can dig a kettle and a couple of cups out of the mess, at least."

Clara's temples began to pound. She had intended to appear at the new neighbor's door later in the week with a plate of homemade *kolacky*, wearing a pretty afternoon dress with a freshly ironed apron that would signal her status as both a hospitable neighbor and meticulous housekeeper, thereby demonstrating that the building's standards were high. Instead, here she was, clutching a ratty old cardigan over her slip and shouting complaints from her window like a Maxwell Street fishwife. It ought to have been Clara extending the first invitation, but this brazen new neighbor had beaten her to it. The situation made Clara feel one-upped, so even though she could have made time for a short visit, and even though a glass of tea might have been just the ticket for her worsening headache, she said stiffly,

"Thank you, but I'll be going to work soon. I work the night shift at Memorial Hospital." She paused, then added, "So during the afternoons, I try to sleep."

"Oh, dear." It was Laurie's turn to look embarrassed. "I'm so sorry. We must have woken you up with all our racket. We'll try to be more quiet. Won't we, Rosalie?"

The little girl pressed her lips together.

"Oh, by the way, have you seen Jerry around?" Laurie said.

"Do you mean Mr. Stevenson?" *Jerry, indeed.* "Not since early this afternoon."

"One of the drains is acting up. He took a look at it earlier, but it's still not working properly."

"Just ring the doorbell to his flat," Clara suggested. "If he's home, he's sure to appear in a jiffy, toolbox in hand." *Especially for a good-looking damsel in distress,* she added silently. Even the woman's name, Laurie Lucas, sounded as if it belonged in lights on a movie marquee.

"It's just that my husband always took care of repairs and things," Laurie said. "I'm afraid I'm not very experienced with tools."

Good luck working in a factory, then. Clara chided herself for the uncharitable thought. She shifted away from the window, eager to move out of the woman's eye. "Yes, well. Just please keep an eye on the child and keep her from running amok."

"Yes, ma'am, I will." Laurie's voice cooled ever so slightly, and her expression tightened. She placed a protective hand on her daughter's shoulder. Little Rosalie looked down at the grass and shuffled her foot.

Back in her shaded bedroom, Clara lay awake and stared at the white plaster ceiling, all hope of slumber gone. *Well. That was a disappointment.* She couldn't help but feel that she ought to have been friendlier to the new neighbor, who after all had no way of knowing that Clara had been trying to sleep. What was wrong with her, anyhow, that she couldn't muster up a simple hello? Her sister's voice floated across the years and pierced unbidden into her memory. *Why can't you be more outgoing, Clara? Always with your nose stuck in a book. You'll never catch a husband that way.*

In spite of all stated intentions to be quiet, moving house was a noisy business, punctuated by thumps and scrapes and the slap of the screen door at the basement entrance as movers came and went. The new neighbor's voice floated up through the radiator as she paced throughout her apartment, directing where each carton and piece of furniture should go. Every once in a while Clara heard Jerry's deep laugh entwined with Mrs. Lucas' lilting one. Clearly she'd found him. Clara set her jaw in frustration. He couldn't possibly be *flirting* with this pretty young woman, could he? The old fool.

Surrendering to the impossibility of sleep, she padded back to the front window and peered out from behind the lace curtain at the new neighbor's possessions, scattered higgledy-piggledy across the neat lawn. There weren't very many things, but what was there looked to be of a modern style, all edges and angles, not a frill in sight. A square gray sofa. A red linoleum table and matching vinyl-padded chairs. A chrome table lamp with a rectangular glass shade. A child-size dresser painted peach and white.

What kind of a young woman lived out on her own, anyway? Didn't Mrs. Lucas have family she could stay with, people who could help her with her daughter? Her soft accent hinted that she had roots in the South somewhere. What was she doing this far north? A basement apartment might be comfortable enough in the summertime, but how would she feel when winter hit and snow piled up around the windows and blocked out all the sunshine?

These and other questions fluttered through Clara's mind as she watched the procession of household goods meander from the van to the basement. After a good twenty minutes, she decided it was useless to figure out what kind of person this Laurie Lucas was based on her household goods. All she knew so far was that the woman was trying to raise a child on her own, without the firm discipline of a father or the steadying influence of grandparents, and was a factory worker who was not handy with tools, none of which boded well.

When Jerry had first mentioned it, Clara had thought it might be pleasant having another woman living in the building. But now, confronted with an actual flesh-and-blood person, she could see they were unlikely to become friends. Being forced to share certain facilities, such as the washing machine and the backyard clothesline, was sure to be a nuisance. Thankfully, with differing work schedules, they would bump into each other only on rare occasions.

If only the basement apartment could have remained empty for a while, or been inhabited by the likes of old Mr. Havlicek, a quiet man who had worked the night shift at the Grant Works and slept during the day, as Clara did. But these days, with factories at full capacity due to war work, housing was scarce and rents were at a premium in industrial towns like Cicero. To let a perfectly good apartment remain empty was practically unpatriotic.

As she turned from the window, Clara thought with a twinge of guilt of how cramped the basement quarters must feel for two people, unlike her own spacious flat, which was more than ample for the needs of a spinster living alone. Her wide front window flooded the living room with late-afternoon light, projecting intricate patterns from the lacy curtains over the dark polished woodwork, cream-colored walls, and hand-me-down furniture, worn but comfortable. When she'd moved in, she'd added a pair of wingback chairs and a good lamp for reading. Everything else had belonged to her parents.

Between the front room and kitchen was an open space meant to be a dining room, which Clara used as a library because she loved books and never had guests to dinner. Here her parents' oak table had been shoved against one wall as a place to store back issues of *National Geographic* and *The American Journal of Nursing*, stacked in tidy, square piles. Her small bedroom and bath opened off the so-called library. An even smaller room—a pantry, really—opened off the kitchen, where she stored her sewing machine and out-of-season clothes and boxes from her childhood home that she'd never taken the time to go through. Everything was neat as a pin, arranged in its place.

Glancing at the clock, she knew there was no point in trying to go back to sleep now. She was standing in the kitchen, fixing herself a simple supper of cheese, crackers, and canned beets, when she suddenly realized who Laurie Lucas reminded her of. Maybe it was because of the day she'd just had, or because of her fractured sleep, or because of the commotion, or all three. It wasn't a true physical resemblance as much as an air about her, a certain spring in her step and sparkle in her eyes. In any case, when Clara looked at Laurie Lucas, the person she saw was Aneta.

5

"Snug as a bug in a rug." Laurie Lucas bent over her daughter and pulled the nubby pink blanket up to Rosalie's chin. "Comfy?"

"Yes, ma'am." Rosalie hugged a brown teddy bear worn shabby by affection. "Can we go shopping for eyeglasses tomorrow?"

"I suppose we'll have to. I keep hoping we'll find them as we unpack. Maybe they fell into one of these boxes."

"I'm sorry."

"I know you are, sugar. Don't you fret. We'll have you back to seeing well, quick as a wink."

"Are you going to read me a story?"

Laurie straightened and glanced around the child's small room, still stacked high with unopened cartons. "I don't know where we'd find your books in all this mess. We were lucky enough to locate your pajamas for tonight, and your toothbrush and Mr. Bear."

"That's all right." Rosalie plucked at the satin edge of the blanket. "We could just talk instead."

"That we can certainly do." Laurie sat on the edge of the bed. "What do you want to talk about?"

"Does Daddy know where we are?"

"I've sent him a letter, telling him our new address."

"Because he'll have to be able to find us when he comes home."

"He'll find us," Laurie said. "But, sugar, it might be a long time before he comes home."

"I know." Rosalie shifted in bed. "Is he where the bombs are?"

"What?"

"The bombs."

"I don't know, sweetheart," Laurie responded, making a mental note to limit listening to war-news broadcasts while Rosalie was awake. "But I'll let you in on a secret. Every time I think of Daddy and miss him or feel scared, I ask God to keep him safe."

Rosalie nodded. "I'll do that, too."

"That's a good girl."

"Do you have to start work tomorrow?"

"No, not until Monday. Tomorrow we'll go over and meet Mrs. Jedlicky, who will be taking care of you while I'm at work."

"Do we have to?"

"You'll like it there, honey. There will be other children to play with. Mrs. Jedlicky cares for several children of factory workers, and she comes highly recommended by the company."

Rosalie rolled on her side. "I wish you didn't have to go to work."

"It's good for us, sugar. Being around new people is good for you and me both, and it makes me feel good to do something to help with the war effort. Things will be different when Daddy gets home."

"Why couldn't we stay with Granny Josephine?"

Laurie's heart ached. She could hardly tell her daughter the truth: *Because we weren't welcome there.*

"Because this is where Mama's job is. Let's talk about something else. How do you like our new little home?"

Rosalie looked around the tiny bedroom, crowded with a bed, a dresser, and a stack of boxes. "It's all right, I guess. It's awful small."

"Three little rooms and a kitchen and bath," Laurie said. "We don't need more than that, do we?"

"I guess not."

"And there's a whole backyard to play in."

"Yeah. As long as I don't step on the flowers." Rosalie studied the hem of the blanket.

"That's true. We'll have to be extra careful around the flowers. Mr. Stevenson says Miss Janacek loves them, especially her roses, and that she's very good at making them bloom."

Rosalie thought for a moment. "Mr. Stevenson is nice. But the flower lady is kind of mean."

Laurie sighed. "We didn't get off to a very good start today, did we? Tomorrow is another day. We can try to make friends, to get a fresh start."

"I don't want to make friends with her. She doesn't like me."

"Oh, Rosalie." Laurie smoothed her daughter's blond hair. "She just doesn't know you yet. Once she does, she'll love you just like everyone else does. Besides, she's probably lonely."

"Doesn't she have any family?"

"I don't know, sugar. But sometimes when people are cranky, it's because they're carrying a lot of sadness. They're hurting. They feel lonely, but then for some reason they do and say things that make people want to stay away, and that makes them even more lonely. Do you understand?"

"I think so."

"But guess what? God can fix things, and we can ask Him to let us help."

Rosalie frowned. "How?"

"We'll be extra kind to her, won't we?"

"Yes, ma'am." Rosalie looked unconvinced.

"In fact, we can go out of our way to be a blessing to her."

"Huh?"

"We'll be a blessing. An encouragement." Laurie snapped her fingers as she hatched a plan. "I know! Whenever she seems grumpy or mean, instead of getting mad back, we'll bombard her with blessings. We'll say something kind in return. We'll give her a smile. We'll do her favors."

"Bombard her with blessings." Rosalie considered this for a moment, then grinned gleefully. "She won't even see them coming. She won't know what hit her."

Laurie laughed. "We'll give our mission a name, like they do in the military. A secret code name, just between us."

Rosalie clapped her hands, eyes shining at the prospect of intrigue. "I love secrets."

"We could call it ... Operation Kindness, or Operation Friendly."

Rosalie shook her head. "Those don't sound very secret." Her forehead puckered in thought. Then she brightened. "Let's call it 'Operation Red Rose,' because she likes roses so much."

They both laughed, then Laurie quickly put a finger to her lips. "Remember, Miss Janacek sleeps during the day because she works at night. So sometimes we'll have to be very quiet as we go about our blessings. All right?"

"All right."

"Now, let's say our prayers."

They clasped hands and closed their eyes. Rosalie recited her nightly prayer.

"Now I lay me down to sleep. I pray the Lord my soul to keep. If I should die before I wake, I pray the Lord my soul to take. God bless Mama and Daddy, and keep Daddy safe and well. Thank you for our new house and for Mama's new job. Bless Granny Josephine and Auntie Melba, and Mr. Stevenson upstairs." She paused.

"And?" Laurie prompted.

Rosalie's forehead puckered. "And the flower lady. I'm sorry that I stepped on her flowers. Help Mama and me think of ways to bomb her with blessings. And please help her not to be such a grump. Amen."

Laurie suppressed a grin. "I suppose that's good enough for the time being. Sleep tight. We have another busy day tomorrow."

She kissed her daughter's forehead and switched off the bedside lamp. Then she went into the other room to unpack a few more boxes before going to bed herself. *Poor Rosalie*, she thought, *dragged from pillar to post because her mother and grandmother don't get along.* It was hard enough to be both father and mother to her, hard enough to raise her to be a good person without Will around. She wouldn't subject her to constant arguing as well.

She switched on the radio with the volume turned very low. Then, remembering that Clara Janacek was at work, she turned it up, just a little, to better hear the jazzy Tommy Dorsey tune. She hummed along and felt her energy returning as she unpacked the familiar leaf-patterned dishes and placed them in a cabinet in the tiny galley kitchen. With a start, she pulled out her husband's favorite coffee mug —a dreadful monstrosity with a scary clown face painted on it. Will had picked it up in a junk shop on a tour of duty in London. He thought it was hilarious, but Laurie hated the thing. The leering face seemed to sneer at her, mock her. But now she gazed at the cup, gently rubbing her thumb over a tiny chip on its brim. A lump formed in her throat. How long would it be before Will would again sip his morning coffee from it, perhaps seated in this very room? Weeks? Months? Years? Laurie had no way of knowing, but the Lord knew. And for now she'd simply have to leave the whole situation in His hands, as the song said.

Firmly she placed the hideous mug on the shelf with the face turned toward the back of the cabinet. Then she reached for the next item in the carton, comforted to pull out an innocuous serving dish covered in a sweet, reassuring pattern of tea roses.

❧ 6 ❧

Clara clung to the strap as the crowded streetcar heaved to a stop in front of Memorial Hospital. She'd spent her commute trying to keep her mind from replaying the clumsy first encounter with the new downstairs neighbor, Mrs. Lucas, with whom Jerry had no problem getting along, it seemed. As annoying as the situation was, Clara had no time to waste thinking about what was happening at home. She had to give full concentration and energy to her job if she were going to impress the review committee and bag that promotion.

As she stepped off the streetcar, she paused to let a speeding ambulance pass, its bell clanging to beat the band as it careened around the corner toward the emergency entrance. Jerry, she knew, would have sent up a prayer for the soul of the ailing person inside, but Clara felt confident that the staff would be able to restore the patient's well being without divine intervention. Memorial had been ranked one of the best hospitals in the state, and she was proud to work there. If such excellent care had been available to Aneta all those years ago, perhaps she ... but no. Clara refused to let her mind go there. Nothing could have been done for Aneta. And Clara had better things to do than to go over that old story again.

In the lingering twilight, she collected her wits and crossed the street toward the hospital. As she passed a large frame bungalow marked with a sign that read *Nurses' Residence*, an animated group of young nurses descended to the sidewalk, giggling and chatting together. Clara nodded a greeting, but they didn't appear to notice her. *This younger generation needs to be taught some manners.* In her day, nurses kept their dignity in public, didn't giggle and guffaw like a pack of hyenas and certainly didn't ignore the presence of a senior nurse.

The nurses' residence had once been the founding doctor's private home and had housed his original clinic back in the 1890s. These days, most students and probationers—first-year nurses—boarded there, but Clara had never done so, opting instead to live at home with her family. Occasionally she wondered if she'd missed out on something by staying home, if she'd have fit in better with the other nurses if she'd lived among them for a few years, sharing late-night confidences over hot cocoa and chafing-dish suppers. Somehow she doubted it. Anyway, she'd had no choice in the matter. Nursing school tuition had been a stretch financially, and the additional expenses of room and board had been out of the question.

Next door to the nurses' residence loomed the hospital, an impressively modern brick building, the tallest for many blocks around. Under normal circumstances its hundreds of lights would have glowed like lighthouse beacons, but now, with wartime blackout regulations in place, the unnaturally darkened building loomed like a ghostly ship against the purple twilight sky. As Clara entered, she inhaled the sharp elixir of disinfectant and floor wax as if it were fine perfume. This was her world, and before long, if things went her way, she might not be simply "Nurse Janacek" but "Head Nurse Janacek." A small shiver of anticipation prickled her skin, and she quickened her pace.

Entering the thirty-bed Women's Medical ward, she spied a gaggle of junior nurses gathered at the central desk. When they saw her coming, they ceased their chatter and rose, as they'd been trained to do in the presence of doctors and senior nurses. If Clara felt slightly embarrassed that they did that, she'd never let on. Procedures must be followed, and she did the same whenever a doctor or Head Nurse Banning came on the scene.

"Good evening, ladies," she said briskly. "I assume all's quiet on the floor, if you've got time to socialize." If Doctor Pratt or any other member of the review committee charged with selecting the next head nurse were to see the nurses on Clara's ward relaxing and having a merry old time, it wouldn't speak well to her managerial skills.

"Oh, Nurse Janacek, Betty Paulson's engaged," giggled one of the younger nurses, her cheeks set aflame by the specter of romance. "Her soldier boy finally popped the question."

"What happy news. Best wishes to you both." Clara smiled at the beaming Betty and dutifully admired the sparkling chip of a diamond on the hand she thrust forward. "My, that's a beauty. Be sure to stash it somewhere safe while you're on duty." Wearing jewelry on the ward, other than a regulation wristwatch for timing pulses, was strictly forbidden under hospital policy.

"I will," promised the grinning nurse.

"Good." Clara's mind scrambled for the sort of thing sociable people said in these situations. "Have you set a date for the wedding?"

"Probably around Christmas, while Tom's home on leave," Betty said. "It will be a small wedding, just family."

Her smile undiminished, Clara said, "Lovely," and silently calculated the number of months left before she'd have to reassign Nurse Paulson's duties. Even though hospital regulations no longer mandated that nurses quit their jobs upon marriage, in Clara's experience, the young brides nearly always did.

"I wish you every happiness, Nurse Paulson," she added. She didn't believe in the recent fashion of calling nurses by their first names, lest it breed over-familiarity. "Now, everyone, let's get back to work. Where is Nurse Kolar?" She glanced around for the nurse in charge, ready for their nightly review of what had happened during the day shift.

"Here I am," sang a cheerful voice as Joy Kolar appeared from around the corner. "Just admiring that lovely cake in the break room. Isn't it marvelous news about our bride-to-be?" She favored Nurse Paulson with a high-wattage smile that almost made Clara want to shield her eyes.

"Yes, Nurse Janacek, there's cake and punch in the break room to celebrate," said Cindy Novak, a petite blonde with a high-pitched, squeaky voice. "We hope you'll join us."

"That's very kind of you," Clara said, "but I'm afraid I have a great many tasks on my schedule. But you all enjoy yourselves. During your regularly scheduled break time, of course. Meanwhile, we have sick people to take care of."

The nurses scurried off to their duties, their enthusiasm somewhat dampened. Clara wished she had sealed her mouth after "enjoy yourselves." On the other hand, there was a time for work and a time for play. A busy hospital ward was no place for socializing, engagement or no engagement, especially when a member of the review committee might be observing and evaluating at any moment.

As she listened to Nurse Kolar's report with half an ear, Clara wondered what it might have felt like to walk into work one day and announce that she'd become engaged. To hear the squealing and the hearty congratulations at being offered a proposal of marriage from a young man, someone who had chosen her, Clara Janacek, to be his bride. To have someone to go home to, other priorities that took precedence over the job. For Clara, of course, the job was the priority, and she never expected it to be any other way. She didn't feel jealous of Nurse Paulson exactly, but what *did* she feel? Some sort of regret, perhaps, of loss, knowing that her own season for romance was long past, if it had ever been there to begin with. Even that was in doubt. Clara had never been the sort of girl men romanced. She was so different from Aneta, who'd collected beaux the way other girls collected butterflies.

With a sigh, Clara shook her head to clear it and forced herself to focus on the task at hand. Love and romance were not meant for women like her. She and the daytime charge nurse finished reviewing the report. Not long after Joy Kolar had left for home, Kathleen Jenkins, superintendent of the School of Nursing, appeared at Clara's side with a young nurse in tow.

"Nurse Janacek, may I introduce Miss Melvina Hyde? Nurse Hyde has just passed her board examinations, has accepted employment with Memorial Hospital, and has been assigned to your ward and shift." Kathleen's ingratiating smile silently added, *Isn't that wonderful news?*

"Welcome, Nurse Hyde." Clara turned her mouth up at the corners and extended her hand. Would there be no end to the interruptions tonight?

"H-how do you do?" Melvina Hyde's pale blue eyes, set in a face every bit as white as her starched uniform, held an expression akin to terror. Clara sighed. Clearly it was going to be a long night.

"Nurse Janacek has been here at Memorial for thirty years," Kathleen told Melvina. "She knows this job, and this ward, backwards and forwards. She's the absolute best person to show you the ropes."

Clara knew the superintendent was just trying to butter her up. She resented that it always fell to the long-term nurses to take new nurses under their wings and teach them things they didn't know, day in and day out. Things they should have learned in nursing school.

Even so, she enjoyed hearing the praise. And she should be happy for a new nurse. The hospital was experiencing a shortage of nurses, with so many joining up to serve in military hospitals overseas. Besides, it wasn't the girl's fault she'd been assigned to Clara's shift. With startling clarity Clara recalled her own first terrifying days at Memorial Hospital and felt a brief but powerful wave of empathy for the young nurse.

"Well, let's get started, shall we?" she said in as cheerful a voice as she could muster. As she did so, she heard a voice from her past echoed in her words. *Well, how about that?* she mused. *Seems after all these years, I've transformed into old Nurse Blair after all.*

✵ 7 ✵

As charge nurse on the night shift, Clara was second-in-command to Head Nurse Bernice Banning, who in turn reported directly to the formidable nursing superintendent, Olivia Kent. The layers of hierarchy had expanded with the growth of the hospital. Now Clara's duties included assigning the caseloads of the other nurses, maintaining the schedule, answering questions, solving problems, keeping a watchful eye on the most critically ill patients, and doing whatever it took to maintain a smooth-running ward, then writing up a report for the day shift. She had no time to shepherd a probie around, so earlier in the evening, she'd pawned off Melvina Hyde as soon as she could.

"Oh, Nurse Paulson," she'd called with relief as Betty passed by. She made quick introductions, then said, "Will you please see that Miss Hyde here gets settled in, and let her accompany you on your rounds? That would be most helpful."

Melvina's face collapsed into lines of confusion as Betty spirited her away. Clara adjusted her reading glasses, glanced once again at Joy's report, then set it aside and went to check in on the patients.

Women's Medical currently housed mostly geriatric women, which Clara supposed qualified as her area of specialty, if she had one. If she could have chosen a specialty, it would have been cardiology. She'd always been fascinated by the workings of the heart. But caring for her parents in their later years had given her ample experience in attending to the needs of the elderly, and she was skilled at deciphering their genuine physical needs from their endless complaints about drafts and diets. This was a hospital, after all, not a vacation resort.

Mrs. Bradley was first on her rounds. Gall bladder. Clara picked up a chart from a hook at the end of the bed and studied it.

"How are you feeling tonight, Mrs. Bradley?" she said.

"Terrible," the patient snapped. "If I have to eat one more bowl of gelatin, I'll scream. When will I be served some decent food?"

Clara neatly penned a note on the chart in red ink. Red ink for the night shift, blue ink for the day shift—a tidy system Clara had inaugurated to keep the recordkeeping straight. She hoped the review committee was aware of her meaningful contribution to efficiency.

"Sounds like your appetite is coming back. That's a good sign."

The patient harrumphed. "Where's that nice, pretty nurse with the freckles? She always makes sure my tea is hot."

"Nurse Kolar has gone for the day," Clara said calmly. She was used to patients preferring Joy Kolar to her because the day nurse frittered away time on socializing and chit-chatting instead of doing her duty. If she'd keep her mind on the tasks that really mattered, she'd get more work done and not leave so much for the overworked night shift.

Clara set the chart down, then picked up Mrs. Bradley's wrist and timed her pulse against the sweeping second hand of her wristwatch. After a few more brief comments, she moved along to the next patient, an elderly and frail woman recovering from pneumonia who had been newly assigned to Women's Medical.

"How do you do, Mrs. Kremel. I'm Nurse Janacek," Clara said. "Let's check those lungs, shall we?" She held the end of a stethoscope to the old woman's chest and listened carefully. "Breathe in, please. Out. Again." As she listened carefully, a swift, sharp memory sliced across Clara's mind, a decades-old memory of other lungs—gasping, drowning lungs—filled with dirty river water, and the terrible wheezing, rattling sound of a pulmotor machine. She quickly removed the stethoscope and made a note on the chart. Goodness, what was *wrong* with her tonight?

"The doctor will have the final say, of course," she said briskly, "but I imagine you'll be right as rain in a day or two."

"Oh, how lovely," the patient said in a fluttery voice. Her eyes held a faraway look and a dreamy smile. It was a relief to have such a docile, agreeable patient for once. Clara checked her temperature and other vital signs. Finding no signs of trouble such as fever or dehydration, she jotted a note on the chart and moved along to the next bed.

As she consulted charts, checked vital signs, delivered medicine, and issued instructions to the other nurses, Clara's mind kept flitting back to Betty Paulson's engagement. Perhaps she'd come across a bit harshly, declining to come to their little party. She couldn't shake the feeling that she'd thrown cold water on the celebration. After all, the best sort of head nurse must be not only respected, but liked as well, and a good supervisor must take a personal interest in those she supervises. At least she thought she'd read something like that once, in a back issue of the *American Journal of Nursing*.

Betty's voice floated over the curtained partition as she introduced Miss Hyde to the finer points of ward life. "Some of the day-shift nurses think the night shift has it easy because the patients are asleep, but that's not true," Clara heard her say. "Many of them sleep all day and stay awake all night. Sometimes they try to get out of bed and hurt themselves. And even on a slow night, we're stuck picking up the slack left by the day shift, and there are a lot fewer of us on duty. It can feel pretty lonely sometimes."

What Betty called loneliness was exactly what Clara liked best about the night shift: less pressure to socialize. She stayed on the fringes of the group, by her own choice. Part of her longed to join in the fun, to accept the invitations to bridge parties and bridal showers, but a bigger part wanted to remain separate, to calmly and peacefully get her work done without interruption, to not have to interact. She knew the nurses found her aloof and standoffish. It was probably better that way, she reasoned, if she was to maintain any authority at all.

Still, maybe she would stop in at their little party after all, just for a minute, and enjoy a piece of cake. Just to prove to the girls that she did know how to have fun, that she wasn't a complete wet blanket. The review committee would look favorably upon a demonstration of camaraderie to the troops.

A small cluster of nurses from the various wards headed down the hall toward the break room. Lingering behind them, Clara heard one of them mutter, "Look sharp, girls. Banning's on the prowl."

Nurse Banning blew into the ward like a ship at full sail. Her silver hair was scraped back into a bun under her starched white cap, and her ramrod posture and unsmiling mouth gave the impression that she would put up with no nonsense. The younger nurses were terrified of her, and with good reason. Clara knew that to be an effective head nurse, she'd have to be tough.

Nurse Banning's piercing blue eyes swept the ward. "Is everything under control here?"

"Everything's ship-shape," Clara said with forced cheer.

"I thought I heard giggling." Head Nurse Banning peered more closely. "Is that a *ring* you're wearing, Nurse Paulson?"

Clara's heart sank. A rule violation! Betty Paulson's pretty face registered horror as she impulsively thrust her hands behind her back.

"I-I'm sorry, Nurse Banning. I'm afraid I forgot to remove it."

"Well, take it off immediately," the head nurse ordered, shaking her head. "Standards, ladies. Standards." Hastily Betty removed the ring and dropped it into the pocket of her uniform. Nurse Banning cast a glance at Clara and lifted one eyebrow as if to say, *What kind of a ward are you running here?* Then, wordlessly, she walked on.

The nurses stood speechless for a moment. Betty Paulson's face glowed red, and poor Miss Hyde appeared to be teetering at the edge of a swoon. Clara felt as if her lungs were dissolving in her chest. To receive a reprimand in front of everyone, just when it was so critical to make a good impression, was a major blow. As soon as the head nurse was out of earshot, she wheeled on Betty.

"I warned you about the ring, Nurse Paulson. That's one demerit for you."

Standing beside the crestfallen Betty, Cindy Novak gasped. "But it's such a stupid rule. What harm can a ring do?" She placed a hand on Betty's shoulder. "It's her *engagement* ring."

Clara drew herself up. "Are you gunning for a demerit too, Nurse Novak?" She rose heatedly to Nurse Banning's defense. "None of our rules are stupid, even when we don't understand the reasons behind them. Each and every hospital regulation is for our own good and that of our patients. As for jewelry, it may get caught on a piece of equipment, or accidentally scratch a patient when you're moving her, or—"

"Yes, ma'am," Betty Paulson interrupted, her voice thick with unshed tears. "You're right. I'm sorry. I won't do it again."

At the sight of Betty's dismal expression, Clara's heart gave a twinge, but she ignored it. Give these girls an inch and they'd take a mile. "What this ward needs," she pronounced, "is a refresher course on the rules. Spit and polish, girls. I'll be watching."

"Come on, Betty," Cindy said, linking her arm through her friend's. "There's still plenty of break time left. Let's go get you a piece of cake. It's your very favorite kind, chocolate with whipped cream, fresh from Dressel's." Slowly and without meeting Clara's eyes, she and the other nurses drifted toward the break room. She thought she heard one of them mutter something about old spinsters and spoiled parties, but she couldn't be sure.

As she watched them go, Clara felt deflated. Even though it was entirely necessary to a well-run ward, meting out discipline was one of her least favorite tasks. Had she been too harsh on the girl? After all, no real harm had been done by wearing the ring. If Nurse Banning hadn't spied that little chip of a diamond flashing on Betty's finger, it was doubtful that Clara would have forced her to take it off, at least not tonight, when her engagement was so fresh and new. Should she have championed the young nurse? On the other hand, rules were rules, and without them the hospital would run amok. She herself rather liked rules. They made things clear and uncomplicated. Usually.

A voice from her childhood hovered around the edges of her thoughts. *Clara, don't be such a spoilsport. Loosen up a little, why don't you?*

Remembering her sister's long-ago remark called to mind Clara's new neighbor, who resembled Aneta so strongly in personality and demeanor. If Laurie Lucas and that odd child of hers hadn't interrupted Clara's sleep, she wouldn't be so tired tonight and would have perhaps handled things a bit differently. Or not. After all, when it came to authority, it was better to be respected than liked. Wasn't it?

With a sigh, Clara glanced down the hallway toward the break room, then turned away, knowing her presence at the party would no longer be welcome, even though the chocolate whipped cream cake from Dressel's Bakery was her very favorite too.

8

L aurie lay awake in the predawn darkness. She never slept well her first night in a new place. And it didn't help that the summer air was warm and sticky. Not quite as warm and sticky as Arkansas, but close.

On the other side of the thin plywood partition, Rosalie slept soundly, worn out by the excitement and activity of moving. Bone-deep exhaustion dogged Laurie too. Her muscles ached from lugging boxes, and her mind churned from making so many plans and decisions. During the day, the chaos kept her too busy to think about things. But at night she was consumed by an aching loneliness that even prayer couldn't seem to dispel.

"Lord, I came here because I thought You had given me a sign, that this is where Rosalie and I are supposed to make our home and live our lives. At least until Will comes home. If he comes home. I thought this is where I was called to be."

How she missed Will, wished he were here with them now. Her husband, her lover, her companion. Rosalie's daddy.

But then, if Will were with them, they wouldn't be in this position, living in a basement apartment, and she wouldn't be preparing to start a new job in a few days. They'd be back home together in Arkansas, and she'd be happily keeping house and caring for Rosalie. But he was gone for who knew how long, she'd felt bored and useless, so she'd uprooted herself and Rosalie and relocated to Cicero, where there were defense jobs aplenty, on the advice of a cousin, who knew someone who knew someone who'd moved here for that reason. Just for the duration of the war. This stupid, ugly, drawn-out, war.

But it wasn't stupid. Not at all. Drawn-out and ugly, maybe, but not stupid. She and Will and thousands, *millions* of others were fighting for what was right. She was sure of that. And she wanted to help. Which was the other reason she was here.

She turned on her side and punched her pillow. In the gray light coming in through the high, narrow windows, she observed the unfamiliar surroundings. The place wasn't bad for a basement apartment. The landlord clearly had done his best to make it not feel like a basement. All the walls and partitions were painted a bright white, which captured most of whatever light filtered in from the casement windows placed up near the ceiling. The windows were spotless and looked out on the front flower beds, which were a pretty sight, colorful and well cared for. Large, thick area rugs warmed and softened the cement floor. The apartment included a small living area, two sleeping areas, a simple but adequate galley kitchen, and even its own miniscule bathroom with a shower. True, it sat next to a common laundry and storage area that was shared by all the residents, but surely people wouldn't be doing laundry or rooting around in the storage shelves night and day. All in all, it was a perfectly suitable, cozy, affordable place for her and Rosalie to live, and she thanked God for providing it when wartime housing was in such short supply. In fact, she found it remarkable that the building only contained two other residents, the landlord on the top floor and the flower lady in the middle, both of them single and alone. At least Laurie had Rosalie.

Laurie smiled into the filtered gray light. Rosalie had come up with the name "flower lady," which was easier for her to remember than Janacek. Laurie hoped that her daughter would eventually have more and better memories of the neighbor than having been yelled at about trampling her peonies.

The first rays of dawn lit the window and landed on her blanket.

Hot and restless, Laurie threw back the covers, slid her nightgown over her head, and pulled on a pair of shorts and a shirt. Quietly so as not to wake Rosalie, she slipped out through the laundry room, up the stairs, and out the back door to the small wooden fire escape that served double-duty as a back porch. She breathed deeply of the fresh air, then jumped, startled, when a male voice said, "Good morning."

She peered through the misty dawn and saw the landlord on his knees, doing something to the fence surrounding the vegetable garden.

"Goodness! You startled me," she said.

He grinned. "I have that effect on the ladies. Or so I've been told."

She leaned against the railing. "You're up early."

"Always am." He returned to his task. "Told Clara I'd fix this here hole in the fence so the rabbits don't sneak in and eat up all her carrots."

"Clara?"

He nodded toward the building. "Miss Janacek."

"Oh, I see." She hesitated, then said, "We didn't get off to a very good start, she and I."

He glanced up. "Oh? Why's that?"

She told him about the peony incident.

He nodded. "Yeah, she loves them flowers. The peonies, the petunias. Especially them roses. Talks to 'em like they're people."

"I wish ... I hope she'll give us a chance to be friends."

"She will. Just give her time."

"I understand she's a nurse."

"Yep." He squinted at the rising sun as if telling the time. "Works nights. Should be getting home soon."

"Does she have any family nearby?"

He gave the chicken-wire a shake, testing its strength. "How's that drain working for you?"

"Seems fine now. Thank you." The sudden switch of topic made her wonder if she'd said the wrong thing. Asked too many questions. Been too curious.

"Place is comfortable enough?"

"Yes, very. But it's kind of stuffy on these hot nights. I think I'll need to invest in an electric fan."

He stood, wiping his hands on the thighs of his pants. "Think I might have one up in the attic. Lemme check before you go and buy one." He picked up his toolbox and headed for the garage, then stopped and turned around.

"There's a church picnic coming up in a week or so. Me and Clara are going. If you and your girl want to meet some nice people, that might be a place to do it."

"Thank you. I'll think about it."

He continued toward the garage. She went inside her apartment and peeked at Rosalie, who was still asleep. Quietly, Laurie plugged in the electric coffeepot, then took a shower. When she was dressed, she poured a cup and sat at the kitchen table, where she opened her Bible and read a chapter. Then she closed her eyes, clasped her hands, and prayed hard that God would bring her a friend.

❦ 9 ❦

B y the end of Laurie Lucas's second week at Western Electric, she'd gotten the routine down pat. Assigned to an assembly department, she sat at a long bench in a large window-lined room with women of various nationalities: mostly Czech, Polish, and Hungarian, but also Irish, Italian, and Scandinavian. Once she'd gotten the hang of it, the work was not difficult, and Laurie felt she was getting along well with the ladies whose stations surrounded hers. She liked her work. Screwing the tiny electrical components together was simple enough to master but challenging enough to hold her attention.

Her workbench partner, a tall lanky woman named Evelyn Hendrikson, had been especially helpful in clueing Laurie in about the rules, both spoken and unspoken, of life on the factory floor.

"Most of the men here are good eggs," she told Laurie, "but one or two rotten ones resent the presence of women workers on the factory floor. Nothing they can do about it, of course. Many workers have been drafted, just at the time when the factory's taken on more war work. Who else do they think is going to pick up the slack?"

"What do they do that's so rotten?" Laurie asked.

"Oh, you know. Inappropriate comments, crude jokes." Evelyn grimaced. "If anyone bothers you, best thing to do is just ignore him." She didn't offer more details, and Laurie hoped to steer clear of any fellows like that.

"What do you do at the factory all day, Mama?" Rosalie asked one evening as they stood together at the sink, washing and peeling potatoes for supper.

"Well, let's see ... mostly I attach wires to small pieces of metal."

"All day long?" Rosalie handed a scrubbed potato to her mother.

"All day long. Except for lunch, of course. At lunchtime I eat my sandwich in the employee cafeteria with the other workers. And once in a while I take a turn delivering the parts we've finished to the supervisor or running some other errand. I like that, because it gives me a chance to get up and stretch my legs."

"What happens after you stick the wires on the metal?"

"Well, I don't know, really." Laurie set down the peeler, carried the potatoes over to the stove, and slid them into a pot of boiling water. "I turn my finished parts in to the supervisor, and she hands them along to whoever needs to work on them next. This particular project is all very hush-hush."

Rosalie wrinkled her nose. "What's that mean, hush-hush?"

Laurie tried to explain in terms a nine-year-old would understand. "It means that the end result of our work is something that's going to be used in the war to help the Americans win. They don't want the wrong people to find out what we're making. So, you see, I'm only allowed to know about the part of the job that I'm responsible for. I don't get to find out how it's used in the end."

"You mean it's a secret."

Laurie laughed and kissed the top of Rosalie's head. "That's a whole lot simpler way of saying it. Yes, it's a secret."

Rosalie considered this. "But it's something for the soldiers."

"Yes."

The child's face brightened. "Then maybe it'll end up being something that helps Daddy. Maybe Daddy will get to use something you've made."

A lump formed in Laurie's throat. "I never thought of it that way, sugar. But maybe you're right. Maybe whatever I'm making will help Daddy in some way."

Rosalie looked at her mother solemnly. "Then you'd better do a really good job."

Laurie nodded. "Yes. It needs to be perfect. For Daddy and the other soldiers."

That quest for perfection, and the knowledge that whatever she was building at the factory was not only helping the general war effort but her very own husband as well, stayed in Laurie's mind and spurred her on during the longest, most tedious days.

On one such afternoon during the steamy dog days of August, the hours dragged. When the whistle blew signifying lunch time, Laurie stayed behind for a few minutes to finish up the assembly she was working on. Experience taught her that it was best to complete an entire unit at once, not to stop in the middle, lest she get mixed up. Even if it meant being a few minutes late for lunch. Her work had taken on a greater sense of urgency since her conversation with Rosalie, and Will and his fellow soldiers were never far from her mind.

Task finished, she stood up from the bench, stretched her spine, and wandered to the cafeteria, where several of her workmates had gathered at a table near the open windows to catch a whiff of a breeze in the sweltering room.

Evelyn called to her. "Hey, Laurie. Come over here and share our oxygen supply." She shifted to make room at the table.

"Did anyone else listen to Fibber McGee last night?" Theresa Renzi asked. Laurie watched her pull an enormous sandwich out of her lunchbox and unwrap it.

"Oh, darn, I missed it." Patricia Kowalski selected a roll from a passing coffee cart. "I had a date. That's my favorite program. What happened?"

"Fibber and Molly were cranking ice cream by hand. You know, like in the olden days before rationing?" Theresa licked her lips. "Sure made me long for some homemade ice cream, especially on scorching days like this one. But who can justify using up that much milk and sugar on a treat?"

"Darn ration coupons." Patricia sighed. "What I wouldn't give for a chocolate milk shake so thick you have to eat it with a spoon."

"Our troops need ice cream more than we do." Laurie's tone came out harsher than she'd intended. The heat was making her grumpy. Her voice softened. "I'm sorry, Patricia. I didn't mean to snap at you. Of course you all know the point of rationing." She sighed. "A milk shake sounds blissful. Make mine vanilla."

Patricia grinned. "With a cherry on top."

Laurie gave a wry smile. "It's just that I don't mind doing without as long as my husband can get a dish of chocolate-mint-chip now and then." She swallowed hard and gazed wistfully out the window at the sunny courtyard below.

Theresa said gently, "I didn't know your husband was serving overseas, Laurie. Where?"

"Pacific. Somewhere near Japan, I think."

"Mine's in Southern Europe somewhere," Evelyn said.

"Hey, my brother's in the Pacific, too," Theresa said. "Maybe he's met your husband. What's his name?"

"Corporal Will Lucas."

"I'll ask my brother the next time I write to him."

"Wouldn't that be wonderful?" Patricia interjected. "But the military is huge. It would be a miracle if they knew each other."

Evelyn smiled at Laurie. "We'll keep Will in our prayers."

Just then a beefy, middle-aged man sauntered up. "What's this? A hen party? Cluck, cluck." He made flapping motions with his elbows and chuckled at his own joke. "Hate to interrupt your chitchat, ladies, but there's a war on."

"It's our break time," Evelyn grumbled, but even so, the women silently slipped back to their workstations. Having arrived late, Laurie hadn't eaten half her sandwich. Even so, she didn't relish being left alone with this fellow, so she wrapped up the remainder and stood.

Gripping a paper cup filled with coffee, the man sidled up to Laurie.

"Hey, there, Blondie," he said heartily. "You're the new girl, right?"

"The name is Lucas," came Laurie's reply, tinged with frost. "Mrs.

Laurie Lucas." Who was this guy? She didn't remember seeing him around the department.

The man pointed a thumb toward his chest. "Carl Bowman. My team works in the shop next door to yours."

Aren't I the lucky one, she thought wryly. Still, her breeding insisted she be polite. Besides, maybe he was just trying to be friendly.

"How do you do, Mr. Bowman."

"Call me Carl, and I'd be doing a heckuva lot better if you'd let me buy you a beer after work. You know, just a friendly way to say 'welcome to the fold.'"

"No, thank you," Laurie said. "My husband wouldn't like it. And I don't care for beer. Thanks, anyway." She turned to go back to her station, but he stepped forward and blocked her path.

"What are you, one of them teetotalers?" Carl said. "Aw, come on, you're too pretty to go around smashing up bars with a hatchet like those old crones in the WCTU." He leaned forward as if about to reveal a secret. She shrank back from the odor of stale tobacco on his breath. "Tell you what—you go out with me tonight, and I'll have the bartender make you something real special."

She recoiled, bumped into the wall behind her. "No, thank you." He'd backed her into a corner.

"I overheard you telling the ladies that your husband's overseas." His grin revealed several gaps where there'd once been teeth. "No need to act like a nun while he's gone."

A chill ran through her body, though her face felt flaming hot. "I said no. Now if you'll excuse me."

He didn't move. She tried to brush past him, but as she did, he jerked his arm and sloshed his coffee cup, spilling hot liquid down the front of her blouse.

"Aw, gee, what a clumsy oaf. I'm so sorry." The tone of his sneer didn't sound the least bit sorry. He pulled a dingy handkerchief from his back pocket and reached toward her chest. "Here, let me sponge that off for you."

She jerked away. "No. Don't touch me. You've got a lot of nerve."

"Geez, lady, lighten up." He raised his voice loud enough for his workmates to hear. "It was an accident."

The man's laughter followed her as she hurried back to her station. She dabbed furiously at the stain with her handkerchief, to no avail. Her hands shook.

At the station next to hers, Evelyn leaned toward her. "Aw, don't pay any attention to him, honey," she murmured. "He's like that with all the new girls. Come to think of it, the old ones too."

"Like an animal, you mean?" Laurie wished desperately that the whole incident had never happened.

Evelyn grimaced in sympathy. "Look, kid, I know it's awful, but what can you do? Boys will be boys."

"I'd rather not discuss it. I've got to get back to work." Laurie picked up her screwdriver. Evelyn looked at her for a moment, then returned to her own task with no further comments.

Laurie was still having imaginary heated arguments with Carl Bowman that evening as she and Rosalie walked home from the babysitter's house—arguments in which she told him what she *really* thought of him.

"Whatcha thinking about, Mama?" Rosalie's voice burst into her thoughts. "You look mad as fire."

"Do I?" She squeezed her daughter's hand. "I'm not mad, honey."

"Yes, you are. Your forehead is all frowny."

Laurie composed her features. "Well, I'm not mad at *you*. I'm just thinking about something that happened at work today. It's nothing for you to worry about."

When they reached home they found Clara on her knees in the front yard, tending to her roses. Rosalie tugged at Laurie's arm and whispered, "Operation Red Rose, right?"

The reminder of their little mission of cheer lifted the gloom from Laurie's spirits. Her daughter had a way of doing that. "Yes! Operation Red Rose launches *now*," and she banished all thoughts of Carl Bowman to the back of her mind.

❧ 10 ❧

Kneeling before the rose bush in the front yard, Clara watched from the corner of her eye as Laurie Lucas and the child approached. She rather hoped they'd keep on walking, but no such luck.

"Those flowers surely are a gratifying sight for weary eyes, Miss Janacek," Laurie said. "I envy you your green thumb."

"Me too, ma'am," Rosalie added. "They're such a pretty color."

Clara's response came out as a noncommittal grunt, but she selected a bloom, clipped it off the stem, and handed it to Rosalie with a promise. "If you take this inside and float it in a bowl of water, it will last a long time."

Eyes wide, Rosalie breathed a surprised "thank you" and took a deep whiff of the rose's aroma.

"I'm afraid I can't grow a blessed thing," Laurie admitted. "Miss Josephine—that's my mother-in-law—she likes to say I have a black thumb. I murder every plant I touch."

"Growing plants is not that difficult," Clara said. "It just takes patience and a little know-how."

"Is that so? Well, I'd be mighty grateful if you'd show me how sometime," Laurie said. When Clara didn't respond, she added, "But right now I suppose I'd better be getting little Miss Rosalie's supper on the table before she starts gnawing on that lovely flower. You have yourself a pleasant evening now." She hesitated a moment, then added, "Maybe you'd like to come downstairs later for a visit. We could listen to the radio and play dominoes. Rosalie goes to bed at eight."

"I'll be working tonight," Clara said. "But ... thank you."

"Oh, that's right. I keep forgetting you work nights," Laurie said, and Clara thought she detected the slightest note of relief in her voice. "Well, good night."

"Good night." Clara held the woman's gaze another moment, then resumed clipping.

Laurie started to walk away, then turned back. "Oh, wait. There was one other thing I've been meaning to ask you about."

"Yes?"

"I'm looking for a good church for Rosalie and me to start attending. Is there a particular one in the neighborhood that you would recommend?"

Clara sat back on her heels and blew a stray strand of hair out of her eyes. "I'm not a good one to ask," she said. "I'm not a churchgoer."

Laurie's eyes widened. "You're not?" Apparently in her world, everyone went to church, even if only for show. She stared at Clara, awaiting some sort of explanation.

"Never have been. My parents were Freethinkers," Clara said. That seemed simpler than getting into an endless debate, as she tended to do with Jerry, about whether or not God even existed, and if so, what He expected of people, and how He treated them.

Laurie tilted her head like an inquisitive robin. "What are Freethinkers?"

Oh, for Pete's sake. "Back in the Old Country, some people felt bullied into following the state religion. So when they came here to America, they relished their freedom to choose not to follow any religion at all. They called themselves Freethinkers, meaning no priest or minister or other dogmatic authority figure tells them what to think." She paused, then added, "My parents among them."

"Goodness," Laurie said. "I've never heard of that. Well, I guess I'm a freethinker, too, then."

"Oh?"

"Yes. I freely think that Jesus is Lord."

"I see," Clara said, though she didn't see and didn't particularly want to. And what was one supposed to reply to that? "Well, then."

Laurie gave a puzzled frown. "So Bohemians don't go to church?"

"*Some* Bohemians don't," Clara said, wearying of the topic. "Others do. There are plenty of churches. Just look around town—there's Saint Francis of Rome, Our Lady of the Mount, St. Mary of Czestochowa ..."

"Oh, we're not Catholic," Laurie interrupted. "We're Southern Baptist."

Clara rubbed her forehead, likely leaving a smudge on her brow from her muddy gardening glove. Speaking slowly, as if Laurie were slightly impaired, she said, "You might consider asking our landlord for a recommendation. He belongs to some brand of Protestant church, and he's quite fond of it." She thought of the church picnic and how a more neighborly person might bring it up, might say, *Why don't you come along?* But the words would not form, and the moment passed.

"Jerry?" Laurie's face lit up. "Why, sure, I'll ask him. Thank you." She smoothed her daughter's hair. "Ready to go, sugar bear?"

Rosalie nodded in her strange, silent way, her large eyes focused on Clara. *What an odd child*, Clara thought as they disappeared around the corner of the building. With a sigh, she turned back to her roses. *Churchgoers. That's all I need.*

She wondered if she ought to have said something about the coffee stain on the front of Mrs. Lucas's blouse—maybe offered a helpful hint about getting it out— but concluded that commenting on the woman's grooming habits lay well outside the boundaries of neighborly duty.

Thirty minutes later, her task finished, Clara went inside and headed straight for the bathroom, where she sprinkled lavender-scented Epsom salts into the white claw-foot tub and turned on the faucets. She stripped off her sweaty gardening clothes, pinned her hair, and dabbed onto her face a soothing skin tonic with a hopeful name, Moondrop Miracle. Then she slid into the tepid water and sighed with relief. Nothing like a cool bath on a hot day to renew one's spirits and ease aching muscles.

Funny thing about water, she mused, lifting her hand and letting the droplets run through her fingers. On a steamy summer day, water was refreshing and life-giving, but at the same time, a person could drown in it.

Her mind drifted back to a hot summer when she was eleven and Aneta was eight. Clara couldn't remember the name of the lake or the town, but her family had spent two weeks at a summer cabin on the shore of a small, peaceful lake in southwestern Michigan. While she didn't know the exact circumstances that had permitted this luxury, which had never occurred before or since, she remembered it as a glorious time. The days had been drenched in brilliant sunshine, tempered by cool twilight breezes. Both she and Aneta had learned to swim. It felt wonderful to escape the heat and humidity of the city. It had been hot in Michigan, too, but the dense trees and refreshing lake made it easier to bear. Clara swam capably enough, but Aneta excelled. By the end of their stay, she was fearlessly diving off the end of the pier, dunking and being dunked by the children from neighboring cottages, screaming with delight all the while, while Clara stayed a little apart, content to paddle in gentle circles and pretend she was a mermaid.

Even though the Janaceks had never been back to the lake after that summer, Clara had cherished the memory in her heart. Her dearest wish, when she retired, was to buy a cottage at a lake just like that one and live in it every summer. Maybe even all year round. She'd decide that part later. But the delicious truth was, such a decision would be hers and hers alone to make. She wouldn't have to answer to anybody.

11

After her bath Clara toweled off and slipped into clean
undergarments and slip. She'd finish dressing later, after she'd
had a good sleep. She slid gratefully between the clean, crisp
sheets.

Sometime later, Clara bolted upright from her nap as an appalling
racket burst into her bedroom through the open window. Bing Crosby
crooning at high volume, inviting her to swing on stars and collect
moonbeams in jars, and some nonsense about mules.

"Oh, for Pete's sake." Clara flung back the coverlet and stomped to
the window. "Speaking of mules," she muttered and slammed down the
sash.

She crawled back into bed and squeezed her eyes shut, but still she
could hear Bing's cheerful voice ringing up through the radiator pipes.
With a heavy sigh she got up, pulled a housedress over her head, and
thrust her feet into slippers. Heedless of her messy hair and the creases
the pillow had pressed into one side of her face, she stormed down the
back stairs and pounded on Laurie Lucas's door.

"Mrs. Lucas."

From inside she heard an off-key female voice singing along with

Bing, something about not all monkeys being in the zoo. In that moment Clara couldn't have agreed more.

Clearly no one could hear her knock. She turned the knob and gingerly opened the door, calling, "Hello? Hello?" as she stuck her head through the opening.

Laurie, dressed in the same blue dungarees and bandanna headscarf she'd worn on moving day, was pushing a mop around the kitchen linoleum. Not pushing, really—more like dancing with it. She stopped mid-twirl when she saw Clara's head peering around the door. She looked startled for a moment, then grinned and snapped off the radio.

"Oh, hi, there, Miss Janacek. Come in! Sorry, I didn't hear you." She leaned her mop against the wall. "Have you come for that game of dominoes? I've been cleaning all afternoon, and am dying to take a break."

"I should say not," Clara said. "I'm afraid I must ask you *again* to keep the radio volume low in the afternoons."

All at once, a look of dismay crossed Laurie's face. "You were sleeping! Oh, I forgot. Gee, I'm so sorry. I guess I just got carried away."

"I'll say."

Laurie's color rose, and she grinned sheepishly. "Housecleaning is such a bore. I was just trying to make it a little more fun."

"Well, if you could have your fun a 'little more' quietly, I would appreciate it."

Laurie winced. "Sorry. We'll be so quiet, you won't even know we're here."

"Thank you."

An awkward silence fell as the two looked at each other. Clara had expected more of an argument from Laurie and felt something more ought to be said, but she didn't know what. From out of nowhere came the unexpected impulse to accept Laurie's offer of a game of dominoes, but just then Rosalie walked into the kitchen clutching a pale blue bundle that dripped water onto the cement floor.

"Mama, I got most of those clothes rinsed out, but—" She looked up and spotted Clara. "Oh. Hi."

"Let's hold that over the sink, shall we?" Laurie said. "Why, Rosalie, I'm so proud of you! Such a help to your mama." She turned to Clara, eyes sparkling. "Isn't she wonderful, Miss Janacek? Mama's little helper."

Clara failed to see what the fuss was about. "I should hope so," she said. "By the time I was her age, my sister and I were responsible for the family's laundry *and* all the ironing." That was a bit of an exaggeration, but Clara found modern parents entirely too lenient with their offspring. No sense in coddling the little darlings. Hard work built character.

The sparkle in Laurie's eyes faded, and she set her mouth in a hard line.

"Mama." Rosalie tugged on Laurie's arm. "Mama."

"What is it, Rosalie?"

The child held forth the wet blue bundle. "This shirt has a stain on it. I can't get it out."

Laurie examined the shirt. "Oh, piffle. Well, come on, let's go see what we can do about it."

That should have been Clara's cue to leave, but she felt compelled to follow them to a corner under the back stairs, where Jerry had walled off a section as a laundry room to be shared by all residents of the building. The area smelled of damp cement walls, Fels-Naptha soap, starch, and hot cotton. Jerry had installed a modern washing machine, but Clara didn't fully trust it to get things really clean. Thus, for her sake, an old wooden washboard still leaned against a cement washtub, and a hand-cranked wringer loomed like some tool of the Inquisition.

"Sugar, go and check under your bed to make sure there are no dirty socks hiding under there." The child disappeared into their apartment. Laurie turned to Clara. "Since you're such an expert housekeeper, Miss Janacek, maybe you can tell me what to do with this stain on my work blouse," she said, and Clara thought the younger woman's voice carried a faint note of sarcasm. "I was on my break at work, and this man ... well, someone bumped into me and spilled coffee."

"Oh." Politely, Clara leaned forward and peered at the brown stain as if coffee on a blouse were an extraordinary sight. "That's what happens when people get careless."

"I think he might have done it on purpose."

Clara glanced up. "Who?"

"The man who bumped into me. He said it was an accident, but I don't think it was." She pressed her lips together. "No, I *know* it wasn't. He was angry with me for refusing to go out with him."

"Oh, dear." Clara straightened up. "Did you tell him that you're a married woman?"

"Of course I did. What do you think? But it just seemed to make him more determined."

Clara thought of Doctor Pratt and his abusive behavior toward the nurses at the hospital. "Some men are oafs," she said. "Unfortunately, in the workplace, they usually call the shots. Best to just do your job and stay out of his way." Which was exactly the advice that generations of nurses had given one another about abusive doctors—just steer clear as much as you can. It wasn't the most effective solution, Clara acknowledged, but what else could be done without jeopardizing one's job?

"That's easier said than done," Laurie said with an exasperated snort. "In the meantime, do you have any suggestions of what I should do about this blouse?"

"Well, hydrogen peroxide sometimes works well on coffee stains."

"That figures," Laurie muttered, flinging the shirt onto the folding table. "I haven't got any." She raised her voice. "Rosalie, can you please check under the bathroom sink to see if we have any hydrogen peroxide? It would be in a brown bottle."

A faint "Yes, ma'am, I'll check," came through the thin plywood wall that separated the apartment from the laundry area.

Laurie studied the stain. "If not, I guess I'll make a note to pick some up at National."

"Oh, you shouldn't shop at National," Clara said with a sniff. "Waste of money. Grocerland's prices are so much more reasonable, and they offer a much better selection of—"

"Must you find fault with everything I do?" Laurie burst out in exasperation.

Startled, Clara gaped at her as if flames were leaping from Laurie's mouth.

"Find fault? Why, all I said was—"

"You sound exactly like my mother-in-law." Laurie's voice quavered. "I moved here to get away from her. I do housework wrong. I raise my child wrong. And now I even *shop* wrong."

Clara blinked and struggled for words. "But I didn't mean—"

"Oh, never mind." To Clara's horror, Laurie burst into tears. "It's just that I feel so stupid sometimes. Like I'll never do anything right."

Clara froze, not knowing whether she should leave or stay or pat Laurie on the shoulder or keep her hands to herself.

"But you're not stupid," she said at last. "You're not stupid at all."

Laurie sniffed and wiped her eyes with the hem of the stained blouse. "Sorry. It's nothing. Don't mind me." She gently but firmly steered Clara toward the door. "Thank you very much for the hint about hydrogen peroxide. I'll be sure to try it. Good afternoon, Miss Janacek."

"But—"

"Good-bye, now." Laurie closed the door. From the back stairs, Clara heard the clatter as Laurie attacked her mopping with renewed vigor, but she was no longer singing.

"Well." She stared uncertainly at the closed door for a moment, then headed back upstairs.

❧ I 2 ❧

From inside the apartment, Laurie heard Clara's heavy tread on the stairs. She stopped and leaned against her mop, feeling thoroughly defeated. She shook her head and muttered to the empty kitchen, "Hair-trigger temper, one. Operation Red Rose, zero."

Abandoning the housework, she found Rosalie, who had given up her search for the hydrogen peroxide, and settled her at the kitchen table with a snack and a storybook. She snapped on the radio—at low volume this time—then went into her bedroom, closed the door, lay across the quilt, and had herself a good cry.

When her tears were spent, she went into the tiny bathroom. "Laurie Lucas, pull yourself together," she told herself sternly. She splashed cold water on her face, then peered in the mirror over the bathroom sink and patted on some powder to cover the blotches.

When she returned to the kitchen, Rosalie looked at her with huge eyes. "You all right, Mama?"

Laurie picked up the mop and swished it across the floor. "Sure, honey. I'm all right."

"Are you angry with Miss Janacek?"

"Oh, sugar. Sometimes people don't act particularly loveable. Including you and me. But the Bible says we need to love people

71

whether they're acting loveable or not." She sighed. "Sometimes *especially* when they're not."

"I feel sorry for her," Rosalie said.

Laurie stilled the mop. "Why?"

"Because I have you, and you have me, and we have Jesus, and she doesn't have anybody."

Laurie's heart melted in her chest. From the mouths of babes! She set the mop aside and sat at the table across from her daughter. "You're right, sugar. You're absolutely right. Let's pray for her right now."

They held hands across the table, and Laurie spoke.

"Dear Lord, we ask your blessing on Miss Janacek today. I'm sorry I lost my patience. She was only trying to help by giving me advice. Help us learn how to be friends, and above all, we pray that when she looks at us, she will see You instead. In Jesus' name, amen."

"Amen." Rosalie opened her eyes. "Resume Operation Red Rose, sailor?"

"Aye, aye, captain," Laurie said. "Operation Red Rose is back in motion." She squeezed and released her daughter's hands. "I think I saw the mailman come by a little while ago. Why don't you check the mailbox and see if we've received any letters."

Rosalie scampered up the stairs, out the back door, and around the house to the front entrance where the mail was delivered. Minutes later she returned with a few envelopes in her hand and a pout on her face. "No letter from Daddy."

Laurie disguised her own disappointment with a smile as she took the envelopes from Rosalie. "That's okay, sugar. Maybe tomorrow."

"Can I go and read my book now?"

"Of course."

Rosalie went into the bedroom and shut the door. Laurie flipped through the meager stack of mail. A promotional flyer from the Troy Department Store on Cermak Road and some sort of official notice from the Cicero Town Hall. The notice, she saw on second glance, wasn't even addressed to her. It had a man's name on it—a foreign-looking name that looked to be mostly consonants. Dimly she recalled being told that the previous occupant of her apartment had been an elderly man with that sort of Eastern European name. She considered putting it back in the mailbox with a "Return to Sender" note but decided to check with the landlord first.

She walked up the back stairs to Jerry's door and knocked. When he didn't answer, she bent down and slid the envelope under the door.

On her way back down to her own apartment, she passed Clara Janacek's door just as it opened. The older woman's face bore a look of utter surprise and consternation.

Well, Laurie didn't care. She was tired of caring. She lived here, too, and had as much right to use the back stairs as anyone.

"Hello again," she said, forcing a grin.

Miss Janacek nodded stiffly, set a dustbin on the porch, and shut her door.

Laurie sighed as she entered her own apartment. Clearly nothing about Operation Red Rose was going to be easy.

13

At the hospital that night, Clara yawned constantly, barely able to keep her eyes open.

She'd only napped fitfully during the afternoon, mostly due to the hubbub downstairs, not to mention that unfortunate moment when she'd encountered Laurie Lucas coming down the stairs from Jerry's apartment. There were many legitimate reasons, she reminded herself, why a tenant might need to speak to a landlord. But surely said tenant could telephone said landlord and not pay him a visit in his apartment. Even Clara, who was Jerry's good friend, seldom set foot in his apartment. Not since his wife died. It wasn't seemly.

She also could not keep her mind from replaying the afternoon's unfortunate encounter with Mrs. Lucas in the laundry room. She had wanted so much for her dealings with her new neighbor to be, well, neighborly. But, thanks to Mrs. Lucas's incessant noise and disruption, Clara felt anything but cordial. In fact, she and the new tenant seemed constantly at odds. Clearly the fault was the blond woman's. Wasn't it? Clara tried hard to muster up some righteous indignation. After all, she wasn't the one making mistake after mistake. But the truth was, the sensation that poked at her heart felt less like righteousness and more like regret. She hadn't meant to come across as being so critical. She must try harder to be nice.

Women's Medical felt especially steamy in the summer heat. Between the sick and cranky patients, the crabby staff, and her own fatigue, Clara was not looking forward to her shift. Thankfully, it looked like it was going to be a quiet night on the ward. In an effort to keep the place in ship-shape for the review committee, Clara assigned Cindy Novak and Melvina Hyde the task of inventorying the linen and supply cabinets while she and Betty Paulson made the rounds of the patients. Betty started at one end of the ward and Clara at the other.

At Mrs. Kremel's bedside, Clara had to wake the elderly patient to check her lungs and vital signs.

Normally calm and serene, almost childlike, Mrs. Kremel seemed agitated at being woken. She struggled to throw off her covers and get out of bed. "Oh dear," she said. "Is it morning already? I need to get going. I'm late."

"Now, now, Mrs. Kremel," Clara said, gently pressing the patient's shoulders to ease her back into bed. "It isn't morning; it's the middle of the night. And you're not going anywhere."

"But I must! I'm very late, and I'm not even dressed."

"Late for what, dear?"

"The wedding, of course," she said. "Oh, how I do love weddings. Don't you?"

"You must have been dreaming, Mrs. Kremel," Clara said. "There is no wedding for you to get to."

"Oh." A look of perplexity crossed the woman's face. "Isn't Freddy marrying Martha today? Yes, I'm sure of it. Let me up. I need to get to the church before the bride walks down the aisle."

Mrs. Kremel was obviously confused, but Clara assured her that today was not the day for the happy occasion.

"Who are Freddy and Martha?" she asked. But Mrs. Kremel seemed to have lost her train of thought and was gazing into space with her usual contented smile.

Before moving on to the next patient, Clara double-checked the doctor's orders on Mrs. Kremel's chart. Then she verified the contents in a bottle on the bedside table and scrawled some instructions on a piece of paper.

"Nurse Paulson, would you please take this down to the night pharmacy and see that Doctor Pratt's prescription gets filled tonight?"

"Sure thing." After Betty took the paper and left, Clara walked to the central desk and scribbled a note for Nurse Kolar on the day shift, asking her to check with Mrs. Kremel's family about any upcoming wedding plans when they came to visit. It would be nice to reassure Mrs. Kremel that she'd be released from the hospital in time to attend an occasion she was so looking forward to, if that were indeed the case. Then she set down her pen and rubbed her eyes, which felt gritty with fatigue.

From the vantage point of the desk, she could observe Cindy and Melvina working at the linen cabinet. "Nurse Novak—I mean, Cindy," Clara overheard Melvina say in her tentative, mousy voice. "You live at the nurses' residence, don't you? I think I've seen you there."

Cindy nodded. "Do I ever. Although it's getting crowded, three of us girls jammed into a single bedroom. Why?"

The student looked at Cindy with wide eyes. "Well, I've never lived with roommates before. May I ask your opinion about something?"

"Go ahead. Shoot."

"If one of your roommates—that is, if you and she had entirely different ... What I mean is ..." Melvina seemed to struggle to find the words. "My roommate does some things that are making my life difficult. I know she doesn't mean to, but she does. Like inviting people over when I'm trying to sleep, and hogging the bathroom, and leaving her unmentionables draped all over."

Hmm. Roommate troubles sounded a lot like downstairs-neighbor troubles. Clara found herself listening harder, straining to hear Cindy's sage words of advice.

"I know what you mean." Cindy's words were laced with sympathy. "Learning to live with people you aren't related to can be tough. Heck, even the ones you *are* related to can be unreasonable at times. Have you talked to her about it?"

"I've brought the matter to her attention," Melvina said. "I'm afraid I might have spoken a little harshly."

Hard as it was to imagine the timid Miss Hyde raising her voice to anyone, Clara's own cheeks burned as she thought about how harshly she'd spoken to Laurie earlier that day.

"Twelve pillowcases in this stack," Cindy said, straightening the stack on the shelf as Melvina noted the number on a clipboard. "I've had my share of bumps in the road with roommates. But if there's one thing I've learned, it's that a peaceful relationship is more important than being right all the time."

Clara inhaled sharply. The nurses glanced up at her, but she didn't take her eyes off the chart she was pretending to study, and they returned to their task.

But being right *was* important, Clara argued to herself. She *did* think she was right, most of the time, anyway, at least about technical matters, like caring for patients and getting stains out of blouses. But when it came to other things—such as getting along with a neighbor, for example, the relationship part of things—she didn't have a clue what to do. Which was why she was eavesdropping on a conversation between two young, unmarried nurses. A ridiculous thing to do.

The pair finished up with the closet and closed the door.

Cindy turned her direction. "What would you like us to do next, Nurse Janacek?"

Just then a short man with a Napoleonic bearing blew into Women's Medical with the force of a tornado, his white coat snapping behind him.

"Ladies, look alive," Clara said quickly as she rose from the desk.

"That's Doctor Pratt, the chief surgeon," Cindy muttered to Melvina. "Watch out. He eats nurses for breakfast."

"What's going on here?" Dr. Pratt's voice hummed with anger.

Clara stepped back. "Sir?"

He pulled a pill bottle from the pocket of his lab coat and waved it in her face. "I just encountered a nurse down at the pharmacy who was only just now filling a prescription I wrote hours ago. Why was that not done sooner?"

"The medicine wasn't completely gone," Clara said calmly. "There was still one dose left."

"One dose! That's not enough," the doctor thundered. "When I ask for a prescription to be filled, I expect it to be filled immediately. Is that understood?"

"Yes, doctor." Clara said quietly. Inwardly she seethed. Who did Dr. Pratt think he was?

The doctor slammed the bottle onto Mrs. Kremel's bedside table. He gave the patient a quick once-over, then wheeled around to poor Melvina Hyde, quaking in her blue probationer's uniform. "You. Bring me a sponge. For heaven's sake, a monkey could respond faster than you nurses."

Melvina scurried off. Dr. Pratt turned to Clara.

"See here, nurse. The patient is developing a rash."

Clara adjusted the light over the bed and peered at a slightly reddened spot on Mrs. Kremel's arm. The patient gave her a tentative smile. Clara returned the smile with a reassuring pat.

"She might have a sensitivity to the soap or the surgical adhesive. I'll take care of it."

"See that you do."

Melvina returned with a folded washcloth.

"For heaven's sake, nurse," the doctor blustered. "I said a sponge, not a rag. Are you completely incompetent?"

Melvina's eyes filled with tears.

Clara felt torn between standing up for her nurses and going head-to-head with Dr. Pratt. She'd long resented the way Head Nurse Banning always sided with the doctors in this sort of dispute, currying their favor. And yet going head-to-head with Dr. Pratt, thus angering him further, would put her promotion in jeopardy.

In the end she did nothing, and when the belligerent doctor stormed out of the ward, her indecision cost her a chance to do the right thing, whatever it was. In seconds all the starch whooshed out of her resolve. She felt like burnt toast.

"Please mind the ward until Nurse Paulson returns from the pharmacy," she said to Cindy. "I'm going to run an errand."

She went into the restroom to splash cold water on her face. Then she sank down on a leather cot in the corner. *I'll close my eyes for just a minute*, she thought. *Just for a minute. No one will even notice.*

She didn't wake up until Betty Paulson burst in through the swinging door, wild-eyed.

"Nurse Janacek, have you seen Mrs. Kremel?"

Clara flew awake. "Mrs. Kremel? No, why?" Blinking, she leaped to her feet and glanced around quickly, as if the elderly patient might be lurking under the sink. "She shouldn't be out of bed."

"She's gone missing."

Clara shot to her feet. "When? Who saw her last?" she asked over her shoulder as she left the restroom and raced down the hall to the ward, Betty right behind her.

Sure enough, Mrs. Kremel's bed was empty. Clara felt the blood rush to her head as she hurried down the hall, looking in storage closets, private rooms, and other wards. Mrs. Kremel was nowhere to be found.

A hospital-wide search for Mrs. Kremel was launched moments after an inwardly frantic but outwardly composed Clara dialed security on the in-house telephone. Seconds later, a loudspeaker over her head crackled to life, and a calm voice repeated a page for a fictional "Doctor Foster" to report to Women's Medical, a code phrase that alerted all relevant personnel to a missing-patient situation without alarming the general population. At the signal, controlled chaos reigned. Various hospital workers from doctors to janitors moved discreetly to the exit doors. Fortunately there were not many people coming and going in the middle of the night.

Doctor Pratt sailed into the ward and strode straight for Clara.

"A patient has gone missing? How could this have happened?" he demanded.

"I—I don't know," Clara stammered. "It's Mrs. Kremel, doctor. She seemed disoriented when I last checked on her, although I thought she'd fallen back asleep."

Dismissive and curt, his beady eyes bore into her as she described the situation.

"You don't know what to look for, nurse," he said dismissively. "You're not a doctor."

Clara swallowed. "No, I'm not, but I know that—"

"Silence!" He turned to Nurse Paulson. "What did you see?"

"Nothing," Betty said.

Doctor Pratt scowled.

Clara drew herself up and faced Nurse Paulson. "I left you in charge of the ward."

"No you didn't," Betty countered, confusion on her face. "You sent me to the pharmacy, remember? When I came back up, I noticed Mrs. Kremel was gone and went to find you."

Her memory thus jogged, Clara knew Betty was right. But embarrassment kept her from saying so in front of the others. She turned to the other nurses. "Nurse Novak? Miss Hyde? Did you notice Mrs. Kremel up and walking around?" The young women shook their heads. Clara had already asked them this question five or six times but felt she needed to ask again in the presence of Doctor Pratt.

"No, of course you didn't," she said wearily, "because you would have known to stop her and alert someone. Well, someone must have seen her get out of bed."

"We've already asked all the patients and the nurses on the other wards," Cindy said.

"Ask them again."

Doctor Pratt peered at Clara with steely eyes. "Where were *you* when all this was going on, Nurse Janacek?"

Clara hesitated. "I was in the restroom." She didn't dare admit she'd been asleep, and she felt deeply ashamed of her behavior.

Before he could press for more information, an orderly burst into the ward. "We found her." He held the door open, and two security guards entered with a bewildered Mrs. Kremel between then.

"We found her in a stairwell," one of the guards said. "Looks to be all right, although she keeps saying something about needing to get to somebody's wedding."

Clara and Betty rushed forward to collect Mrs. Kremel and get her back in bed—with the rails up this time.

"Good work, gentlemen." Doctor Pratt turned to Clara. "Nurse Janacek, I'm very disappointed in what I witnessed here tonight. I trust you will review the procedures of your ward and make sure something like this never happens again."

"Yes, doctor," Clara said, her relief at Mrs. Kremel's safe return tempered by the humiliation of being dressed down by Doctor Pratt and the knowledge that this incident did not bode well for her chance for promotion.

But maybe that was for the best, she reflected miserably. Any nurse who could fall asleep on the job wasn't head nurse material, after all.

❧ 14 ❧

The morning sun was already baking the pavement when Clara arrived home from work, spent and weary. The neighborhood was quiet with the stillness of Sunday morning, but inside, Clara felt anything but peaceful.

What a night. If she never had to live through another night like that one, it would be too soon. Would Doctor Pratt see to it that any chance she had for promotion were scratched from her record?

For the rest of her shift, she'd done her routine work automatically, dreading what the nursing superintendent would say in the morning. Before going home, Clara entered Nurse Kent's office with trepidation. Her knees threatened to melt under her. Surely she would receive a reprimand, or worse, for allowing Mrs. Kremel to wander off on her watch. But Nurse Kent only asked for Clara's version of what had happened, taking careful notes, and then said, "All right," and sent her home.

Clara wanted to blame Laurie Lucas for disrupting her sleep and thereby setting all the other catastrophes in motion. But she couldn't, not in good conscience. In fact, she couldn't get Cindy Novak's words out of her mind. *A peaceful relationship is more important than being right all the time.* Maybe she should try harder to get along with Mrs. Lucas—

for the sake of that young daughter of hers, if nothing else. Clearly the child needed a stable influence in her life. And she did seem smart as a whip, something Clara grudgingly admired in one so young. If Laurie reminded her of Aneta, Rosalie reminded her of herself. Why did relationships with people have to be so complicated? It was so hard to know what to do. Roses were easy. Soil, air, water, sun. People were not so easy.

She mulled over what she could take to her neighbor as a peace offering. A coffee cake or a plate of homemade cookies would be nice, but the thought of turning on the oven in this heat was more than she could bear, and her butter and sugar rations might not stretch that far. Remembering the coffee stain on Laurie's work blouse, she thought of a way to be helpful. She hunted up a nearly full bottle of hydrogen peroxide in her medicine cabinet, then went downstairs and knocked on Laurie's door. When nobody answered after several minutes, she went back upstairs and grabbed the pad of paper in the kitchen where she wrote her grocery lists. Then she thought better of using scratch paper, moved to the small desk in the living room, and pulled a sheet of pretty flowered stationery from a drawer. In her most careful penmanship she wrote:

"Dear Mrs. Lucas,

This hydrogen peroxide should do the trick to remove the coffee stain on your blouse. Mix a few drops of it with the yolk of an egg and a little warm water and sponge it on the stain. It should not alter the color, but to be on the safe side, test it on an inside seam first.

Sincerely yours, Clara Janacek."

She read over the note, then added, "P. S. You may keep the rest of the bottle. It comes in handy for many uses." She considered listing the uses, then decided not to, not wanting to sound like a housekeeping know-it-all.

She capped the pen. *There.* Maybe now Laurie would think of Clara as a thoughtful neighbor and feel inspired to be thoughtful in return and not blast that infernal radio at all hours of the day.

She taped the note to the bottle, carried it downstairs, and placed it on the cement step in front of Laurie's door. Then she went back upstairs to fix herself a meal. The mention of egg yolks in her note had spurred an appetite for a poached egg on toast.

In the early afternoon, while running her feather duster over the fireplace mantel, Clara glanced out her front window to see Jerry, Laurie, and Rosalie walking together down the sidewalk, side by side, looking for all the world like one of those happy smiling families pictured in the magazine advertisements. The sight of them laughing together made Clara's chest feel tight. As they approached the walkway beneath her open window, she leaned closer to the screen to better hear their conversation.

"So the preacher saw the little boy out fishing on a Sunday," Jerry was saying, "and the preacher said, 'You there, boy. Why are you fishing instead of going to Sunday school? Don't you know the Lord watches everything you do?' And the little boy said, 'Yep, but He can't see nothin' today. It's cloudy out.'"

Laurie burst into laughter, while Rosalie looked confused. Clara rolled her eyes. *Him and his stories.*

"Thank you ever so much, Jerry." Laurie patted her tummy, flat as a college girl's under her narrow-cut skirt. "We haven't eaten that grand a feast in weeks. Have we, Rosalie?"

"And ice cream for dessert! Thank you, Mr. Stevenson," Rosalie added with more enthusiasm than Clara had ever heard tumble from the child's lips.

Jerry chuckled. "You're both very welcome. I hope we can do it again sometime. Maybe next week." He tipped his hat and disappeared from Clara's view under the porch roof while Laurie and Rosalie went around to their door. Soon she heard Jerry's steps on the stairs. He didn't even stop to knock on her door to say hello or ask how she was. She could be lying on the floor, collapsed from a heart attack or heat stroke for all he cared.

Clara returned to her dusting with renewed vigor. So he'd taken Laurie and Rosalie out to lunch, had he? Clara might have liked to go out for lunch, too, instead of eating a boring poached egg all alone in her lonely little kitchen. But then, she didn't have blond curls and a slender waist and the kind of tinkling laugh that made even the lamest of old jokes seem hilarious, causing the chest of the joke-teller to puff out with pride.

That little hussy has her hooks out for him. As she lay on her bed, Clara couldn't help but feel a pang of dismay over her hasty impulse to leave a peace offering at Laurie's door. If anything, Laurie should be making the first move toward reconciliation. But of course it was too late to retrieve it now. Her last thought before drifting off was an uncharitable wish that hydrogen peroxide would fail to work on the coffee stain after all. Maybe even make a permanent white spot on the blouse.

But instead of bringing her satisfaction, this wish only made her feel petty and small and burdened with the knowledge that no garment, coffee-stained or not, would diminish Mrs. Lucas's abundant charms toward the opposite sex.

15

On the day of the church picnic, Clara met Jerry on the front steps of their building. Nervously she glanced at the glass in the front door, eager to catch a reflection of her new hairdo. She had to admit, the wizardry of the beautician's scissors made her look years younger. In honor of the occasion, she'd pinned a small bunch of cherries to the brim of her new straw hat and hoped she wasn't gilding the lily.

No sooner had she greeted Jerry than Laurie and Rosalie emerged from the basement. Rosalie looked like a cute Dutch doll in a Delft-blue gingham sundress with matching hair ribbons. Laurie wore a shoulder-baring shift splashed with island flowers, reminding Clara of one of those fruity tropical drinks made popular by the men coming home from the South Pacific. Not that Clara had ever tasted one, but she'd seen a picture in a magazine, along with a recipe that sounded as if it might have been refreshing, if Clara were the kind of woman to keep bottles of rum in the pantry.

Together they walked to the streetcar stop, Jerry and Laurie ahead, Clara and Rosalie behind. While they waited for the car, Laurie turned to Clara and said, "I've been meaning to thank you for the hydrogen peroxide. You were right. It took the stain out of my blouse."

"I'm glad," Clara said and meant it. She might not be the tropical-foliage type, but at least she could be useful in the things that mattered, like laundry skills.

Clara was familiar with the picnic grove, the community's summer gathering place, where old-timers played chess and told stories in Czech, young couples strolled arm-in-arm along the shady paths, and children scampered and played on the grassy lawns. Although most of the picnickers didn't arrive until noon, men in white aprons had started roasting a pig on a spit early that morning, their well-muscled arms turning it every half-hour or so, their faces red and shining from the heat of the coals. Serving tables groaned under the weight of sausages, sauerkraut, potato salad, and sweet, flaky strudels. Everyone had brought food to share. Women wiped down benches and set table-cloths to billowing across the wooden picnic tables, swatting good-naturedly at the children who wove in and out, looking for a nibble.

Upon their arrival, Rosalie scampered off with some of her class-mates from Sunday school, and Laurie carried her covered cake dish to the serving table and immediately was swept into conversation with women she'd apparently met at church.

Clara stayed close to Jerry as he greeted people he knew. Many of them were familiar faces from around the neighborhood, but she didn't have more than a passing acquaintance with any of them. All of them acted friendly toward her, and she did her best to respond in kind. When Jerry got caught up on a heated political discussion, she strolled off and circulated through the park alone. Feeling out of place, she began to worry that coming to the picnic might not have been such a good idea after all. She watched the people streaming through the park. The women all seemed so sweet and soft and good that she wanted to sink into the grass and disappear. Maybe she should wait until after she learned how to be good before coming to church events regularly.

Her stomach growled and she made her way back to where Jerry, Mrs. Lucas, and Rosalie were seated at a long picnic table, along with a few other people she didn't know. They made room for her and, after what felt to her like an interminable prayer of blessing over the food, she dug into a plate of pork, dumplings, and sauerkraut. No matter how uncomfortable and awkward she felt, Clara's appetite remained hearty. A lively conversation about jobs and families and children swirled around her, but she didn't join in unless someone asked her a question directly, which they seldom did. Small talk had never come easily to her.

After eating, a sleepy sense of peace settled over the adults. Clara continued her peaceful walk around the park, observing rather than being observed. Old people pulled out the dominoes, reminisced, recalled picnics of their youth, and talked about visiting the old country one more time. The children went right back to playing, Rosalie among them, turning dessert into competition about who could eat the most poppy-seed cake or spit watermelon seeds the farthest. A local politician walked among the tables, chit-chatting in a mixture of Czech and English, nodding, shaking hands, smiling.

Clara found an empty folding chair and seated herself in the shade among the older women, clustered near the wooden dance floor in a corner of the picnic grove. From this vantage point, they could hear the music, observe the dancing, and dream about their own long-past dancing days while keeping an eye on the propriety of the younger folk.

In the late afternoon, a band of musicians set up. A man held a mother-of-pearl accordion in his lap. Others tuned a bass, a violin, and a guitar-like instrument. With wide grins they launched into a fast-paced polka, putting their whole bodies into the act. The older people got dreamy-eyed, mouthing all the words. A group of folk dancers picked their way out onto the floor, the women costumed in lace blouses, richly embroidered skirts and aprons, and black vests trimmed with red silk ribbons, the men wearing yellow knee britches, short jackets, blue stockings, and buckled shoes. Gradually more dancers joined them, circling to the plunky-sounding rhythms of the old country: a waltz, a mazurka, another polka. A group of women joined a circle dance, arms intertwined, hopping and twirling through the ancient steps their grandmothers had danced, and their grandmothers' grandmothers.

"Clara Janacek." Elzbieta Soucek, a woman who'd just introduced herself, had a voice heavily accented and creaky with age. "Are you any relation to Emil and Anna Janacek?"

"They are my parents," Clara replied. "Were."

Elzbieta clucked her tongue. "Ah, yes. I was sorry to hear of their passing. I knew your mother from our lodge. Of course, she couldn't participate as much as she would have liked, due to her health, but I remember one time when we ..." And she headed off down Memory Lane at a rapid clip.

Clara listened with half an ear. Thoughts of her mother filled her with mixed emotions. There'd been happy times before Aneta's death, to be sure, but these memories faded, submerged in the years of sorrow that followed. Now she equated her mother mainly with dim rooms, drawn blinds, and rebuffed gestures of kindness.

She slapped at a mosquito and glanced around to see what Jerry was up to. He had not settled in for dominoes and horseshoes among the older men. Finally she caught a glimpse of him on the far side of the dance floor, demonstrating the polka to a group of children.

"You can't go out on the dance floor until you get it right," he shouted at them over the music. "You're liable to get run over. Now remember, nothing moves from the waist up." He demonstrated with his arms. "No twisting, no charging around the floor like a herd of buffalo. You move from the waist down, like this. You glide." He glided, and Clara's heart warmed at the way the children tried to follow his footsteps in their clumsy coltish way.

"You were a good daughter to care for them both," Elzbieta croaked in her ear, and Clara struggled to pick up the thread of their conversation. "My own daughter, she can scarcely be bothered to come and visit her old mother. I'd go to visit her, but now with my rheumatism and my ..."

Only half listening to old Elzbieta's organ recital, Clara observed Laurie socializing with the other ladies of the church. She reminded Clara of a butterfly, a watermelon-and-mango colored butterfly, flitting from table to table, the sunlight glinting off her golden hair. It seemed as if Clara were watching Aneta, those many years ago. Aneta, always the butterfly, and Clara, observing from the shadows. Some things never changed.

Her mind drifted back to earlier picnics at this same grove. Not church picnics, but those held by the fraternal organization her father and mother belonged to. The organization had, for the elder Janaceks, stood in as a sort of substitute for church, but Clara hadn't kept up with it after their deaths. She wasn't a joiner.

Now, watching Laurie, Clara could picture Aneta seated on top of a picnic table in the sunshine, surrounded by admirers, looking every inch like Scarlett O'Hara on the veranda, deciding which suitor would take her to the barbecue, in that Civil War movie that had made such a splash a few years back. Jerry's wife had still been alive then, and the pair of them had dragged Clara to see it at the Olympic. She'd enjoyed the story more than she'd thought she would, and at least during movies one wasn't forced to make conversation. But, yes, now that she thought about it, Aneta certainly had been the Scarlett O'Hara of Cicero, young men buzzing around her like flies to honey. Clara, on the other hand, had usually endured picnics sitting in the shade, making polite conversation with her parents and their friends, and wishing she'd brought along a book. She'd spent picnics much as she was now, listening to old Elzbieta prattle on about her rheumatism and her gout.

"... but of course they were never the same after your sister died." Elzbieta was peering at her, obviously expecting some kind of response.

"Hmm?" Clara said.

"Your mother and father. They never were the same after your sister died."

Clara stared at Elzbieta. Had the old woman been reading her thoughts? Just as she struggled to formulate a reply, a child's frantic screams echoed across the park.

"Help! Help, somebody! Albert's been hurt!"

"Excuse me." Clara stood and hurried toward the sound of the screams, along with several parents. A young boy lay on the ground, grasping his ankle and fighting back tears.

"Albert! What happened to you?" cried his anxious mother bent over him.

"I fell down," the boy said through clenched teeth.

"Oh, my poor darling! It's all right. Mother's here."

"Please, let me through," Clara said, elbowing her way through the assembled crowd. "I'm a nurse." She knelt and examined the boy's ankle. "It doesn't appear broken, just a sprain. It's painful, but it will heal." She untied her scarf, briskly wrapped it around Albert's ankle to stabilize it, and glanced up at his mother. "Try to keep the leg elevated and apply ice to it. That will help reduce the swelling." She turned to Albert and tried her best to sound cheerful in spite of the bad news. "And no running for you for a while, young man."

Albert gulped and nodded. Clara had to admire the boy's fortitude.

"I still don't understand what happened." His mother glanced around the circle of wide-eyed children who were watching the spectacle. "Did any of you see what happened?"

"We were racing for that tree, and Albert tripped and fell," Rosalie said, pointing.

"Rosalie was winning," another child reported. "Albert couldn't keep up."

Albert's mother looked annoyed. "Young ladies should not be running races."

Now Clara was annoyed. "Nonsense. What else should they be doing at a picnic? Embroidering tea-towels?"

The boy's mother sniffed. "They certainly should not be racing against the boys."

Clara rose to her feet. "Or beating them, is what you really mean."

Albert let out a groan, and for a moment his mother looked as if she wouldn't have minded beating Clara.

Just then, Jerry stepped forward and grasped Clara's arm, steering her away from a brewing argument.

"Thank you for looking after the boy so quickly, Clara," he said loud enough to make sure all the mothers overheard. "What a blessing to have a nurse present at times like these."

Clara waffled. "Well, of course, I—"

"What do you say we take a turn on the dance floor?"

"Jerry Stevenson, you know I can't polka. My knees—"

"Your knees are fine. And it's not a polka, it's a waltz. Come on."

When they reached the dance floor and starting circling, looking for an opening among the swirling couples, Jerry's face crinkled into a smile. "Are you off your rocker?"

"What do you mean?"

"Trying to pick a fight with Albert's mother."

"I wasn't picking a fight." Clara said, appalled. "I only said—"

"You would have lost for sure," he said with a wry grin. "That woman has forearms the size of ham hocks."

Clara giggled nervously, feeling like a very confused schoolgirl. She liked Jerry very much. She enjoyed his company. Maybe under other circumstances, if life had turned out differently, if he hadn't been her good friend's husband—but no. That path had been closed a long time ago. Romantic feelings would only complicate a deep, abiding friendship. And, she reasoned, if she and Jerry were not romantically linked and never would be, why not stand aside and let him have fun with some other woman who did want him?

"You don't have to dance with me," she said abruptly. "I enjoy listening to the music. You can dance with Mrs. Lucas if you want to."

His dark eyes met hers. "I don't want to. I want to dance with you." He extended his hand to her in invitation, and they walked onto the floor for a slow dance. She noticed that he pulled her a little closer than usual, and she let him. It felt nice, unaccustomed as she was to being held at all, by anyone. She felt content in his arms.

He propelled her around the floor. "Listen," he said, "they're playing our song."

We have a song? Clara thought. But as she felt his firm grip around her body, the years melted away, and she felt an old familiar thrill.

"'Let me call you sweetheart, I'm in love with you.'" Jerry sang along softly with the band in his delightfully off-key baritone voice.

Over Jerry's shoulder Clara caught Rosalie's eye. The child smiled and waved. Clara smiled and waved back. And just for a moment, she felt as if she were twenty years old again. Twenty years old and dancing around the living room with her younger sister.

Suddenly her throat swelled and her eyes welled up with inexplicable tears. "Hey, what's the matter with you?" Jerry said gently, watching her with a look of concern. "Look, don't worry. The kid's going to be okay." His arm tightened around her waist.

Clara nodded, her throat tight with a sweet sadness. She never cried. For the life of her, she could not explain the reason for her tears. But she knew for a fact it had nothing to do with anybody's sprained ankle.

❧ 16 ❧

May 1915

"What's the matter, Clara? Did you turn your ankle?" Aneta stared at me, her blue eyes round as lollipops.

"I'm fine." I smoothed my skirt, trying to recover my dignity, which now lay shredded on the slippery wooden floor I'd just skidded across in my stocking feet.

On the warm spring evening, a breath of lilacs wafted in through the open windows of the front room of our childhood home. My sister and I had the whole house to ourselves, our parents having gone to some event at their fraternal lodge. Without their repeated admonitions to turn down the volume on the Victrola, and with the rug rolled up and stashed against a wall, Aneta decided it was as good a time as any to teach me the latest dance craze. She flung her arm around my waist as if hoisting a sack of flour. With her other hand, she grabbed mine and lifted it into the air.

"Clara, *do* try to keep up. Let's start again. One, two, three, four, five six, seven, eight."

With the furrowed brow of an Olympic competitor, Aneta steered me around the bare wooden floor as Scott Joplin's "Maple Leaf Rag" poured forth from the Victrola.

"Step, hop, step, hop. Walk, walk, hips. Walk, walk, hips. Come on, Clara, stick out your backside, like this!" She contorted her body into what looked like a paralytic spasm.

I dropped my arms and stepped back. "I will *not* stick out my backside. That looks perfectly ridiculous."

"Of course it looks ridiculous," she said with strained patience. "It's meant to. It's the Turkey Trot. You're supposed to imitate the way a turkey walks."

"Whatever it is, it's not for me." I collapsed onto the sofa and fanned my perspiring face with a back issue of *Denni Hlasatel*, the local Czech-language newspaper.

Aneta crossed her arms over her pintucked bodice, her cheeks pink with exertion and annoyance.

"Everyone's doing it."

"Who's everyone?"

She reached down to tug my arm. "Come on, I have to practice. Marguerite can do it blindfolded."

I evaded her grasp. "That must be an edifying sight."

"There's a dance at Sokol this weekend. I need to be ready."

I quirked an eyebrow. "A dance? Do Mama and Papa know?"

"Yesssss," she hissed darkly. She stomped over to the Victrola and silenced the music, then folded herself onto the sofa beside me. "They're coming along as chaperones, if you can believe that. I'm utterly humiliated, but Papa said that's the only way they'll let me go."

"I see. Well, after all, you are only seventeen."

"And you're twenty. Big deal."

"A lot of growing up happens between seventeen and twenty."

"Yeah. Like being allowed to put up your hair and wear your skirts down to the floor."

"A lot more than that," I said. "The working world's a lot different from high school. You have to take on heavier responsibilities, learn to get along with all sorts of people, without depending on Mama and Papa so much."

She flung her head back against the sofa cushion. "Nobody else's parents keep watch over their every move. Were they this strict with you?"

"I suppose they were," I said lightly. But they hadn't been, because I hadn't given them any reason to. My high school years hadn't included endless, dizzying social rounds the way my sister's did. Studious, quiet, likely to be tucked at home with my nose in a book, I naturally caused my parents few headaches. Even fewer now that my newly launched career as a nurse left me with little time for frivolity.

But Aneta was another story. Steeped as they were in the mores and traditions of the Old Country, Mama and Papa didn't always know what to make of their younger daughter's steady stream of comings and goings, her dances and parties and theater outings and trips to the beach.

But, no mistake, she was the light of their lives. Of all our lives.

I grasped her slender hand in mine. "All right. I'll admit that dancing's not my favorite activity."

She snorted. "That's because you've got two left feet."

I laughed. "Guilty. But here's the deal. I'll help you practice your dancing, provided we can switch to something more dignified. No more Chicken Strut, or whatever it is."

"Turkey Trot." She cast a look of disdain upon my hopeless ignorance of popular culture but hopped off the sofa and switched the records. When our parents returned a quarter of an hour later, they smiled at the sight of their daughters clomping around to the sedate strains of *Let Me Call You Sweetheart*. Grinning, Papa gently nudged me aside, then swept a laughing Aneta into a waltz worthy of the Hofburg Palace.

I followed Mama into the kitchen to ease my parched throat with a drink of water. Part of me wished Papa had chosen me as his dancing partner. But the other part—the part with two left feet—was relieved to be let off the hook. At least for the time being.

September 1944

O
n Monday afternoon a few weeks after the church picnic, Laurie set down her screwdriver and stretched her cramped muscles.

"If I tighten one more bolt, my eyes will go buggy," she said.

Evelyn smiled.

Ted Palmer poked his head in the door of the workroom. "I need one of you girls to run down to supply," he said in his usual gruff manner.

"I'll do it, Mr. Palmer," Laurie said. "It'll feel good to stretch my legs."

Mr. Palmer gave her a scrap of paper with some part numbers written on it. "Make sure they give you the right ones."

"I will."

On her way back from the parts department, she passed a small group of men standing near the entrance to the workroom.

"Excuse me, Mrs. Lucas, may I speak to you for a moment?" one of them said.

Laurie's stomach tightened. Carl Bowman did not normally speak this nicely. Something was up. "What is it? I'm in a hurry."

"This won't take long," he said, glancing around at his mates. "We have a question we think you might be able to answer."

Laurie moved cautiously over to where he stood. Maybe he'd finally gotten the message that she wasn't interested in dating him and they could continue with a smooth working relationship.

"What's your question?"

"We fellas need you to help settle a question about weights."

"Me? I don't know anything about weights."

"Sure you do." Carl glanced around at a few of his friends, who stood listening to the conversation. Shouldn't he be asking one of them? "Our question is, what gets easier to pick up the heavier it gets?"

What kind of a question was that? "I don't know. What?"

"Women!" All around her, men broke into laughter. She could feel her face redden. Without a word, she walked the few feet to Ted Palmer's office, suspecting he'd overheard the whole exchange.

"Here are the parts you wanted. I made sure they were correct." She slammed the paper bag onto the desk with a thud.

"What's the matter with you?"

"Carl Bowman. Can't you do something to make him stop?"

"What? He's just having fun. It just means he likes you." So Ted had overheard. Laurie's resentment deepened. "Come on, Lucas. If you can't take a joke, you'll never get very far in this world."

She walked back to her station, feeling the men's eyes on her. She slid onto her stool and muttered, "I can't believe he said that to me. And that Mr. Palmer thinks it's okay."

"Honey, don't let it bother you," Evelyn said. "Bowman's like that to all the girls, especially the new ones. Be glad you don't report directly to him."

"But why does he take such pleasure in humiliating me?"

Evelyn shrugged. "Men will be men. You should hear what they said to me when I first started working here. I just hope things are different for our daughters when they grow up."

Laurie tried to shake it off, but it bothered her the rest of the afternoon.

After such a long, trying day, Laurie felt tired and frazzled as she dragged herself to Mrs. Jedlicky's house to pick up Rosalie, hoping the sitter wouldn't be annoyed that she was a few minutes late.

When no one responded to her knock, she opened the door and walked in.

"Hello? Mrs. Jedlicky?" she called. "It's Laurie Lucas."

The house was quiet. Too quiet. She walked through the empty rooms, poking her head into each doorway she passed.

"Rosalie? Mrs. Jedlicky?" Her voice rose in pitch. "Anybody?"

Her mind scrolled through possible scenarios. Hide-and-seek? An outing? A trip to the park or the zoo? Laurie couldn't remember Mrs. Jedlicky mentioning taking the children on such an outing, and it was unlike her to do such things spontaneously. And surely in any case, if they had gone out, they'd be back well before pick-up time. Wouldn't they? Unless, of course, there'd been some kind of an accident, or—?

Willing herself not to overreact, Laurie hurried through the kitchen, where a plate of cookies and a pitcher of juice sat on the table, untouched. She bolted out the kitchen door into the backyard. The swing set and sandbox sat empty. Where could they have gone?

"Mama!"

Laurie spun around and followed her daughter's voice to the yard next door. There sat Rosalie on the next-door neighbor's back porch, nibbling a cookie as pretty as you please. Laurie ran to the fence that separated the two yards.

"Rosalie Ann Lucas, what, pray tell, are you doing over there? Where's Mrs. Jedlicky?"

"She fell," Rosalie said around a mouthful of cookie.

"What? Stay there, I'm coming over." Laurie navigated two rusty-hinged gates to reach the neighbor's yard, then climbed the back steps. "What happened?"

A tall woman with a broad Slavic face came onto the porch wiping her hands on her apron. Without preamble she said, "Are you Sally's mother?"

"You mean Rosalie," Laurie said. "Yes, I'm her mother."

"You're late. I was told all children would be picked up by five-thirty sharp."

"Sorry. Where's Mrs. Jedlicky?"

"She fell and was taken to the hospital. Broken hip, I hear. I was asked to watch the children for the rest of the day, and I agreed, of course, even though I had a great many things on my schedule today."

"Oh, I see. The poor thing."

"I notice all the other parents were able to come on time."

"Yes, I'm sorry," Laurie repeated. "Well, thank you, Mrs.—"

"Nemecek."

"Mrs. Nemecek." Laurie took Rosalie's hand, and they started down the steps. She turned back. "How long do you suppose you'll be filling in for Mrs. Jedlicky?"

The woman drew herself up. "I am not filling in for Mrs. Jedlicky after today. I was willing to help in an emergency, but good grief, daily child care is too much to ask. You'll have to make other arrangements for Sheila."

"Rosalie." Laurie tried to keep her plastic smile in place. "I see. Well ... thank you."

On the walk home, only half-listening to Rosalie's long-winded prattle about how the untimely presentation of a garter snake by one of the boys in Mrs. Jedlicky's care may have played a part in her fall, Laurie wondered where she would find another babysitter on short notice.

When they got home, she sent Rosalie into their basement apartment while she climbed the back stairs to Clara's kitchen door to ask to borrow the telephone. A split second before knocking, she remembered the woman's sleep schedule. Rather than risk, once again, incurring her neighbor's wrath, she climbed another flight of stairs to Jerry's back door. Fortunately he was home and directed her to the old-fashioned telephone hanging on the kitchen wall.

"Gee, I'd love to help," Evelyn said when Laurie reached her, "but my babysitter's roster is all filled up. She's allowing people to put their names on a waiting list, but that's all. But I'll be glad to ask her if she can recommend someone else."

"I appreciate that." As Laurie replaced the receiver on the hook, Jerry said, "I couldn't help but overhear. You need someone to watch Rosalie?"

Laurie nodded. "Mrs. Jedlicky broke her hip."

"How much time?"

"Just a couple of hours after school, plus a few more on Saturday morning. Why? Are you offering?"

Jerry blushed. "Aw, a young girl don't want to tag after an old man all day. No, I was thinking, why don't you ask Clara?"

Laurie sputtered. "Miss Janacek? You're joking with me, right?"

Jerry looked hurt. "I can totally vouch for her character. I've never met a woman with a deeper sense of responsibility. And she's a nurse, so she's used to taking care of people."

"I suppose she is," Laurie said slowly.

"She's home in the afternoons," he continued, "and you get home around five-thirty, right? She doesn't start her shift until seven. As for Saturday mornings, well, maybe me and her could take turns."

Laurie was touched. "You'd be willing to do that? Give up your Saturday mornings?"

"Sure. I'm crazy about Rosalie. We both are."

Laurie gave an unladylike snort. "I'm pretty sure Miss Janacek isn't."

"Aw, she's a softie. She's just got a different way of showing it."

"A very different way." Laurie weighed the factors in her mind. At last she said, "Well, I'm desperate. Maybe we can try it on a temporary basis. Just until Mrs. Jedlicky's back at work or I can work out some other more permanent arrangement. Will you ask Miss Janacek about it?"

Jerry held up his hands. "Oh, no. I think it's gotta come from you. But don't worry," he added. "It's like what they say about a dog who eats nothing but garlic."

"What do they say?"

"Her bark is worse than her bite. She may spend more time telling you what you've done wrong than what you've done right, but in reality, she sees the good in you too. It's just hard for her to express it."

Moments later, Laurie was still chuckling about Jerry's lame joke as she walked down the back stairs. Just as she passed the first-floor apartment, the door swung open and Miss Janacek stepped out, wastebasket in hand. The two women looked at each other.

"Hello," Laurie chirped. "Lovely day out, isn't it?" *Operation Red Rose*, she reminded herself.

The neighbor nodded, set the wastebasket on the back porch, and retreated back inside.

Laurie swallowed her irritation. And Jerry wanted her to ask this unfriendly woman to watch Rosalie after school?

But really, what choice did she have?

❧ 18 ❧

The next morning, as Clara washed up her breakfast dishes, she wondered what in the world Mrs. Lucas had been laughing about and why she'd been laughing about it up in Jerry's apartment and if he'd been laughing too. And the pictures that ran through her imagination made her forget to turn off the tap until the sensation of hot water nearly scalding her hands brought her back to her senses.

When she'd finished with the dishes, Clara lugged her laundry basket to the backyard and pinned her clean laundry to the clothesline strung between the house and the garage. She found the task soothing to her frazzled nerves. Something about the way her white, bleach-scented uniforms snapped and flapped in the breezy sunshine along-side her sturdy aprons, practical housedresses, and sensible white cotton towels lifted her spirits. She could have had her uniforms laundered at the hospital, as most of the other nurses did. But the hospital laundry never used quite enough starch for her liking.

Indeed, this morning she felt something akin to contentment. But she knew better. How could she possibly feel content when her very job was on the line? Tomorrow she'd have to sit in Olivia Kent's office and listen to whatever fallout came from the Mrs. Kremel situation, and it likely wouldn't be pretty.

To add further insult, Jerry's attention had been captured by someone other than herself. A young, pretty, vivacious someone. Someone next to whom Clara felt about as vivacious as a bowl of oatmeal.

It had been hard enough during the years when he'd been married. Clara had been friends with both him and his wife, and she'd listened as she praised him to the skies. Clara had admired how Jerry had cared for her so faithfully in her final months before she'd succumbed to illness. But ever since he'd been widowed, Clara felt she and Jerry had reached something of an understanding between them, that they would always be boon companions. Not a romantic involvement, goodness knew—they were both too old for that sort of thing. More like kindred spirits of a sort, drawn together out of mutual loneliness into a steadfast friendship. Though to be perfectly honest, not a word had been spoken to make her feel that way. She had absolutely no right to consider him hers or lay claim to his loyalty. No right at all.

A gloomy cloud descended on her heart. Clara shrugged it off. And a lucky thing Jerry *wasn't* hers, if this was the way he was going to act, his handsome silver head swiveling like a nail to a magnet in the direction of every pretty young thing that crossed his path.

A shadow fell across the snowy bed sheets as the aging Lothario emerged from the garage, toting his toolbox.

"Hello there, beautiful" he said heartily.

"Hello yourself."

Jerry lifted his face toward the sun and inhaled deeply. "Looks like you've got yourself a fine day for hanging the wash."

"Yes." Clara snapped a clothespin to the line with unnecessary force.

"Nice to have a cooler morning for once after all the heat we've been having. Fall is in the air."

"That's usually the way, come September." Clara started to lift a girdle out of the basket, then reconsidered and chose a pillowcase instead. Present company did not need to view her undergarments, which she would hang discreetly between the bed linens later, after he'd continued on his way.

She threw him a sidelong glance. "Did you come out here to give me a weather report?"

"Nope," he said. "Came out to get my tools."

"And now I see you've gotten them, so ..."

He looked puzzled. "What's eating you?"

"Nothing." She pinned the pillowcase to the line and gave it a hearty tug.

When he didn't move, she said, "Isn't there somewhere you have to be?"

"Not particularly. Why?"

Clara gestured toward the toolbox. "I thought Mrs. Lucas might be requiring your services again."

"Who? Laurie? No. I was just going to fix those loose tiles in the entryway before one of us trips and breaks our neck."

"I see."

He shuffled his feet. "Well, I'd better get to it. If you're sure you're all right."

"Perfectly fine. Never better."

"All right." He started to walk away, glancing back over his shoulder at her with a puzzled expression.

"What?"

"I don't know. You're acting weird."

Clara took a deep breath. "It's just that you've been spending a lot of time with her," Clara blurted.

"With who?"

"Laurie. Mrs. Lucas."

"When?"

"Like last Sunday. You two had a date for lunch. I saw you walking home."

"What? Oh, that. Well, I'd hardly call it a date. She and Rosalie have started attending my church. I invited them to lunch after the service, seeing as how they are newcomers and all. Seemed the neighborly thing to do."

"I see."

"She's nice." He paused. "Why don't you like her?"

"I don't *dis*like her. I just ..." Clara felt hard-pressed to come up with an answer that sounded reasonable, even to her own ears.

"Have a little compassion," Jerry urged. "She's mighty lonely and misses her husband."

"I suppose so."

He started to walk away, then turned back. "It was nice, having you at the picnic the other day. Fun, wasn't it?"

"Yes." She waited until he'd gone inside, then quickly hung her girdle amid the pillowcases. Then she picked up the empty laundry basket and headed indoors. Already the day seemed just a tiny bit brighter.

19

L
ater that day, after Clara had taken a good, long nap but before she needed to get ready for work, she kneeled at the edge of the vegetable garden, pulling rich golden carrots out of the soil and admiring their color as she heaped them in a basket. A pair of dirty saddle shoes appeared at her side, and a shadow with long braids fell across the grass. Clara looked up, lifting her arm to shield her eyes from the sun.

"Hello, Rosalie."

"Whatcha doin'?" the child asked.

"Harvesting carrots."

"Can I try one?"

"Yes, you *may* try one." Clara selected a carrot from the basket and handed it to Rosalie. "Rinse it under the spigot first."

Rosalie obeyed, then came back, munching. "Mmm. Those are really good. *May* I have another?"

Clara sat back on her heels and said, not unkindly, "If you're going to eat me out of house and home, the least you can do is help. You'll find an extra pair of gloves in the shed."

Rosalie's face lit up. Eagerly she scampered to the shed and back, her small hands swimming in adult-sized gloves of flowered canvas. Clara suppressed a smile and pointed.

"You can start at that end."

Rosalie grasped a carrot top and yanked. The top broke off in her hands.

"Not like that," Clara said. "You're pulling much too hard."

At the child's stricken expression, she softened her voice. It was just a carrot, after all.

"It's all right, there's no harm done. Now, see, you just grasp the top firmly and tug at it gently." Rosalie tried it, but the carrot didn't budge. "A little harder. Yes, that's it," she said approvingly as the stalk came smoothly from the soil, carrot still firmly attached.

"That's right. Now, if a stubborn one gives you trouble and doesn't want to come out, you just take the trowel and dig up the carrot like this, see?"

Clara demonstrated. Rosalie carefully pried up another orange root and gently laid it in the basket.

The girl grinned and reached for another stalk.

Clara returned to her own patch.

After a few minutes Rosalie said, "That was swell, what you did for Albert at the picnic. Some kids at school were talking about it. Nobody else knew what to do about his ankle, but you knew."

"Well, it was only a sprain," Clara said, a bit flustered. "And I'm always a nurse, even when I'm not wearing my uniform. I have a duty to help."

"Albert came back to school today. He had a crutch and was showing off to the other boys."

"Boys do that sort of thing."

Rosalie placed a carrot in the basket as carefully as if it were fine china. "He didn't cry when it happened. If it were me, I would have cried."

"Most people cry when they're hurt." *I should know*, Clara thought. She'd witnessed enough crying to last a lifetime. Several lifetimes.

"Boys don't."

"Sure, they do. They just do it when nobody's watching."

Rosalie shook her braids. "Albert doesn't. He makes other people cry."

"Like who?"

"He picks on the smaller kids. And the girls."

"Has he picked on you?"

"Yes. But he hasn't made me cry."

Clara sat back on her heels and looked at the girl. "That's not all right. Have you told your teacher?"

Rosalie shrugged. "Telling the teacher makes it worse. If she yells at Albert or gives him detention, then later he seeks revenge on whoever told."

"You're still right to tell a teacher, so she can go and inform the young man's parents." Clara recalled Albert's mother from the church picnic, and her spirited defense of her son. It wouldn't have surprised her if the teacher *had* tried to get through to the woman, and failed.

They pulled carrots in silence for a few minutes, Clara wracking her brain for some bit of wisdom to pass along and coming up short. As a child herself, she'd been largely ignored by other children, but never bullied by them, so she had no personal experience to share.

Rosalie broke the silence. "In *Anne of Green Gables*, there's this boy in Anne's class who calls her 'Carrots' because of her red hair."

An unexpected spark of joy jolted Clara. "*Anne of Green Gables* was one of my favorite books when I was young."

"Mine, too." Rosalie gazed at Clara with fresh admiration.

"I hadn't thought about Anne in ages," Clara mused. "Have you read any of the other books by L. M. Montgomery?"

Rosalie screwed up her face. "Ellen Montgomery?"

"L. M. For Lucy Maud."

"Oh. My grandma's name was Lucy. Her middle name wasn't Maud, though, I don't think."

"I thought your grandma's name was Josephine." Clara recalled Laurie saying they'd lived with a Josephine back in Arkansas.

"That's my other grandma. Grandma Lucy died. Mama cried for a long time."

Something constricted in Clara's chest. "I'm sorry to hear that."

"Then Daddy went to war and said we should move in with Granny Josephine while he was gone."

"I see."

"But Granny Josephine didn't like us living with her. She yelled a lot at Mama. And at me. But mostly at Mama. So Mama got a job up here. So we wouldn't be a burden, she said." Rosalie looked up from the carrots.

"I see," Clara repeated, feeling that she was perhaps learning more about the Lucases' personal business than she should.

Rosalie dropped another carrot in the basket. "Mama's job at the factory is very hush-hush."

"And so it shall stay," Clara said. "Well, anyway, if you enjoyed *Anne of Green Gables*, you should look for some other books by Lucy Maud Montgomery. She wrote many. I'm sure the public library must have several of them."

Rosalie kicked the dirt with her saddle-shod toe. "I've never been to the public library."

"You haven't?" An outrage. "Well, then you and I must go there together."

An astonished silence hung over the garden as Clara contemplated what she'd just said. Had she, Clara Janacek, actually offered to take the child on an outing? Perhaps she'd been out in the sun too long. It was softening her brain.

Rosalie grinned. "I'd like that. When will we go?"

"Oh." Clara stammered. "Uh, well, that is—"

Laurie emerged from the house, still dressed in her work clothes. She trudged over to where they were kneeling. "Rosalie, you shouldn't bother Miss Janacek when she's gardening." She turned eyes toward Clara. "I hope she's not being a nuisance."

"Not at all," Clara said, startled to realize it was true. In spite of the admittedly callous way she'd been treating them, Mrs. Lucas and her daughter were among the kindest people she'd ever met.

Laurie held out a hand to Rosalie. "Come on, sugar, let's get washed up for dinner." Weariness dripped from her voice.

Clara suddenly found herself reluctant to see them go.

"The carrots are at their peak. Will you take some?"

Laurie turned back. "Are you sure?"

Clara waved her hand over the vegetable patch. "There's far more here than I can use. Please, take plenty." She held up the basket of harvested carrots, and Laurie pulled out several stalks.

"Thank you. That solves the vegetable question for tonight."

Clara noticed the dark circles under her eyes. "Rough day at work?"

Laurie gave Clara a curious look, clearly surprised by the chattiness in her neighbor. "Oh, you know. No more than usual."

"Is that man still bothering you? The one who spilled coffee on you?"

Laurie let go of Rosalie's hand. "Run along inside and set the table, would you, sugar?" When Rosalie was gone, she said, "He's left me alone the last couple of days. Probably moved on to some other poor girl."

"Well, remember what I told you. His type is all bluff and bluster but no substance. You gals just need to stick together."

"I'll remember." She exhaled. "By the way, do you know of anyone reputable in the neighborhood who looks after children? Rosalie's after-school sitter, Mrs. Jedlicky, broke her hip and won't be able to care for Rosalie while she's recovering."

Clara thought for a moment. "I believe Mrs. O'Malley down the block does some babysitting."

"I asked her, but she's only accepting infants. Now that school's started, we'd only need someone in the late afternoons until I get home from work."

Clara frowned. "I can't think of anyone else. Of course, I'm not very plugged in to that sort of thing."

"Sure. Well, if you think of someone ..." Laurie hesitated, as if wanting to say something else, then turned to head back inside.

Before she knew what was happening, Clara heard her own voice saying, "I'll do it."

Laurie turned back. "I beg your pardon?"

"I can watch Rosalie. I'm home in the afternoons anyway."

Relief mixed with gratitude washed over Laurie's face. "You sure you wouldn't mind? I can't pay you very much."

"That doesn't matter."

"It would only be temporary, until Mrs. Jedlicky's well again."

"That would suit me just fine."

"All right, then. Thank you."

Clara nodded and turned back to her carrots. She braced herself for some feeling to descend—regret at speaking so hastily, perhaps, or annoyance at the loss of her free afternoons—but, remarkably, the only thing she felt was peace.

❧ 20 ❧

The child was due to arrive home from school at any moment. Clara paced in the kitchen. Her gaze moved from the clock to the window and back again. The minutes ticked by slowly. 3:21. 3:22. Laurie had told her that the school let out at 3:15, so the child could show up on her doorstep at any minute. Already, neighborhood children were drifting down the back alley from the direction of the school in pairs and threesomes, scuffling their feet along the sidewalk. Normally Clara paid scant attention to passersby, but today she seemed riveted to the window.

Would the girl be on time? What if she didn't show up at all? How long would Clara wait before going to the school to find her? What route did Rosalie take home from school? What if she had been kept late by the teacher? What if she got to playing with the other children and forgot she was supposed to go to Clara's? What if she were walking along the sidewalk and a car pulled over to the curb and a man leaned out the open window and said, *Excuse me, little girl, want some candy?* What if—

Clara's increasingly distressing list of what-ifs was cut short by the ringing of the doorbell, a shrill sound so seldom heard that Clara nearly jumped out of her apron. She patted her hair, walked to the front door, and opened it. The child stood on the doorstep, a beanie perched atop her blond braids, a book bag in her arms. Relief that she was safe poured through Clara, followed immediately by the consternation of realizing she'd now have to actually interact with her.

"Hello, Rosalie. I expected you to come in the back door," she said nonsensically. There was no particular reason the child should have come in the back way, only that that was how Clara had always done it when she was growing up.

A brisk September breeze whirled in through the open door. She stepped aside. "Well, come in. Wipe your feet. You may leave your things here." She gestured to a coat rack in the entryway. Dutifully, the child scuffed the soles of her saddle shoes over the bristled mat. She set her book bag on the floor and hung her cardigan on a hook. Then she stared through her round eyeglasses at Clara's spotless front room.

Feeling under inspection, Clara found herself straightening a doily that was already perfectly straight.

"Your mother suggested that you might want a snack," she said stiffly. "I used to want one after school when I was your age." She cringed at the sound of her own voice. How she'd hated those when-I-was-your-age stories from her elders when she was young. And now here she was, repeating those same words to the child. Maybe that was how all adults spoke to children when they had no idea what else to say to them.

The girl didn't smile but said, "Yes, please," in a solemn little voice. She pushed her glasses up the bridge of her nose.

"Follow me."

Rosalie trailed her through the apartment to the kitchen. "Sit there," Clara directed, a little more forcefully than she'd intended. The child sat at the kitchen table, where Clara had neatly laid out a placemat and a small china plate bearing an oatmeal cookie and a peach *kolacky*. And a napkin. She assumed the child knew how to use a napkin. She'd baked the cookies that morning, thinking that oatmeal would provide suitable nutrition for a growing girl. As for the *kolacky* ... well, Clara's kitchen almost always contained fresh *kolacky*. Jerry loved them so.

"I've just made some fresh coffee. Would you like some?"

The girl wrinkled her nose.

"No," Clara said, feeling foolish. "I suppose you'd prefer a glass of milk."

Rosalie nodded.

Clara opened the icebox, poured some milk into a glass tumbler, and set it on the table.

While Rosalie nibbled the cookie, Clara ambled around the kitchen, swiping now and then at nonexistent crumbs, refolding the dishtowel on its hook. She sifted her brain for some morsel of conversation to offer the child.

"How was your day at school?" she said finally.

"Fine." Rosalie took a swig of milk.

"That's good."

The girl gave the *kolacky* a suspicious poke with her finger.

"Don't you know what that is?"

Rosalie shook her braids.

"It's a *kolacky*. Have you had it before?"

The child shook her head again, more slowly.

"Oh. Well, it's a kind of pastry. My mother used to make them, and her mother back in the Old Country. Have you ever heard of Prague?" The girl regarded her intently but made no reaction. "Well, anyway, it's quite good. Try it."

The girl broke off a tiny bite of the pastry and looked at it thoughtfully. She put it in her mouth. Then she took another bite. And another. When she looked up at Clara, her eyes were shining.

"Ith goot," she said around a mouthful of pastry.

"Of course it's good," Clara said gruffly, even though her heart warmed. "I told you it would be."

When Rosalie finished her snack, Clara picked up the dishes, carried them to the sink, and turned on the tap. What had she and Aneta done after school, all those years ago? Clara couldn't remember. Chores, she supposed, but she couldn't imagine asking Rosalie to do chores. She ought to have had a game ready, some plan in mind for how to fill the time. But Clara didn't play games. She thought there might be a deck of cards somewhere in the apartment, but she couldn't remember where she'd last seen them.

She turned and looked at the child. The child looked back. Each waited for the other to say something.

"I suppose you have some homework to do," Clara said at last.

Rosalie nodded.

"Very well. Go and fetch your book bag. You may come back here to the table or sit in the front room. It's warmer in here."

When the child slid off her chair and left the kitchen, Clara sighed. What did one say to children? What were they capable of talking about?

Moments later Rosalie returned, wearing her cardigan. She set her book bag on the floor, pulled out a book, and opened it. Relieved not to have to make conversation, Clara dickered over whether to stay in the kitchen or sit in another room. Surely it was safe to leave the child unsupervised. Or would it seem unfriendly or negligent if she were to go to the front room to read a novel or work on her latest knitting project, a scarf for Jerry?

Undecided, she wiped off the counters that didn't need wiping. She filled a small watering can at the tap and carried it throughout the house, watering the plants. She returned to the kitchen and fussed at rearranging silverware in a drawer. Ordinarily she'd be sleeping now, resting up for work, but she'd done that earlier in anticipation of Rosalie's visit. Perhaps she should go into the front room and see what was on the radio and leave the child to do her work in peace.

Rosalie frowned at the book before her, swinging her legs back and forth under the table. She pushed her glasses up the bridge of her nose and sniffed.

Clara folded the dishtowel and was about to tiptoe out to the front room when the child suddenly looked up at her.

"What's treacle?"

"Hmm?" Clara said, caught off-guard.

"What's treacle?" Rosalie pointed at a page. "The children in the story are eating treacle on bread with their tea."

"Oh. Well, I suppose it's sort of like jam."

"Have you ever tasted it?"

"Treacle? No. Jam, yes." Clara hesitated. "There was peach jam on your *kolacky* today. Would you like another one tomorrow?"

Rosalie looked up again, her expression brighter. "Yes, please. With tea?"

Clara blinked. "You'd like tea? Instead of milk?"

The girl shrugged. "It's what the children in the story are drinking after school."

"I see." Clara thought for a moment. Was tea considered appropriate for American children nowadays? "Well, I'll ask your mother. But I don't see why not."

For the first time since she'd arrived, the child smiled. Clara felt an unexpected rush of warmth.

"It sounds—your story sounds like it's set in England."

"Yes, it is." The girl sounded impressed. "How did you know?"

"Deductive reasoning. Children drinking afternoon tea, and treacle and all." Clara pulled out the chair opposite Rosalie and sat. "What is the name of your book?"

"*The Railway Children*." Rosalie showed her the cover.

Delight surged through Clara. "Oh! I love that book!"

"You do?"

"Yes! By Edith Nesbit, as I recall."

Rosalie examined the cover. "It says E. Nesbit."

"E stands for Edith."

Rosalie stared at Clara with a look of wonder, as though she'd pronounced Edith Nesbit a close cousin.

"Are you enjoying it?" Clara ventured, a bit hesitantly lest the child say no. She couldn't bear to have that bit of her childhood smudged by a negative comment.

"I am. Mostly. But ..." Rosalie stared at the book, looking a bit doubtful.

"But what?" What could the child possibly not like about such a delightful story?

"I don't understand all the words. Like *treacle*." She sounded frustrated.

"Oh. Well, that's just a word the English use that Americans don't. Like *lorry* for truck, and *loo* for bathroom."

Rosalie giggled. "They say *loo* for bathroom?"

Clara warmed to her subject. "Yes. It comes from the French

phrase, *gardez l'eau*. French and English got a little mixed together, you see, during the Norman conquest. So the French phrase for—"

"Norman who?"

Clara stopped short. "Well ... Norman isn't a who, it's a what."

"Oh." Rosalie paused. "There's a boy in my class named Norman. His last name is Johnson."

"I see." Clara briefly considered launching an explanation of the Norman conquest and decided she didn't have the energy. "Anyway, *gardez l'eau* means *look out for the water*. In medieval times housewives used to ... well, they used to empty the chamber pots into the street."

"What's a chamber pot?"

"It's like a toilet. Before toilets were invented." Clara began to regret bringing up the subject.

Rosalie wrinkled her nose.

"They emptied their toilets into the street?" Her owlish expression reflected horror mixed with fascination.

"More or less." Clara cleared her throat. "Anyway, they'd shout '*Gardez l'eau!*' to warn the people walking by to get out of the way so they wouldn't get hit by anything ... unpleasant. Only, being English, they pronounced it more like 'gardey loo.' And that's where *loo* comes from. Supposedly." She straightened in her chair, eager to leave the subject behind. "Now, let's get back to *The Railway Children*. How far have you gotten?"

Rosalie slumped and pushed her glasses up her nose. "Not very far. It's too hard. There are too many strange words."

"Nonsense. An unfamiliar word is simply ... simply a friend you haven't met yet," she said, awkwardly appropriating one of Jerry's phrases concerning strangers. Rosalie looked unconvinced, so Clara shifted her chair so they could both see the book. "You read aloud, and I'll listen. We'll go through it together."

Rosalie began sounding out the words. The child was quite a competent reader. She just needed a bit of help here and there, which Clara was happy to provide.

Before long, a rap at the kitchen door startled them both. Through the curtain, Clara spotted Laurie on the back porch.

"Goodness. That time already?" Clara went to the door and opened it to Laurie's bright smile.

With an expression of infinite relief, Rosalie stood and ran to give her mother a hug.

Something tugged inside Clara's chest.

"Go get your things, sweetie," Laurie said. She smiled at Clara. "Thanks so much for looking after her. Did everything go all right?"

"Fine. Just fine," Clara said, surprised to find her words were true. She looked at Rosalie, hoping the child felt the same.

"What do you say to Miss Janacek?" her mother prompted.

"Thank you. Good-bye." The girl gave her glasses a push.

"Good-bye," Clara responded. "See you tomorrow."

After they'd gone down the back stairs to their own apartment, Clara looked around her kitchen, which felt oddly empty. She opened the icebox in search of supper, then decided she wasn't hungry. She went into the book room and scanned the shelves until she found a dictionary. She flipped it open and looked up *treacle*. The entry read, "a syrup made of molasses and sugar." Goodness. She'd have to correct that with Rosalie tomorrow, lest the child go around thinking that treacle was the same as jam. In fact, she decided to keep the dictionary handy and encourage Rosalie to use it for the hard words, instead of relying on Clara's off-the-cuff guesses.

She set the dictionary on the table and continued scanning the rows of books until she found her own dog-eared copy of *The Railway Children*. Pulling it out, she noticed that, naturally, it was an older edition than the one Rosalie had been reading with an antique cover illustration. Perhaps the girl would be amused by it. Clara resolved to show it to her.

She flipped open the cover, and her heart skipped a beat. There on the flyleaf, her own neatly penciled name had been scratched out and the name "Aneta Janacek" scrawled across it in large, looping letters of brilliant peacock-blue ink. *How like Aneta*, she thought with a sudden flash of annoyance, *to obliterate my name with hers*. No sooner did the thought cross her mind than it was shoved aside by a rush of guilt and self-chastisement. What kind of horrible person was she to think such uncharitable thoughts about her poor, dead sister?

Meekly she replaced *The Railway Children* on the shelf and chose an Agatha Christie mystery to savor for an hour before she had to leave for work. Enough time had passed since she'd last read it that she couldn't quite remember the ending. Even if she did remember, she enjoyed rereading favorite books. Old books, like old friends, brought comfort and familiarity.

As she headed for her favorite wingback, she thought about Rosalie. The girl seemed a bit lonely, having to navigate a new school with no siblings, a working mother, and a father off fighting the war. And there was that troubling information about the bully at school— Clara meant to ask about that. But as long as Rosalie had books to keep her company, she'd be all right.

If nothing else, Clara determined, she'd make sure that the girl had books.

✢ 21 ✢

Seated at her workbench, Laurie set her tools aside, straightened her back, and stretched her arms overhead to relieve the ache in her shoulders. Sometimes she got so absorbed in her work, making sure each miniscule screw and slender wire was assembled with faultless precision, that she forgot to change her position now and then. She paid the price later in the form of stiff, sore muscles.

The large clock on the wall told her she had an hour to go until quitting time. Throat parched, she rose and walked over to the drinking fountain, limping slightly as her leg muscles unkinked from long hours of inactivity. As she bent to take her drink, a long, low whistle sounded behind her.

"Well, wouldja look at that, fellas."

She straightened and turned to see Carl Bowman snickering with his sidekicks. He widened his eyes in mock innocence when she glared at him.

"What's the matter, Blondie? Just admiring the view."

"Oh ... take a powder, why don't you," she spat with as much force as she could muster, sorry she couldn't think of a stronger putdown.

"Somebody should shut that fellow up," she muttered to Evelyn when she got back to her workstation.

"Agreed," Evelyn said. "But what can you do? It's not like we have any authority."

"No, but someone does. And I'm fed up."

Laurie found the foreman, Ted Palmer, sitting in his glass-walled lair, hunched over a ledger. He glanced up when he saw her.

"Yeah, Lucas?"

"I don't know if you're aware, Mr. Palmer, but Carl Bowman and his friends are trying to intimidate me. And not only me, but many of the women in our section."

The wooden office chair squeaked as Mr. Palmer leaned back. "Oh, yeah? How so?"

"They make off-color jokes. Sometimes we find crude drawings posted on our lockers or on our workbench."

Mr. Palmer's eyes narrowed. "You seen him do it?"

"The jokes, yes. The pictures, no, but I'm sure it's him. Who else would do such a thing?"

He squinted at her. "I don't think you really want me to intervene."

"Why not?"

"Come on, Lucas. Boys have been teasing girls since elementary school. Usually means they like 'em. You should be flattered."

She stiffened. "It's insulting. That's what it is."

"Sounds like it's a problem between you and him. Work it out."

"But it's not only me," she protested. "Other women have complained of being picked on, too."

"Can't you see Carl is just teasing you? Men will be men. Look, Lucas. This ain't a ladies' tearoom. If you ladies are gonna work in a factory, you gotta learn to stick up for yourself. Believe me, plenty of fellows get razzed, too, when they're new on the job."

Laurie stood aghast. "And you're saying that's all right?"

"I'm saying you have to toughen up." Mr. Palmer shrugged. "The sooner you show you're a good sport, the sooner they'll let up."

"Or move on to another victim," she muttered.

He rubbed his eyes. "You're a good worker, Lucas. I'd be sorry to see you go. But if you can't hack it—"

"If *I* can't hack it?" she sputtered.

"You can always give your notice," Mr. Palmer finished calmly.

Laurie sealed her mouth, even though inwardly she fumed. When she got back to the workbench, Evelyn lifted an eyebrow in her direction, but she didn't want to talk about it.

As the weeks passed, Clara and Rosalie's after-school visits fell into something of a routine. The girl would show up at Clara's door after school, eat a snack, and then do her homework until her mother arrived to pick her up.

One afternoon in October, Clara responded as usual to a quiet knock at the back door. She opened it, and there stood the child.

"You know, Rosalie," Clara said. "You've been coming here for some weeks now. You might as well come right in without bothering to knock. This is your home, too, in the afternoons."

Rosalie said nothing, and pushed on her glasses. Clara stepped aside.

"Well, come on in. Your snack is waiting for you."

As usual, the child ate her *kolacky* and drank her milk (after deciding, upon an experimental taste, that the English children could keep the tea on their side of the pond). When she'd finished, she drew her hand across her mouth. Clara handed her a napkin from the rack on the table.

"Shall I do my schoolwork now?"

"If you have some." Clara picked up the dishes and put them in the sink.

The girl pulled a book out of her book bag.

"What are you reading now?"

"*Black Beauty.*"

"Oh, I read that as a girl," Clara said.

Rosalie nodded politely and pushed her glasses up.

The following Friday, Clara made good on her promise to introduce Rosalie to the public library. They each returned with armloads of books.

"Why don't we sit in the front room?" she said. "The chairs are more comfortable in there, and I've turned up the radiator."

They snuggled into chairs set companionably on either side of the radiator, which hissed and clanked in a reassuring way.

After that, their reading time became a ritual. Sometimes Clara read stories aloud. Sometimes they read in silence, each in her own chair. And nearly every Friday, they visited the public library to return their books and borrow new ones.

By late October, Clara was joining the child in her snack and asking about her day at school. She was even starting to recognize some of the names of her classmates. To her surprise, she actually started to miss Rosalie on weekends when they didn't get to visit. That's how Clara came to think of their time together—as visits more than babysitting stints. She enjoyed Rosalie's company as much as, or perhaps more than, most adults'.

So when the day came that Mrs. Lucas announced that Mrs. Jedlicky had made a full recovery and was ready to care for Rosalie again, Clara begged to keep their current arrangement a little longer.

"At least until Christmas," she suggested, and Mrs. Lucas agreed.

Clara didn't mention how the hours spent with the girl took her mind off the stress of working at the hospital. No announcement had yet been made about the head-nurse position, and even though Clara was reasonably sure she had it in the bag, it made her antsy not to know for sure. In addition, when the promotion did come through, it meant her working schedule would change and she would no longer be able to care for Rosalie after school. Then there'd be no choice but to send her back to Mrs. Jedlicky's. But in the meantime, Clara aimed to make the most of their time together.

23

Late one Friday afternoon in November, Carl stopped by Laurie's worktable.

"Hey, Lucas," he said, grinning. She braced herself for a rude remark or a vulgar joke, but he only said, "Palmer told me to tell you to go to up to the die works and pick up some parts. Here's a list." He handed her a piece of paper with numbers scribbled on it.

"Why didn't he ask me himself?" Laurie couldn't help the suspicion that laced her voice. While it was nothing unusual for Mr. Palmer to send her or one of the other ladies on errands to other parts of the building, he didn't usually ask Carl to pass his messages along. And she didn't trust Carl.

"He's got busy on a call. Some bigwig from over at the Jersey plant."

Laurie glanced through the glass wall of the foreman's office. Sure enough, he looked embroiled in a telephone conversation, and not a pleasant one, judging by the way he was pacing to and fro as far as the cord would allow.

"All right," she sighed. "Where's the die works department located?"

She followed Carl's instructions to a remote part of the plant.

Funny, nobody seemed to be working there. Perhaps she'd made a wrong turn.

She found herself at the end of a long, dim corridor. Here and there, shafts of weak light broke through an open door or frosted glass transom. She felt around on the wall for a light switch but found none.

Most of the enormous plant bustled with workers and machinery running at peak capacity to supply the war effort, but this section was apparently unused, even forgotten, as silent as an empty church. Perhaps, she reasoned, this was some kind of a shortcut, known only to those familiar with the layout of the plant. She would have asked for directions, had there been anyone to ask, but there was no one. The hallway looked to have once been a suite of offices. Some of the rooms contained old, shabby wooden furniture, but no papers or other signs of recent habitation.

Goosebumps crept up her arms. The paper in her hand grew damp in her clammy palm. But she'd look very foolish if she returned without the requested parts. She determined not to let her fears get the better of her and breathed a quick prayer for courage as she continued down the musty corridor. Trusting she'd find the die works at the far end, she soldiered on, her footsteps creaking on the dusty wooden floorboards.

A sudden loud *whoosh* overhead stopped her dead in her tracks, heart thumping. But further inspection showed it was only the sound of water rushing through a pipe. She released a long, slow breath.

Behind her, a floorboard creaked.

She felt as if she were being watched, but when she turned around, no one was there. She gulped.

"Hello? Is someone there?" Her voice sounded shrill and tinny in the high-ceilinged space. Hearing only silence, she chastened herself. *Old buildings creak, you goose. Stop being such a scaredy-cat.*

She took a few more steps. Then she picked up the pace and hurried down the corridor, eager to reach the safe harbor of the die works department. At last she reached the closed door at the end of the hallway, certain it led to the Promised Land, or at least to a different corridor, one well lit and populated by other human beings.

She grasped the knob and yanked open the door. More darkness.

Disappointed, she stood still a moment as her eyes adjusted. Then she let out an involuntary shriek. There, strapped to an old office chair, was a skeleton like the kind used in medical schools. Probably some decoration left over from Halloween.

From far down the corridor came an uproar of men's laughter.

A prank. It had only been a prank.

How dare they? Mustering her dignity, she turned and walked calmly back to where she'd started, seething but not willing to give Carl and the other men the satisfaction of seeing they'd rattled her with their stupid joke.

"Die works. Get it? *Die* works!" Carl crowed, laughing at his own razor-sharp wit.

"Very funny, Bowman," she said coldly. "You're in my way."

The other men parted before her, still chuckling among themselves.

"I don't know about you boys," she said as she passed, "but I have a job to do." She strode back to her work area with her coworkers straggling behind.

"Aw, Laurie, don't be sore," one of them said, his voice kind. "We didn't mean no harm."

"We was just joshing you," said another. "You gotta admit, it was pretty funny."

She'd admit no such thing. And Carl Bowman wouldn't give it up, even after the other men had gone ahead and returned to their work.

"Who could it have been?" he said, his voice exaggeratedly deep and ominous, like a radio announcer sharing a tragic news broadcast. "Ladies and gentlemen, a skeleton was found in the factory today. Some poor soul from the *Eastland*, maybe."

Laurie refused to look at him. She entered the workroom with as much dignity as she could rustle up. The next thing she knew, Evelyn was standing beside her, touching her elbow.

"Never mind him," she murmured in Laurie's ear.

Several other women had joined them, forming a protective semicircle around her. They didn't say anything to Carl, didn't egg him on. They simply stared at him.

No longer surrounded by his cronies, he seemed to shrink. "Stupid dames," he muttered, stomping off.

"Thanks," Laurie breathed as they made their way back to the workstation.

"I had a feeling Bowman was up to no good, especially since he and his two henchmen disappeared at the same time you did," Evelyn said. "I went to check on you, but I had no idea where you'd gone."

"Thanks anyway. I'm glad you tried."

Before they could resume their places at the workbench, the whistle blew. Quitting time.

As they clocked out and then walked together to Evelyn's streetcar stop, Laurie related the whole story to her friend. "I don't want to be a poor sport, but I have to admit, it troubles me that he'd put that much effort into carrying out a prank. Does he dislike me that much?"

"He doesn't dislike you. More likely the opposite," Evelyn said. "His pride was hurt when you refused to go out with him, which was absolutely the right thing to do. But now he wants to even the score. That's my theory, anyway."

It was a sound theory, but Laurie didn't know what she could do about it. Carl's injured feelings weren't her problem. "And where was Mr. Palmer while all this mischief was going on?" she snapped. "Why wasn't he harping at Carl and the others to stick to their work, the way he's always harping at us?"

"Dunno." Evelyn shrugged. "Palmer's been off somewhere else most of the afternoon."

"What's the *Eastland*?" Laurie asked suddenly.

Evelyn glanced at her, brows raised. "What?"

"The *Eastland*. When Bowman was teasing me about the skeleton, he said something about the *Eastland*. What did he mean?"

"A dark blot on the company's past." Evelyn squinted in the direction of the streetcar as it rattled around the corner.

"What do you mean?" Laurie pressed.

"A terrible accident, a long time ago. Lots of people died." Evelyn took a step forward as the streetcar screeched to a stop. "My ride's here. See you Monday."

"That's ... that's horrible," Laurie stuttered, unwilling to end the conversation. "I'm surprised I haven't heard of it already."

Evelyn waited while several other people boarded the vehicle. "As I said, it happened a long time ago. Thirty years. Nobody likes to think about it. Or talk about it."

"But if it really happened, then—"

"Of course it really happened." Evelyn grasped the railing and swung herself aboard. "Ask anybody. Ask your neighbor lady, or your landlord. You said they've been living in Cicero a long time. Ask them."

"But—"

"Please, Laurie, it's a gruesome story. Let it go." The doors shut and the streetcar ambled down the street, leaving Laurie standing on the curb.

On the walk home, her thoughts kept returning to Evelyn's words. An accident. What on earth had gone wrong that day? A fire? An explosion in the factory? Whatever it was, it seemed to upset her friend. She'd have to ask someone else.

But maybe she didn't really want to know.

24

On the day before Thanksgiving, Rosalie seemed restless, picking up her book and putting it down. Clara glanced up from her own book.

"What's the matter? Don't you like what you're reading?"

"It's boring," Rosalie said.

"Life is too short to read boring books." Clara gestured to the bookcase. "Go and see if you can find something you like better."

"I have to read it for school." Nevertheless, Rosalie set the book aside and wandered over to Clara's bookcase and browsed the shelves. She ran across Clara's copy of *The Railway Children*. She examined the old-fashioned cover illustration and leafed through the pages, then pointed to the flyleaf, where the name *Clara Janacek* had been written over and cancelled out by Aneta's brilliant signature.

"Who did that?" she demanded.

From her seat across the room, Clara squinted at the page Rosalie was holding up. "My sister."

"She crossed your name out. Why would she do such a thing?"

Clara closed her own book over her thumb to hold her place. "Well, as the older sister, I had the book first, and she would have received it as a hand-me-down. I suppose she was staking her claim."

Rosalie regarded the page. "I didn't know you had a sister."

"I did."

"Where is she now?"

"She died a long time ago."

Rosalie's head tilted to the side. She gave her glasses a push. "Her name was Aneta?"

"Yes. Only it's pronounced *Ann-etta*, not *Ann*-ita."

"It looks more like Anita."

"It's the Czech spelling."

Rosalie traced the name with her finger. "She had nice handwriting. What was she like? Ann-*ett*-aah."

Clara thought. "Well, let's see ... she was blond, like you, and very pretty." She regarded the girl. "Like you," she added.

Rosalie's face pinked, but she looked pleased. "Did she like to read?"

"Not as much as I did."

"Did she like dolls?"

"We both liked dolls."

"How did she die?"

"In an accident. She drowned." Suddenly thinking it would be wise to redirect the child's morbid line of questioning, Clara pointed to Rosalie's abandoned book. "Now get to reading or you'll fall behind."

Rosalie slid *The Railway Children* back into its spot on the shelf and returned to her chair. Dutifully she picked up her own book, but after a short while, she set it down and stretched her thin arms over her head. "Tell me about when you were my age."

Startled, Clara groped for words. "Oh. Well, I'm sure it wasn't that different from childhood now. Except we didn't have as many cars. Or the radio. Or electric refrigerators." It occurred to Clara that her childhood must seem exotic indeed to a modern child. She lifted a bookmark from the table, slid it between the pages of her own book, and set it aside. "What would you like to know?"

Rosalie shrugged. "Everything. Where did you live?"

"I grew up just a few blocks away from here, in a white house with a green door and a wide front porch."

"With your family?"

"Of course. My mother and father and Aneta."

"Did you like it there?"

Surprised at the question, Clara thought for a moment, then said, "Yes. Most of the time, while I was growing up." Not so much in adulthood. But the child didn't need to know all that.

Rosalie looked as if she were going to ask another question, but Clara glanced at the clock on the mantel. "Goodness! You'd better gather up your things," she said, standing. "Your mother will be here any minute."

"Aw."

"Tomorrow is another day. We'll talk then."

"Promise?"

Clara nodded, warmed by the child's interest in her story. But several minutes later, as she closed the kitchen door behind mother and daughter, she had second thoughts.

She fixed herself a simple supper of a grilled cheese sandwich and coffee, then dressed for work. On the streetcar, she told herself that Rosalie's interest in those long-ago days was just a passing fancy, which she'd forget about by tomorrow. But now that the door to the past had been cracked open, Clara could think of little else. She tried to think of other things, but Rosalie's questions nagged at her mind. Even on the streetcar, she couldn't keep her mind from spooling out the memories she'd tried for so many years to forget.

25

June 1915

"Aneta, you eat so fast, you make yourself sick," Mama scolded in her thick Eastern European accent. "Slow down."

"I've got to hurry, Mama," my sister said. "The gang will be here any minute. There's a new play opening at the Colonial tonight, and we don't want to be late."

"Your friends will wait," Papa said mildly. "Now, eat your soup."

Aneta's pretty mouth turned down at the corners, and she dramatically pushed her bowl away. "It's too hot out for all this heavy food, anyway. Who eats liver dumpling soup and roast pork in the middle of June? At Marguerite's house, they're having cold shrimp salad and iced tea."

My sister and I didn't see eye-to-eye on very many things, but on the matter of the menu, I had to agree. Normally a hearty eater, I felt my appetite wither in the heat and could only pick at the food on my plate.

Mama clucked her tongue. "Cold salad no stick to your ribs. You'll be hungry again in an hour."

"You girls will eat what is placed before you," Papa said, gesturing toward Aneta's bowl as if she were seven instead of seventeen. With a great show of reluctance, she sighed and picked up her spoon.

"Chilled food is the way *proper* Americans eat when it's this hot outside."

Aneta had a knack for turning virtually any topic into a lesson for our parents on the American style of doing things. The stubborn way they clung to their old-country ways embarrassed her deeply. I didn't mind it as much, except when it came to some of my mother's silly superstitions, another old-country leftover. My training was in science. I had no patience for superstition, but a streak of mischief inspired me to make a joke of it now, just to annoy my sister.

"You're not going to the *Colonial*, are you?" I stage-whispered to Aneta, with a sidelong glance at Mama to make sure she heard. "Didn't the Colonial used to be the *Iroquois*? Where that terrible fire happened years ago and all those people *died?*"

Mama's hand flew to her mouth. "Fire? There was a fire in the theater? You no go, Aneta. Is bad luck."

My sister scowled at me. "Thanks a lot," she muttered. To Mama she said, "It'll be fine. The fire was a very long time ago, and they've completely rebuilt the theater with all kinds of safety equipment."

I tried to stifle my laughter, but it burst out as a snort.

With her forehead still furrowed, Mama glanced at me and realized she was being teased. She jabbed a finger toward my plate.

"Eat."

I ate.

"Papa," Aneta said, idly stirring her soup, "have you heard anything more about the company picnic? A lot of my friends are going."

Papa nodded. "The picnic has been a big topic of conversation at the plant."

"Not to mention around the Janacek dinner table," I muttered. Aneta had been bringing it up at least once a day.

"The Hawthorne Club has been pushing ticket sales at the plant," Papa said.

I turned to him. "So did you buy some? Are we going? If so, I'll ask for the day off."

He shook his head. "You young people might enjoy it, maybe, but I don't think Mama and I will go. It will be very crowded. Besides, I think that as long as the plant will be closed, it might be a good weekend to go see Mama's sister in Wisconsin." He buttered a thick piece of rye bread. "Speaking of Minnie, Anna, have you had more news?"

"I receive letter from her today. She is not good." Mama frowned and patted her chest. "Her lungs. The doctors move her to hospital near Milwaukee. Wisconsin State ... something."

"Wisconsin State Sanatorium, probably." I reached over and put my hand on Mama's. "I'm sorry. I didn't realize Aunt Minnie was that sick. But the sanatorium has a good reputation. She'll be well cared for there."

Mama smiled and squeezed my hand. "You are nurse, you would know."

"I'm just barely a nurse. But trust me, I've heard very good things about Wisconsin San."

"Is good." Mama stood and busied herself clearing dishes from the table.

"Don't you worry, Anna," Papa said. "We go visit." He turned to Aneta. "But there's no reason you girls can't go to the big picnic. You want I should buy tickets for you?"

Aneta shook her head. "Not yet. I'm pretty sure somebody is going to invite me."

Papa raised a bushy eyebrow. "Oh? And who is that?"

Aneta blushed. "Just somebody."

"Well, you'd better bring this 'somebody' by to meet your parents before you go off to a picnic with him."

"Oh, Papa." Aneta glanced toward the ceiling and exhaled sharply. "You're so old-fashioned."

"What about you, Clara? Shall I buy you a ticket?"

"I don't think so," I said. "I'm with Mama. Too many people for my taste. Besides, I'll probably have to work."

The doorbell rang, and Aneta shot to her feet. "That'll be Marguerite and Lil."

"What about the dishes?" I protested.

Aneta dimpled at me. "Be a dear and take my turn? I'll take your turn tomorrow night. Promise."

"Sure." I stood and gathered dishes, knowing I'd be doing the same thing the following night, but there was no use arguing. Aneta had a busy, active social life and I, well, didn't.

While washing the dishes, Mama asked about my day at the hospital.

"It was all right." I dried a plate with a dishcloth and set it in the cabinet. "A lot of routine surgeries and things lately. Not very exciting. I'm hoping maybe they'll move me to another ward soon."

"Maybe they put you with the children next."

I took a wet glass from her hand and polished it with the towel. "I don't know, Mama. It must cause a lot of wear and tear on the heart, working with sick children. And what if they don't get better? Losing a child must be the worst thing in the world."

"You have tender heart. You will be good mother." Mama patted my shoulder. "I know."

"I don't think I'll marry, Mama. Aneta gets all the beaux. The boys don't look at me twice."

"You no need many, how you say, beau. It only take one." Mama patted my hand. "You could make a little more effort, Clara. There are nice boys at hospital, no?"

"They keep us too busy to socialize." Knowing Mama would keep up this line of questioning, I changed the subject. The truth was, I would have welcomed some male attention, had it come my way. But it hadn't, at least not yet, and I felt I needed to be content with that.

I spent the evening curled up on the overstuffed sofa in the front room, deeply immersed in *Ruggles of Red Gap*, with recordings of Debussy and Ravel popping and hissing on the Victrola. My parents had already gone upstairs to bed by the time Aneta and her friends clattered noisily onto the porch after their outing to the theater. Through the open window I could hear that, sometime during the evening, several young men had been added to the group—a typical occurrence where my pretty sister was concerned. Her energetic chatter floated through the screens.

"Edward McAuley, if you take me to another play by that dreary

Norwegian, I swear I'll never speak to you again." Her words seemed harsh, but her tone was laughing, and I could picture her swatting playfully at a good-looking, red-haired youth, the latest in a long string of gentlemen callers. I tried to concentrate on my book.

"Yeah. Next time, make it a musical, huh?" droned a nasal voice I recognized as belonging to Lil Drummond. "Or let's skip the pictures altogether and go to Wrigley Field."

"A girl who likes baseball?" said a male voice. "Be still my heart!"

Aneta spoke up. "I'll have you know that Lil here is a pitcher for the Western Electric ladies' softball team."

"The Bloomer Girls," Lil added.

"Well, you can pitch my heart anytime," said the young man.

I rolled my eyes, stuck a bookmark in my novel, and was about to switch off the Victrola when I noticed Mama peeking around the corner, wrapped in her bathrobe, her long braid trailing over one shoulder. She was gesturing wildly in my direction.

"What is it?"

She motioned toward the porch. "Take them some refreshments."

"What? Now?"

"Well, *I* no go out there looking like this!" she hissed. She had a point. I went into the kitchen. She pulled open the wooden door of the icebox. "You bring them some of this nice strawberry ice cream that Papa churned this afternoon."

"Oh, for Pete's sake," I said but found myself dutifully balancing a tray loaded with pink ice cream in glass dishes. Papa and Mama encouraged us to bring our friends home, no matter how late, as they preferred that we be safe under their roof and not "running around the neighborhood until all hours," as Papa put it. This, of course, was more of an issue with Aneta than with me.

I elbowed open the screen door and stepped out onto the porch. As usual, Aneta was the center of attention, holding court while her friends buzzed around her like fireflies, especially the young men. For one brief moment, they buzzed around me—for as long as it took to snatch dishes of ice cream from the tray in my hands.

"Clara, you know Marguerite and Lil, of course," Aneta said. "And you've met Mr. Edward McAuley, and this is Mr. Martin Husker and

Mr. Leon Tabat. And that's Mr. Jaroslav Stepnicka over there. Everyone, this is my sister, Clara."

The men murmured their hellos. Amid the sound of clanking spoons and exclamations over the ice cream, I noticed the fellow called Jaroslav looking at me. The porch light shone on his dark, brilliantined hair, and though his face was in shadow, I sensed his eyes were dark as well. *The Arab* was my first thought, having recently seen the swashbuckling movie, and immediately I felt embarrassed at the comparison to dashing film star Edgar Selwin, though I'd said nothing out loud. He accepted a dish of ice cream from Lil but kept his eyes on me, averting his gaze only when he noticed me looking back.

Flustered, I set the tray on a wicker table and returned inside to the safe haven of my sofa and my book. But I could no longer concentrate, keenly aware of the mysterious dark-eyed man sitting just on the other side of the windowsill from me, so close I could touch him if the screen weren't in the way. Never before had I paid attention to any of Aneta's friends, and I didn't know why I did so now. I reached over and restarted the Victrola, turning up the volume as if to drown out the sound of my own thoughts.

I didn't know how much time had passed when the screen door slapped open. I looked up to see the man I'd been trying to forget about walk in carrying the tray, spoons rattling in the empty glass dishes.

"Where do you want I should put this?" he said politely.

I leaped up from the sofa. "Here, you don't need to do that," I said. "I'll take it into the kitchen."

"It's no trouble," he said. "Just show me where."

I led him into the kitchen, and he set the tray on the drain board.

"Thank you," I said, impressed by his thoughtfulness. We walked back to the front room, and I expected him to continue back out onto the porch, but instead he stopped near the Victrola.

"Nice music," he said. "I was listening through the window." He stood, looking unsure, and I noticed how his long arms protruded from his too-short shirtsleeves. "It's Debussy. Am I right?"

"Why, yes," I said, surprised. Aneta's crowd's taste in music tended toward ragtime and the occasional sentimental waltz, so the fact that he recognized one of my favorite classical pieces impressed me. He even pronounced the name correctly.

He nodded. "I like it."

"So do I." Was he hinting that he'd like to stay inside and listen? I was so hopeless at picking up on hints.

His dark eyes met mine. I had to resist a sudden bizarre urge to reach up and touch his cheek. Horrified at myself, abruptly I turned away.

"Mr. ... Stepnicka, is it?"

"Jaroslav. Please." He suddenly whisked off his hat, as if he'd forgotten he was wearing it indoors. "And I hope you'll let me call you Clara."

"Yes."

I turned back. We looked at each other awkwardly for a moment. Then I remembered my manners. "Won't you sit down?"

We perched at opposite ends of the overstuffed sofa. His hands toyed with the brim of his hat, turning it over and over like a wheel.

"Your sister tells me you're a nurse."

"Yes, at Memorial Hospital."

"You must be a very smart girl. Er, woman. Lady."

I found his verbal stumbling endearing. Why, he felt as nervous as I did! My insides relaxed a little.

"I don't know about that," I said, hoping the subdued lighting hid my blush. "I always worked hard in school."

He gave his hat a spin. "I left school after eighth grade to help support the family."

"Oh." Leaving school that early wasn't uncommon for a working man. "What do you do?"

"I'm a welder over at the Western." He jerked his head in the general direction of the factory.

"Perhaps you know our father, Emil Janacek. He works there, too."

"No." He paused, then added, "It's a big place."

"Yes, it is."

The room fell silent except for the scratchy recording and the muted chatter of Aneta and her friends outside.

Suddenly, my sister burst through the screen door. "I can't take this anymore," she said, hurrying to the Victrola and shuffling through the nearby stack of recordings. "I'm going to put on something *lively*, something we can dance to."

She selected the Peerless Quartet. Soon the strains of *Let Me Call You Sweetheart* wafted through the still air, accompanied by much giggling and shuffling from the porch as the crowd paired off to dance.

Jaroslav looked at me with uncertainty. "Would you care to come out and dance?"

My pulse pounded. "I'm afraid I have two left feet."

Relief washed over his face. "So do I."

"We could just listen. It seems that you enjoy music."

"Oh, yes. My folks played lots of music in the house. Piano, violin ..." He twirled his hat. "I-I don't have a Victrola at home, like you do. But sometimes I go to the symphony."

I gasped. "The symphony? The *Chicago* Symphony?"

"Yes." He sat forward eagerly. "Would ... would you like to go with me sometime?" His dark eyes widened, as if the words had flown straight out of his mouth before he could stop them.

"Would I ever!" I blurted before remembering that a lady tempers her enthusiasm.

"How about Saturday night?"

"S-Saturday?" I found myself ever more intrigued by this man.

"It's the last concert of the season," he explained, sounding almost apologetic. "If we miss it, we'll have to wait until the new season begins in the fall."

I found myself at a loss for words.

In the silence his face colored, and he gripped his hat. "Maybe you are too busy ..."

"Oh, no. I mean yes," I collected my wits. "Of course. Yes, I'd love to go."

"Wonderful." He had a very appealing smile. "I will call for you at seven o'clock on Saturday night."

"Aneta! Clara!" Papa's deep voice boomed from the top of the staircase. "Turn off that racket. You'll wake the neighbors."

I stopped grinning at Jaroslav long enough to lift the needle from the record and silence the Victrola. He and I joined the others on the porch as the party broke up amid much laughter and noisy promises to see each other soon.

"Where did you disappear to?" Edward said, bumping into Jaroslav with his shoulder.

Jaroslav didn't reply but bowed to me slightly and tipped his hat.

"Saturday," he said.

"Saturday," I replied, as though it were a secret code word between us.

My heart hammered as I watched him walk with the others toward a pair of jalopies parked at the curb.

For the first time in my life, I had a real date.

As the sound of chugging motors faded in the distance, Aneta and I went upstairs to our shared room and got ready for bed. Aneta chattered on about the evening's events, but my mind was fixed on a pair of dark eyes and a bowler hat.

"Are you listening to me?" Aneta's voice pierced my reverie.

"Sorry. What?"

"I *said*, look at the beautiful brooch Edward gave me. Isn't it lovely?"

Proudly she held forth a little black box, within which nestled a piece of jewelry. *Beautiful brooch* seemed a bit of a stretch for the painted tin bauble that looked as if it had been purchased at the five-and-dime. Nonetheless, it was a sweet gesture on Edward's part.

"That was nice of him. Did he know roses are your favorite flower?"

"I may have mentioned it once or twice," she said coyly.

If she was happy, I was happy. Aneta certainly seemed smitten with the young man. He was a couple of years older than she was, already out of school and working at the Western.

Aneta snapped the box shut and slipped it into her jewelry box amid a jumbled heap of hair ribbons, tangled necklaces, and school attendance badges. Then she opened her dresser drawer, in a similar state of disarray, and pulled out a nightgown.

"I don't know why you had to hide inside the house all evening," she chided as she slipped the faded, flower-sprigged garment over her head. "Why can't you be more outgoing, Clara? Always with your nose stuck in a book. You'll never catch a husband that way."

"Who says I'm trying to catch a husband?"

She looked at me and sighed. "If you aren't even trying, then you really are hopeless. You'll end up *alone*." She emphasized the word as if it were a fatal disease.

"Alone doesn't sound so bad. It beats sharing a bedroom with a bossy sister." I smiled at her to take the sting out of my words, but I needn't have bothered. Criticism slid off Aneta like water off a duck's back. "Besides, work takes up all my time. I'm around people the whole day long, sometimes all night, too, and when I have a little spare time, I just like to read and relax. Is that so terrible?"

She yawned. "I noticed you were talking to that Jaroslav fellow. What were you talking about?"

"Music, mostly."

Aneta rolled her eyes in apparent disgust. "Well, *that* should set his heart on fire. Really, Clara, could you be any more boring?"

"I wasn't trying to set anything on fire. I'd never even met the man before."

"Me neither, until tonight." She yanked the coverlet down to the end of the bed. I grabbed it and folded it. "Edward brought him. He recently joined Edward's work team at the Western." She wrinkled her nose. "He seems like a cold fish to me. Sort of stand-offish."

Mentally I filled in the blanks. *You mean he didn't instantly fall for your charms like every other boy since the first grade.*

"I don't know," I said, trying to sound noncommittal. "I thought he seemed nice."

"I suppose. But I hope he doesn't keep hanging around all the time. He doesn't even dance." She sat on the edge of the bed and kicked off her house slippers. "You're inexperienced. First your life was consumed with nursing school. Then you studied around the clock until you took your boards."

"And passed them," I added.

"Of course you did. Then you got hired by Memorial and started working grueling hours."

I shrugged. "That's what it takes to be a nurse."

Aneta switched off the bedside lamp. "Well, let's hope you meet some nice doctor at that hospital. Because if you're going to be working, working, working day and night, then that'll be your only chance." In the glow from the streetlamp through the window, I saw the white of her smile.

"I hope he invites me to the company picnic. Lil told me more about it tonight. Did you know it's in Michigan City, and they've chartered boats to cross the lake."

"Same as last year," I reminded her. "And we didn't get to go then, either, because of Mama's fear of boats."

"Well, she won't stop me this year," Aneta said. "I can't wait to get on that boat and sail all the way to Michigan City. With Edward." She snuggled down under the sheet. "I wouldn't be at all surprised if he popped the question, right there on the deck of the steamship. Wouldn't that be romantic? Like in the movies."

I turned toward her and rested my head on my arm. "It sure would. But it's an excursion boat, not an oceangoing vessel. I don't imagine you'll be cruising aboard the likes of the *Aquitania* just to get across Lake Michigan."

I bit my lip. I'd almost slipped and said *Lusitania*, the sister Cunard ship that had been destroyed by a German torpedo off the coast of Ireland only a few weeks earlier. And I didn't even want to think about *Titanic*, with its tremendous loss of life, which had only happened three years earlier and remained fresh in people's minds. Well, in most people's minds. Not my sister's, apparently.

"If he asks you and you accept, Mama will hit the roof," I added.

"Fiddlesticks. Mama likes Edward."

"Edward's not the problem. Your crossing Lake Michigan on a boat is," I replied, to which Aneta only huffed. "In any case, the end of July's a long way off. You have a few weeks to think about it."

Our mother, who'd endured a rough crossing from Prague when she'd immigrated to the United States as a teenager, now wouldn't step onto a boat for love nor money. I doubted that she would want Aneta to go on the boat. But if Papa gave his permission, she'd acquiesce. My parents always had trouble setting firm limits where Aneta was concerned. They didn't tend to be so easily charmed in my case, even though I seldom gave them reason to pull rank. There was only so much trouble an introspective, bookish daughter with a dearth of suitors could get into.

Except now I had a suitor—maybe. I considered telling Aneta that Jaroslav had invited me to a concert at Orchestra Hall. Then I thought the better of it. She'd only laugh and call it dull, and while I hadn't yet sorted out my feelings about the dark-eyed young man, I knew they weren't something to be laughed at. And they were anything but dull.

❦ 26 ❧

December 1944

I n spite of her determination to keep her stories to herself, by the time the school year paused for Christmas vacation, Clara had ended up telling Rosalie, bit by bit, the whole story of her childhood, her school years, her family, even her short-lived goldfish, and finally how she met Jaroslav. Goodness, she hadn't meant to blather on about her youth, least of all about her love life, but she'd gotten swept up in the tide of memories. It had been so long since she'd discussed the olden days with anyone. Her parents had refused to discuss the past. And Rosalie seemed quite fascinated. Still, Clara reasoned to herself, it wouldn't do either of them any good to dredge up too many memories.

The word "dredge" stopped her cold. The ugly word suddenly brought to her unwilling mind a snippet of memory. Helmeted divers plunging again and again into the murky river, bringing up body after body, some showing signs of life, but many—far too many—limp and lifeless in their sodden lace dresses and waterlogged Sunday suit jackets. No, Clara decided firmly. She wouldn't revisit those memories. Certainly not with a nine-year-old child. Not even with herself.

Christmas passed quietly, as it always did for Clara. Laurie and Rosalie traveled back to Arkansas for a week to spend the holidays with Laurie's mother-in-law. A few months earlier, Clara would have jumped at the chance to have been free of the Lucas duo for an entire week. Now the building just felt silent and empty with only herself and Jerry rattling around.

One thing out of the ordinary was that Clara went to church with Jerry on Christmas Eve. In past years, he'd always asked and she'd always refused. But for some reason, this year felt different. Maybe some of Rosalie's Sunday-school chatter was rubbing off on her.

"I suppose it won't kill me," was her ungracious response when Jerry invited her. But in truth, she didn't relish the idea of being alone on a night meant for families. To her surprise, she found in the festive yet reverent atmosphere of the church a comfort she hadn't felt in years, almost as if she were being inexplicably drawn toward something. The sensation made her feel unsettled, excited, and wistful all at once, and she wished she knew what caused it. It was just the sentimentality of the old familiar carols learned in grammar school, she decided, and the scent of pine boughs. Even though her family had not been Christ-followers, they'd celebrated Christmas in secular ways, with trees and holly sprigs and feasting. At least, they'd done these things as long as Aneta was still alive. After that, Christmas, along with every other holiday, was no longer observed in the Janacek household.

Clara and Jerry had gone to the early service, which ended in plenty of time for her to begin her shift at the hospital. As she always did, she'd volunteered to work Christmas Eve so others could spend that evening and the following morning with their families.

"Come down for lunch tomorrow?" she said to Jerry at the streetcar stop. She lifted the collar of her coat, shivering in the cold December air as she waited for his answer. She knew he had nowhere else to spend Christmas Day, but she didn't want to make assumptions.

"I'd be honored." He touched the brim of his hat and bowed slightly, which amused her. He could act so formal one minute, like a gentleman transported from the Gilded Age, and the next be found sprawled in his easy chair, sipping a root beer in shirtsleeves and suspenders, burping loudly. If nothing else, he kept her guessing.

On this night, Women's Medical was blessedly silent. For once, most of the patients slept soundly. Clara made her rounds with her flashlight, her rubber soles softly squeaking on the tile floor. A bright moon spilling through the windows illuminated the ward as she moved softly from bed to bed. Here and there, tinsel garlands glittered in the moonlight. They'd been hung by the younger nurses in a determined attempt to add holiday cheer to the ward. For Clara, tinsel, wreaths, and ornaments did little to dispel her feelings of being an outsider looking in. But if decorations pleased the patients unlucky enough to be stuck in the hospital over Christmas, she supposed there was no harm in them.

Hours after beginning her shift, she still felt unsettled by the odd sensation that had come over her earlier in church. At her break time, she left another nurse in charge and took the elevator upstairs to the hospital chapel. *There is some reason people come here*, she thought as she sat alone in a wooden pew in the tiny, dimly lit space. *They get something out of the experience. They find some comfort, or strength, or power that helps them deal with the illness of their loved one. Something draws them here. I don't get it.* She gazed around as if the answer she sought could be found in the stained glass windows or the metal cross hanging at the front of the room. What was it? She didn't know. But for the first time in her life, she wanted to.

Her break time nearly over, she stood to leave. At the last moment, she picked up a small Bible from the rack and took it with her. Jerry seemed to think the Bible contained all the answers. So, apparently, did Laurie. She planned to take it home, read what it had to say, and then return it to its place when she was finished.

When she got home in the morning, she pulled the Bible out of her purse and set it on the table by her reading chair, then promptly forgot about it as she went to prepare a simple but hearty Christmas lunch for herself and Jerry.

He came downstairs around noon, dressed in his Sunday best and carrying a bottle of apple cider. Clara had made an effort, too, and put on one of her nicer dresses. While she didn't put up a tree or decorate the apartment, she enjoyed making an occasion of the meal, even if they were the only two present.

After their simple but festive lunch of roasted chicken and carrots, followed by pumpkin pie, Jerry went into the parlor, sat in one of the wingbacks, and lit his pipe. Clara followed, leaving the dishes for later.

Puffing on his pipe, he spotted the Bible and raised one bushy eyebrow. "What's this?" He picked it up.

"It's a Bible."

"I can see that. What's it doing here?"

"I'm going to read it."

He examined the cover. "It says *Property of Memorial Hospital.*"

"I only borrowed it. I'm going to put it back." She lifted her chin, indignant.

His smile was kind. Genuine. "I'm glad, Clara. Start with the Gospels."

"What?"

"Matthew, Mark, Luke, and John. If you want to learn about Jesus, that's the place to start."

"Who said I wanted to know about Jesus?" She gestured to the Bible. "I just think I should read it, is all. It's a classic. A foundation of Western thought and philosophy."

He shrugged. "If you say so. In any case, if you start at the beginning and go straight through, you're likely to get bogged down. Read the Gospels first. Then later you can go back and catch up, so to speak."

"I see." She stood, ready to change the subject. "I think the coffee's ready."

She went to the kitchen and poured two cups, one black, one with cream and sugar. She set them on a tray with a few cookies and carried it back to the front room.

In the waning afternoon light, Jerry had turned on the table lamp and was still leafing through the Bible. She began to wish she hadn't left it lying there. Seeing it in her home might raise his hopes, and she didn't know if he should be raising his hopes about anything. She was only going to read the thing. That was all. No big deal.

"Perhaps there's something good on the radio." She walked over to the Philco and switched it on. Soft orchestral strains of an old carol drifted from the speaker and wrapped themselves around the room.

She sat in the other wingback and sipped her coffee. Outside the large front window, snow had begun to fall. Thankfully, she didn't have to go out in it. Her next shift wasn't for two days. It comforted her, somehow, watching the crystalline flakes dance through the frozen blue air, while inside, she and Jerry sat with full bellies in the cozy warmth generated by the hissing radiator. They were friends, and they were together. What could a person ask for more than this?

Her reverie was interrupted by words being spoken. At first she thought the voice came from the radio, a narrator reading something over the quiet instrumental music.

"And in the sixth month the angel Gabriel was sent from God unto a city of Galilee, named Nazareth, to a virgin espoused to a man whose name was Joseph, of the house of David; and the virgin's name was Mary."

It wasn't the radio. It was Jerry, reading aloud from the Bible she'd swiped from the hospital. She watched him a moment. There was something incongruent about hearing the King's English filtered through his flat working-class vowels. Incongruent, but pleasant.

She swallowed. There was also something incongruent about having a purloined Bible in her house. Clara Janacek wasn't a thief. She vowed to return it to the hospital chapel on Monday.

But for now, she lay her head against the back of the chair, closed her eyes, and listened.

❧ 27 ❧

On New Year's Eve, toward the end of her shift, Clara completed her rounds and returned to the nurses' desk. Seated in the comforting circle of lamplight, she began compiling the night report to share with Joy Kolar at the change of shifts. She wasn't the least bit sleepy. She'd been asked by the nursing superintendent to meet in her office before she went home. Clara couldn't help but feel that this was the moment she'd be informed of her promotion. Every time she thought of it, her insides contracted in a pleasant way.

A few hours later, after turning over the ward to Joy, she went to the superintendent's office. Nurse Kent stood to greet her.

"Take a seat, please."

Here it comes, the news I've been waiting for. Clara sat gingerly on a chair and smoothed her skirt with damp palms.

Nurse Kent walked around the desk and perched on the edge. "Nurse Janacek, why did you become a nurse?"

Clara blinked in surprise. "Pardon me?"

"When you were young. What made you want to become a nurse?"

"Oh." Faced with this odd and unexpected question, she quickly threw some thoughts together. "Well, I suppose I always wanted to be one. I loved science in high school, and my science teacher suggested nursing as a likely career path for a girl who loved science. It seemed as good a choice as any."

She paused. Nurse Kent waited, then said, "Anything else?"

"Well." Clara thought. "As an unmarried woman, I needed to earn my own keep, so why not earn it doing something I enjoy? And I suppose I wanted to make myself useful. To help those less fortunate."

"I see." Nurse Kent nodded. "That makes sense."

She stood and paced to the window. "I'll get straight to the point, Clara. Nurse Banning is retiring, and you've applied for her position. As you know, the head nurse position calls for a number of qualities including technical proficiency, medical knowledge, dutiful patient care, and the ability to lead a staff. All of which you've shown yourself to excel at."

Clara felt the tiny seed of hope unfurl like a rosebud. "Thank you."

"You have a reputation for being a stickler for details, for following procedures, and for doing things by the book," Nurse Kent continued. "You're loyal, hardworking, and dedicated."

Clara felt herself blush. "I try my best."

"And, of course, a head nurse must also get along well with people. She must prove herself to be a wise and excellent leader and competent administrator, with the ability to get along well with staff and patients alike."

Clara did her best to look wise and competent.

The administrator cleared her throat and continued. "It is for these reasons that we have decided to promote Joy Kolar to the position of head nurse."

As if by a giant vacuum, all the air was sucked out of the room.

"Joy Kolar?" Clara managed to utter. Had she heard correctly? "But ... but I've been here thirty years," she sputtered. "Joy's only ... Why, she—"

"I understand you must be disappointed," the administrator said evenly. "But surely you understand our position. You are a technically proficient nurse, and a valued member of our staff. But to be frank, your people skills are lacking. You have a reputation for being very tough on the nurses under your authority."

And that was a bad thing? Clara scrambled to formulate a response. "They need to learn to either sink or swim, just like I had to when I was a brand-new nurse. Just like we all had to."

"There's a difference between being strong and being unreasonably rigid."

Clara could barely find words over the rushing sound in her head. At last she spoke, her voice sounding unfamiliar to her own ears, high-pitched and reedy with suppressed rage. "My job is to mentor them, not spoon-feed them. I'm trusting that they have a basic level of knowledge and skills. Instead of hovering over their shoulders every single minute and telling them what to do, I try to give them guidance."

"The general consensus is that you are too intimidating."

General consensus? Since when were important decisions made by general consensus?

"Is this because Mrs. Kremel went missing?" Clara asked, almost in a whisper.

"While that was a very serious situation, it turned out well. Mistakes happen, as you know, and we're not here to assign blame." Nurse Kent settled back into her chair. "It was not that incident alone that determined the committee's decision. But it does illustrate my point. You tried to blame the incident on Nurse Paulson when it was actually your responsibility. You passed off the blame to someone else. And as we discussed at the time, that is not what a true leader would do."

Clara felt as if the world were crumbling around her. "But ... thirty years ..."

"I'm afraid that the accumulation of seniority alone is not what makes someone head-nurse material. Rest assured that you are still a very valued member of our team." The administrator stood, indicating that the conversation was over.

Never had Clara been so relieved to go home. Somehow she managed to clock out and navigate the locker room with a smile pasted to her face. Not until she was safely on the streetcar did she let herself feel her feelings. Clara rarely cried, but at times like these, she wished she could.

"I just can't believe it," she kept repeating to Jerry over pancakes and coffee at the Seneca Restaurant later that morning. He'd insisted on taking her there after coming across her standing in the snow in the front yard, paralyzed, staring at her dormant rose bush as if shell-shocked.

"No news is so bad that good coffee and a plate of pannycakes won't fix it," he'd insisted as he'd steered her gently but firmly down the sidewalk toward Cermak Road. But now she left her breakfast uneaten, her appetite withered by disappointment and humiliation.

"So whatcha gonna do?" Jerry asked. "Appeal the decision? File a complaint?"

Clara shook her head slowly. "That wouldn't do any good. The administration has a right to choose whomever they want. Their minds are made up. Happy New Year to me." She picked up her coffee cup, stared at it, put it back down.

"Are you gonna quit, then?"

"I've never wanted to quit something so badly in my life," she confessed. "But I'm not going to. I've never been a quitter. Besides, I'd never find another job. Not at my age."

"Age, schmage. If you're unhappy, you should do something else," Jerry picked up his coffee cup, sipped, and sat back in the booth. "Look at me. Twenty years as a welder until the back started giving me trouble. Switched to buying and selling real estate, built a whole second career for myself."

"You were a lot younger when you made that move than I am now," Clara reminded him.

"Even so. It's never too late to make a change, if you really want to."

"You make it sound so easy."

He regarded her steadily for a moment. Then he set down his cup. "Look, Clara. You know me. I'm not gonna tell you what to do." He leaned forward. "I know you don't like it much when I pray out loud. But will you let me pray for you now?"

What good would that do? But she shrugged. "Go ahead, if you want to. I don't suppose it could do any harm."

He reached across the table and took her hand in his. He bowed his head and closed his eyes.

She didn't.

"Dear Lord," he said. "We know You are in charge of the whole universe. You are in control of everything, even those things—*especially* those things—that we don't understand."

All at once the words she'd read that morning before sleep scrolled through her mind. *I am the Way, the Truth, and the Life. No one comes to the Father except through me.*

"We come before you now to ask for guidance," Jerry continued. "Please show Clara the way You want her to go. Show her the gifts You've given her, the ways You've equipped her to serve You. Above all, make her understand that you never intended for Your children to go it alone."

No one comes to the Father.

"Show her that she, like all of Your children, needs a Savior, and that Savior is You. Amen."

Except through me.

By the time Jerry opened his eyes, she had closed her own. Not out of reverence but so he wouldn't see they were filling with tears. Something deep inside her had shifted. She didn't yet understand what the words meant. Only that they were important.

Jerry released her hand and picked up his fork. "Speaking of New Year's, what do you think the Lord has in store for us in 1945? What do you hope will happen?"

Now that Clara was no longer anticipating a promotion, she felt off balance yet oddly free at the same time. She sensed a world opening up —a world filled with new possibilities she couldn't quite grasp yet. But she'd wanted that one thing for so long, she had no idea what else to hope for instead.

"I hope this stupid war ends," she said at last.

❧ 28 ❧

On the second of January, Clara was running a feather duster over an end table in the front room when she heard rustling at the mailboxes in the foyer. She flung open her door in happy anticipation. Sure enough, there stood Laurie and Rosalie, whom she'd missed more than she'd ever thought possible.

Laurie, flipping anxiously through the mail that had accumulated during their week away, barely glanced her way. "We're home," she said absently. She seemed to be eagerly looking for something.

Still wearing her snow-flecked coat and hat, Rosalie flung her arms around Clara and gave her a hug.

"Oh, Miss Clara, I missed you so much!"

"Well. I missed you, too," Clara said, patting the top of Rosalie's head. She didn't know when "Miss Janacek" had softened into "Miss Clara," but she liked it. Overcoming her awkwardness with the unfamiliar gesture, she circled her arms around the child's back and pulled her close.

"I'm glad you're home," she said to Laurie over Rosalie's head.

"Thank you. And Happy New Year." Laurie seemed subdued,

preoccupied with the letters in her hand. Not her usual bubbly self. Perhaps she was tuckered out from the long journey.

Clara stepped back from the door, making room. "Have you time for a cup of tea?"

"Thank you, but Rosalie and I should go downstairs and get unpacked. School starts tomorrow." And yet she didn't move.

"All right, then." Clara closed the throat of her cardigan against the chill of the foyer. "How are things in the Land of the Ozarks?"

"Pine Bluff isn't in the Ozarks," Laurie said, apropos of nothing.

Then she looked at Clara, gave a little sort of hiccup, and burst into tears.

Gently yet firmly, as if she were steadying a wobbly patient, Clara led Laurie into her apartment and onto the sofa. She took the stack of letters and set them on an end table. She removed Laurie's coat from around her shoulders, pulled her boots off, and stowed both in the foyer to dry off.

"Rosalie, honey," she directed, "there are fresh cookies in the jar in the kitchen. You know where to find them. Go and fix yourself a snack while I talk to your mother."

"She's been this way on and off ever since we left Granny Josephine's," Rosalie said solemnly. She hung up her own coat and hat, then did as she was told.

Clara never knew what to do with emotions. So she sat in a wing-back chair, folded her hands, and listened.

"I was ... I was sure there'd be a letter waiting from Will," Laurie choked out between sobs. "It's been so long since he's written. His mother was so ... so awful while we were down there, always talking about horrible things she'd heard about the war, rumors passed along from neighbors and such. She hadn't gotten any recent letters, either. I know she's as worried about Will as I am, and I'd hoped we could comfort and encourage each another, but all her speculations just made me feel even worse."

She paused, pulled a handkerchief from her purse and wiped her nose.

"Some thoughts are best kept to oneself, especially the negative ones," Clara said.

"You see? I knew you'd understand," Laurie said, and Clara felt an unexpected warmth spreading in her chest. "I told myself there was nothing to worry about, that as soon as I got home there'd be a letter from him telling me so. But now—" Laurie waved helplessly at the pile of letters on the end table, then buried her face in her hands.

Clara watched her, troubled. Too often her own response to heartache had been to pull away from other people, to crawl into her shell, as Jerry called it. So she had no business trying to advise Laurie. She only knew it would be a shame if that sweet, kind woman closed herself off and allowed sadness to take over her entire life, the way Clara's parents had.

"S-s-sorry," Laurie sniffled. "I just—I miss Will so much."

"I know you do." Clara reached over and patted her awkwardly on the shoulder. "Well, you're home now," Clara said firmly. "Everything's going to be all right. Besides, maybe no news is good news. You don't know for sure that anything bad has happened to Will."

She was grasping at straws, but apparently hit on the right words, for to Clara's relief, Laurie's tears subsided and she mopped her face.

"H-How was your Christmas?" she asked in a choked voice. Clara recognized the desire to change the subject, to talk about more pleasant things.

"Better than yours, I think," Clara said quietly. She paused, searching for the right words to describe her experience. "I went to church with Jerry."

Laurie's red-rimmed eyes brightened. "You did?

Clara nodded. "And I-I've started reading the Bible."

A grin broke through on Laurie's face. "Oh, Clara. I'm glad to hear it."

Clara struggled to put her strange new feelings into words. "It's hard to explain, but when I read the Bible and pray, I feel like something—or Someone—is ironing out the wrinkles in my soul." She paused to gather her thoughts. "There's so much I don't understand," she said finally. "But I want to learn."

Laurie squeezed her hand. "And I will help you. I will help you all I can."

❧ 29 ❧

Later that week, following a heavy snowstorm, Clara stood in her coat and boots in the backyard, clearing snow off the bird feeders.

Laurie and Rosalie came around the house, accompanied by another woman and a girl who looked to be about Rosalie's age. On their way to the entrance to the Lucases' apartment, they paused.

"Clara, I'd like to introduce you to my friend from work, Evelyn Hendrikson, and her daughter, Debbie," Laurie called. "They've come by for a visit. Evelyn, this is my friend and neighbor, Clara Janacek."

My friend. Clara's heart warmed. "How do you do."

The woman named Evelyn nodded and smiled. She was holding a white cardboard bakery box tied with string.

"The girls won't bother you if they play outside, will they?" Laurie continued. "It's such a bright, sunny day, and they've been cooped up so long."

"I don't mind. It's her backyard as much as mine." Clara went back to cleaning the feeders.

"Would you care to join Evelyn and me for a cup of tea? And a cinnamon bun?"

"No, thank you." Clara cast a second, longing glance at the white box. "Well, maybe in a little while. Gotta get these bird feeders squared away."

"I'm sure the birds will appreciate it," Laurie said. "Come inside when you're finished."

As the women disappeared into the building, the girl called Debbie flopped down on her back in the snow, and Rosalie followed suit.

"Here's how you do it," Debbie said, and began flapping her arms and legs. Clara realized with a start that Rosalie's childhood in the South hadn't exposed her to snow. Not this much of it, anyway. She finished with the feeders and tromped over to the girls.

"Look, Miss Clara! We're making snow angels!" Rosalie's eyes were bright with enthusiasm.

"So I see. Have you girls ever built a snowman?"

Both girls sat up and looked eagerly at Clara.

"Here, let me show you."

Soon, all three were bent over, rolling giant snowballs. Clara showed the children how to stack the balls one on top of the other to form a snowman—actually a snow-lady, they determined—with arms made of sticks and eyes and mouth made of small stones that they found in the alley. Clara borrowed Jerry's lawn-mowing hat from the garage—she was certain he wouldn't mind—and placed it on the snow-lady's head. Finally she unwrapped her own scarf from around her neck and donated it to the cause.

Rosalie and Debbie clapped their mittened hands.

"It's wonderful!" Debbie exclaimed. "It's the best snow-lady there ever was."

Rosalie's wide grin said it all. She gave her steamed-up glasses a push and slipped her other hand into Clara's.

"And now we shall go inside and have something warm to drink," Clara said, feeling a bit like Mary Poppins.

"May we stay outside a little longer?" Rosalie begged. "I want to make more snow angels."

"Me too," Debbie said.

"Well, I suppose it's all right with me, if it's all right with your mothers. Don't stay out too long, though."

As the squealing girls flopped down in the snow, Clara made her way to the basement apartment, feeling a grin that started way down in her belly.

She couldn't remember the last time she'd had that much fun.

30

Meanwhile, seated in the Lucases' small living room, Laurie and Evelyn were enjoying some good girl-talk. As they sipped their tea and chatted about the joys of motherhood and the strain of being married to soldiers on active duty, Laurie vowed to invite Evelyn and Debbie to come over more often. Both she and Rosalie needed more fun in their lives.

By the time Clara entered and removed her coat, they'd moved on to the topic of work. She took a seat, and Laurie went to the kitchen to fetch another teacup.

"I was just telling Laurie some news that our foreman let slip," Evelyn confided to Clara. "He said our team stands a good chance of earning this month's commendation for exceeding our quota."

"And this in spite of Carl Bowman trying to trip us up every chance he gets," Laurie added, pouring tea into Clara's cup. "Carl's the fellow I've told you about."

"The heckler?" Clara huffed. "Is that oaf still bothering you ladies?"

"I've told you about the skeleton, haven't I?" Laurie asked, and both she and Evelyn tittered.

"No, I don't believe you have," Clara said. "I think I'd remember something like that."

In vivid, dramatic detail, Laurie related the story of the skeleton. By the end, all three were laughing.

"It wasn't funny then, but it's sure funny now," Laurie said, wiping her eyes.

"It's funniest the way *you* tell it," Evelyn said.

Laurie turned to Clara. "But the best thing about it was how Evelyn and the other ladies helped me out simply by gathering around and letting me know they were looking out for me."

"He backed off when he realized he was outnumbered," Evelyn said. "He's really a big chicken when he doesn't have his pack of coyotes to back him up."

"He still makes rude remarks to us sometimes," Laurie said, "but he never pulled a prank on that scale again. I really felt like we solidified as a team that day."

"Don't let him get to you," Clara advised. "Men might run things, but women form the backbone of Western Electric. Always have, even back in my father's day."

Evelyn nodded. "You can say that again."

"Isn't that a bit unusual?" Laurie asked.

"Nonsense. Western Electric isn't like most other factories," Clara explained. "A lot of jobs there require fine motor coordination, not brute strength. Women are perfectly suited to do the work."

"Tell that to the likes of Carl Bowman," Evelyn said ruefully. "But it helps a lot to have friends like Laurie and the rest of our team. We girls need to stick together."

"But if we're *too* strong, we run the risk of not being liked," Laurie said, thinking of what Ted Palmer had told her. In any case, she'd been raised to get along, to be gentle, not strong. To acquiesce to men, not to argue with them.

"I'm used to people not liking me," Clara said matter-of-factly. "One gets used to it. It's not the end of the world."

"Well, *I* like you," Laurie said stoutly. "And Rosalie adores you."

Clara said nothing but looked for a moment as if she'd been struck by lightning, stunned and glassy-eyed.

"And I like you, too," Evelyn added. "Even though I don't know you yet."

Their laughter broke the tension. Clara turned to Evelyn, "Tell me more. What did you mean about you girls sticking together?"

"Oh, you know. Being on each other's team. Sticking up for one another. One for all and all for one and all that *Three Musketeers* stuff."

"I see." Clara sat back and took a bite of a cookie and chewed it thoughtfully.

Evelyn continued. "It's sort of like how our daughters have learned to handle bullies on the playground at school."

Laurie snapped to attention. "What do you mean?" she asked, alarmed. "What bullies? Rosalie hasn't mentioned any bullies to me."

"Probably because she's got it handled," Evelyn said in a soothing tone. "Oh, they're not in any real danger. Just boys teasing them on the playground, acting stupid, wanting attention. That sort of thing. Anyway, Debbie told me how she and her friends—including your Rosalie—stand up to them."

"How?" Laurie couldn't imagine her gentle, soft-spoken Rosalie standing up to anyone, much less someone being mean to her. The very thought of it cracked her heart open.

"It's the cleverest thing," Evelyn said, leaning forward and speaking quietly, as if she didn't want the girls to overhear, even though they were still playing out in the yard. "If one of them is getting picked on, the others pass around a code phrase to all the other girls. As the word gets around, the girls all stop whatever they're doing and come and form a circle around the one who's being picked on. They stare the bully down until he backs off. Or she." She sat back with an expression of distaste. "Not all the bullies are boys."

"They do all that? They band together and stick up for each other?" Laurie's heart swelled with pride in her daughter. "Why, that's so ... so *mature!*"

"More mature than the way most nurses behave at the hospital," Clara remarked. "Many of them seem prepared to shove each other under the bus at any moment."

"That's not right," Laurie said, indignation rising in her chest. "Like Evelyn said, women in the workplace ought to stick together."

"That's what I think," Evelyn said. "If a scheme like that worked so well on the playground, it might work for us, too. So I got the ladies at our workstation together, and we came up with our own plan. That's how we all banded together with you against Carl Bowman when he played that prank on you."

Clara made no comment but seemed interested in what the younger women were saying.

Laurie turned to Evelyn. "I'm so curious," she said. "Did Debbie happen to tell you the code phrase they use at school?"

Evelyn smiled. "It's the cutest thing. But you must never reveal that I told you." She leaned forward conspiratorially. "I have no idea where they picked it up, but the code phrase is 'Operation Red Rose.'"

Laurie's heart swelled as she realized it was her own daughter who'd instigated the plan.

"But we didn't want to steal the code from the children, so we modified it," Evelyn continued. "Ours is 'Operation Yellow Rose.'" She smiled at Clara. "Because Laurie's from Texas."

"I'm from Arkansas," Laurie reminded her. But she was deeply touched just the same.

The late afternoon sun was slanting through the high windows when she stood and picked up the empty teapot. "More tea, ladies?"

"I have time for one more cup," Evelyn said, glancing at her wristwatch.

"Me, too," Clara said. "I'm off duty tonight."

As Laurie moved toward the tiny kitchen, Evelyn turned toward Clara. "Miss Janacek, you mentioned your father worked at the Western."

"It's Clara, please. And, yes," she replied. "He was a switchboard assembler. Worked there his whole career."

"My father did, too. And my uncle." Evelyn paused, then said quietly, "So your father would have been there in 1915."

From the kitchen Laurie heard a slight hesitation on Clara's part, then a quiet, "Yes."

Laurie strained to hear what they were talking about.

She heard Evelyn ask, "Was your family there? Were *you* there that day?"

Clara hesitated as if weighing her words. "I wasn't on the boat, no. My parents were out of town that weekend. And I had to work." To

Laurie's ears, Clara's answers sounded short, almost curt. Maybe this event, whatever it was, wasn't something Evelyn should be probing her about.

Evelyn released her breath in a rush. "That was a blessing. I'm afraid my family wasn't so lucky."

Laurie returned from the kitchen with a fresh pot of tea. "What boat?" she asked as she filled the cups. "What are you two talking about?"

But before anyone could answer her, Rosalie and Debbie came clattering into the room from the backyard.

෴

CLARA SHIVERED AND BUTTONED HER CARDIGAN AS A COLD DRAFT from the back door swept through Laurie's apartment

"Hello, sugar." Laurie bent and kissed Rosalie's cheeks, bright pink from the cold. "Look at your face! I see you brought me roses."

Rosalie lifted her hands and touched her cheeks. "Oh, Mama. You always say that." But Clara could see that she was pleased. Clara felt a stab of pain that she would never have small rosy cheeks like that to kiss. But she was happy for Laurie and Rosalie. She had to be content with that.

"Honey, you're dripping all over the floor," Laurie said. "You and Debbie go and take off your coat and boots in the laundry room so they can dry." Rosalie grabbed Debbie's hand and scampered off.

Evelyn called after them. "Debbie, leave yours on. We need to be on our way." She stood. "Sorry, Laurie. I just remembered we need to get to the grocery before it closes. Thank you for a wonderful afternoon."

After everyone said their good-byes and the guests had left, Clara said reluctantly, "I guess I should be going too." In fact, she wanted to stay and hear more about Operation Yellow Rose. Her mind was stuck on her own earlier remark about nurses shoving each other under the bus. She suffered a stab of regret, remembering her own behavior and knowing she'd done more than her share of shoving over the years.

"Can you stay for dinner?" Laurie asked. "There's plenty of soup and bread to go around. And you already said you don't have to work tonight."

Rosalie tugged on her arm. "Please, Miss Clara? I want to hear more about Jaroslav."

Laurie cocked her head. "Who's Jaroslav?"

Clara felt herself blush. "I've been telling Rosalie some stories about my girlhood."

"Ah. So Jaroslav is someone from your youth? A brother, perhaps?"

Clara's blush deepened. "I don't have a brother."

"Oh?" Laurie's voice took on a new, more interested tone. "Well, go on, then. I want to hear about this Jaroslav, too."

Would they never stop with their questions? "It was a long time ago."

"Please?" Rosalie begged.

Clara acquiesced, her resolve softened by the thought of soup, bread, and warm company on a cold evening. Then maybe later she and Laurie could get back to their earlier topic. She picked up her teacup and took a sip. "Very well. Let's see, where did I leave off?"

"The concert," Rosalie prompted.

"Oh, yes. The concert."

❧ 31 ❧

June 1915

On the evening of the concert at Orchestra Hall, Jaroslav came by the house early to pick me up and meet my parents, who acted pleased if vaguely mystified that their ugly-duckling daughter had actually landed a potential suitor. Aneta's dates swarmed through the parlor with regularity, but I'd only had one date, a skinny, awkward boy from the neighborhood who'd been shanghaied by both our mothers to take me to an eighth-grade graduation dance. After that humiliation, I swore off arranged dates forever, even if it meant being left at home with a good book, which it usually did.

Jaroslav shook my father's hand and charmed my mother by speaking a few sentences in Czech. Seated on the overstuffed sofa, he and Papa swapped stories about Western Electric while Mama served cherry cordial in the fine crystal glasses from Bohemia that she reserved for company. I didn't think they would ever let us leave, but finally Jaroslav smiled at me and said, "I guess we'd better make it snappy if we're going to get to the concert on time."

We rode the streetcar to the Loop, then walked along Michigan

Avenue to Orchestra Hall. Stars twinkled in the darkening sky as a perfect summer breeze off the lake ruffled our hair.

I'd never been inside Orchestra Hall, and its opulence took my breath away. The lobby teemed with members of Chicago high society. The women's elaborate evening gowns rustled, and diamonds hanging from chains sparkled as the men in dark suits flocked around them like penguins. Jaroslav and I, skulking along the wall, were markedly underdressed.

"Follow me," he murmured in my ear. He took my hand and led me through a nearly invisible side door.

"Where are we going?"

"My friend Arnie works backstage," he said. "Come on, he's waiting for us."

I followed him through narrow passages until we were behind the stage. He guided me through the dark, past the ropes and pulleys, to a small booth where an engineer sat.

"Arnie, this is Clara. I mean, Miss Janacek," Jaroslav said.

"Clara, please," I said as I shook Arnie's hand.

Jaroslav took me aside. "Clara, I'm sorry," he said, his voice hoarse with embarrassment. "This is the last concert of the season, and the only tickets that were available were the ones I couldn't afford. Arnie's an old friend. He often lets me listen from backstage. Do you mind?"

"Mind? Of course not." Indeed, I was charmed. It felt special, being able to watch the behind-the-scenes production of a professional symphony orchestra concert. Arnie pointed out some interesting architectural features of the world-famous concert hall. When he needed to focus on his job, Jaroslav and I sat on work stools and chattered about music and books and life until the random tuning-up sounds of the orchestra stopped. We watched from behind as the grand curtain parted and spotlights bathed the orchestra. From the right side of the stage, the conductor entered. The audience burst into applause, and my pulse pounded with the thrill of it. When the music started, it swept me away.

Jaroslav took my hand in his and held it tight. I sneaked an occasional sidelong glance at his profile. Never before had I known someone whose interests and personality meshed so perfectly with mine. With Jaroslav I didn't feel weird or strange. Instead, I felt comfortable and at ease. I loved being able to discuss books and music with someone without feeling foolish. After so many years spent in Aneta's shadow, socially speaking, it was an exhilarating feeling for a young man to take a specific interest in me.

After the concert, over milkshakes at a nearby ice cream parlor, we talked about the music and how much we'd enjoyed it.

"Next time I will get us real seats. I promise," Jaroslav said. He took a long sip of his milkshake.

"I hope not," I said, and I meant it. "Sitting backstage felt almost like being part of the production. Except the stool did get hard after a while." I winced to underscore my point.

He laughed. "I'll try to remember to bring cushions next time."

Next time. I liked the sound of that.

Eventually the conversation turned, and I found myself asking about his friend Edward.

"He sure seems to have fallen for Aneta," I said. "No surprise there. She's the belle of the ball."

"No, she's not."

I glanced at him, surprised. His eyes held an earnest look. I'd only made a truthful observation about my sister and hoped he didn't think I was fishing for compliments. Unsure of what to say next, I picked up my spoon and swirled it in the glass of thick, creamy liquid.

"I mean, sure, she's pretty and lively," he continued. "She's a good kid. Edward's sure sweet on her. " His head tilted to the side as he studied me. "But there's something about you. The minute I set eyes on you, I said to myself, 'She's different. That girl's different.'" He sat back in the booth and smiled. "I don't know when I've enjoyed anything so much as just sitting here, talking to you."

"I think that's the nicest thing anybody's ever said to me," I blurted. Embarrassed, I dipped my head and focused on the milkshake. I hadn't meant to say that out loud.

But he only laughed in a kindly way. "You deserve to have nice things said to you."

I couldn't meet his gaze, so I looked at his hands resting on the table. Strong hands. Hardworking hands, nicked and scarred. Alarmed at a sudden impulse to touch him, to feel the warmth of his touch in return, I clasped my hands in my lap.

"I should get you home," he said finally, sounding reluctant. He pulled some coins from his wallet and set them on the marble-topped table.

On the streetcar ride back to Cicero, we were mostly quiet, but comfortably so. I appreciated a man who was easy to talk to and yet could be comfortable in silence, too. That seemed to be all too rare a combination.

He walked me from the streetcar stop to my door.

I turned to him and extended my hand. "Thank you for a wonderful evening," I said. "I had a wonderful time." Inwardly I cringed. I was a well read person. Could I think of no more creative adjective than *wonderful?*

He didn't seem to notice as he clasped my hand warmly in his. For a moment I thought—*hoped*—that he would kiss me goodnight.

We gazed at one another for a moment. "Well, thank you again."

He released my hand, tipped his hat, and said, "I look forward to seeing you again soon."

But when? But when? I longed to say, eager to pin him down to another date.

But he was gone.

January 1945

LATER THAT EVENING CLARA CLIMBED WEARILY TO HER OWN apartment, spent by the effort of storytelling. On the one hand, it felt good to unleash the memories that had been pent up inside her heart for so many years. On the other hand, she had a feeling of having said too much. Of having wanted too much. Of daring to have needs of her own when others' needs were so much more pressing.

"What happened to Jaroslav?" Rosalie had asked as Clara had prepared to leave. "Did he die, like Aneta?"

"Rosalie! Mind your manners," Laurie interjected. Then, stricken,

"Aneta died?" Her eyes had gone round with sorrow and disbelief. Clara realized Laurie had missed out on the brief context she'd given to Rosalie months earlier.

"Jaroslav and I went our separate ways," was all Clara said, too exhausted to say more than that.

The last thing she wanted was their pity.

❧ 32 ❧

February 1945

Laurie sensed from the minute she stepped onto the factory floor that something was wrong. The air crackled with tension. All the women at her work station looked somber, downcast. No one returned her sunny greeting.

"What's wrong with everybody?" she said finally.

Patricia glanced up. "Our team's been called out," she said. "Our last batch of parts was found to be defective. We have to do all of them over."

Laurie's heart sank. "Oh, no. How can that be? We're always so careful." Now they'd have to work doubly hard to meet their quota. And they could kiss that commendation good-bye.

"Are we?" Theresa said sharply. She refused to meet Laurie's questioning gaze.

Evelyn pulled Laurie aside. "Look," she whispered. "Were you having trouble with your tools yesterday? Was something not working right? Because if you're having trouble, you need to tell someone."

Laurie backed away, defensive. "Everything was just fine."

Just then, Mr. Palmer bellowed from his cubicle, "Lucas! In here, now!"

When she reached his desk, hot with embarrassment and confusion, he held up a board with wires screwed to it.

"What do you call this?"

"It's—it's one of our components, sir."

"And what do you call this?" He gave a gentle tug to one of the wires. It slipped easily from its screw as if it had been barely attached at all.

"I—I don't know, sir."

"That's shoddy work, Lucas," he barked. "These screws are much too loose. And look at this." He picked up another component. "This one has the black wire attached where the red wire should go, and vice versa."

She stood mute. She couldn't believe she'd made such careless mistakes. She was always so careful about her work.

"Luckily the next department caught these. Do you have any idea what would have happened if poorly assembled parts were installed in our military equipment? People could die, Lucas, that's what."

Laurie stood mortified. "I-I'm sorry, sir."

"I'm warning you, Lucas. You screw up like this again and you're out."

"Yes, sir."

Hot tears stung the backs of her eyelids as she returned to the work station. She felt like everyone was looking at her. Silently she sat on her stool and picked up her tools.

Evelyn reached over and touched her forearm. "Operation Yellow Rose," she whispered.

But at that moment, Laurie didn't feel as if anyone, including her closest workmates, were acting the least bit supportive.

33

February 1945

A s sleet pelted the windows, Clara perched on a stool in the little room off the kitchen she ambitiously called her sewing room but really used for storage, and wondered where to begin. All around her stood neat stacks of unopened boxes. She thought she had some more books from her childhood that would interest Rosalie, but she had no idea which of the several cartons marked "Books" contained the ones she was looking for. And several more boxes, those she had lugged from her parents' attic without opening, held no clue whatsoever to what they contained. Why was she hanging on to all this stuff? She needed to call the Purple Heart Veterans at the first opportunity and make a donation.

She selected a box and opened it. In it she found her high school diploma and nursing school certificate, along with some yellowed paperwork from the Illinois Training School for Nurses and several old nursing textbooks. Why had she hung on to those? She flipped through a couple, marveling at how far medical technology and patient-care techniques had advanced over the past thirty years.

She set that box aside and picked up another one. This one looked more promising, filled with books that had once taken up several shelves in her parents' home. She spotted one book in particular that had a piece of paper sticking out from between its pages, apparently serving as a makeshift bookmark. When she pulled it out and unfolded it, an old sepia-toned photograph dropped into her lap. She picked it up and saw a small, light-colored house surrounded by trees. She recognized it as the cottage her family had visited that one summer when she was eleven, where she and Aneta had learned to swim. Nostalgia and regret made her chest contract. It was exactly the sort of cottage she'd dreamed of owning one day, a dream that felt out of reach now that she'd missed out on the promotion that was going to fund it.

Buzzing around the edges of her mind was the reason *why* she'd lost the promotion—her lack of comradely care for the nurses under her supervision. That wrinkle would require a lot more reflection before she could come to terms with it. For as long as she could remember, she'd always had trouble relating to people and their emotional needs. She recognized this as a flaw in her character, but didn't know if it was something she was capable of fixing.

She studied the photograph of the cottage, then opened the accompanying paper. It was a faded letter dated 1906, written in Czech, addressed to her mother, Anna, and signed by her mother's sister, Minnie. Clara's Czech was very rusty, just good enough to pick out a word here and there. But that was enough to tell her that the letter contained an invitation, a suggestion that the Janaceks make use of a cottage that Minnie and her husband had rented for the summer. They would need to vacate it for a couple of weeks due to Uncle Harvey's surgery, and Minnie thought it would be a shame to let it sit empty. Her aunt added a line that perhaps the girls would enjoy swimming in the lake.

Clara smiled. "The girls"—she and Aneta—had indeed enjoyed swimming that summer. The mystery of how her family had been able to enjoy that one-and-only vacation had finally been resolved. Generous Aunt Minnie had been behind it. Clara should have guessed.

She looked again at the photograph, then turned it over. Neatly penciled in her aunt's handwriting were the words "Bluebird's Nest" and the name and address of a realty company.

Aunt Minnie and Uncle Harvey had passed away many years ago. There was no point in keeping the letter. Or the photo, for that matter. She set both aside, and plunged further into the carton, where she found what she was looking for: several children's books, including *Alice's Adventures in Wonderland* and *The Wonderful Wizard of Oz*. She pulled them out to give to Rosalie that afternoon.

At the bottom of the carton, she found a small black box. She opened it, and the sight took her breath away. It was a rose pin that had belonged to Aneta. One of her favorites, as Edward had given it to her as a present the summer she—.

Clara held the brooch up to the light. The red enamel had nearly worn off, and the cheap metal had tarnished. It held no value, nothing of beauty. How like her parents to keep reminders of their sorrow all around them, no matter how worthless and ugly. They'd been so engulfed by their grief, they couldn't bear to part with anything associated with the daughter they'd lost.

Clara snapped the box shut, gathered up all her finds, and carried them to her bedroom. There she spread them out on the dresser. She discarded the letter from Aunt Minnie. She almost discarded the photo as well, but at the last minute, pulled it out of the wastebasket and slid it into the frame surrounding the mirror. It would be refreshing to have something pleasant to look at, a reminder of one happy memory in the midst of so many painful ones.

She fingered the small black box, on the verge of throwing it into the trash as well. What use had she for a battered, beat-up brooch? What good would it do her besides bring up sad memories? But she hesitated, finally tossing it into a dresser drawer and slamming the drawer shut. As she did, she heard the back door open. She and Rosalie had long ago dispensed with formalities like knocking. Rosalie now came and went from Clara's apartment as she pleased, as if it were her own.

The girl was delighted with the books when Clara showed them to her.

"Oh, thank you!" she breathed, clutching *The Wonderful Wizard of Oz* to her chest. "Mama took me to see the movie when we lived back in Arkansas, but I've never read the book."

"And I've not seen the movie," Clara admitted.

Rosalie looked at her, pop-eyed. "You haven't?"

Clara shook her head. "I don't get to the movies very often. The books are usually better than the movie versions, anyway. Or so I've been told. After you've read it, you must tell me what you think."

"I will." Rosalie started paging through the book. Then she set it aside, wiggled around on the sofa until she sat with her legs tucked underneath her, and turned to Clara.

"Tell me more about you and Jaroslav. Did he call you again after you went to the concert?"

"Don't you want to read your book?"

"I'd much rather hear your stories, if you don't mind."

Clara didn't mind. Not this part of the story, anyway.

34

June 1915

I spent the next week reliving my delightful evening with Jaroslav, hoping he'd call, wondering about our next meeting, and longing to be with him again. All through my shifts at the hospital and through long evenings at home, I rehearsed what sparkling, witty things I'd say to him, and what he'd say back, and what I'd say, and what he'd—

"Nurse Janacek, watch what you're doing. My, your head is in the clouds these days." Nurse Blair frowned as she sidestepped the cartload of medicine bottles with which I'd nearly knocked her over.

"So sorry, Nurse Blair." I practically curtsied. Mortified, I vowed to pay more attention to my job, Jaroslav or no Jaroslav. There was no excuse for sloppiness in my line of work.

As the days passed with no call or note from him, I began to doubt his interest in me. I combed through our conversation. Had I said something wrong? Had I acted too forward—or not forward enough? Did he think I wasn't interested? Had I ruined everything without even knowing it?

At last he did call. He had to use a public telephone, so it was a hurried conversation with a lot of noise in the background. But I was so relieved to hear his voice that I nearly melted.

We chitchatted about the concert we'd gone to and then about the weather. I felt increasingly impatient for him to get to the point. Was he going to ask me out for another date or not?

"Well, I guess I'd better be going," I said finally.

"Wait," he said. "I was wondering if—you, see the Hawthorne Club is sponsoring ballroom dance classes. I thought maybe, you know, we might go and, well, since we both have two left feet ... that is, if you think ..."

My heart leaped in my chest. So I hadn't ruined everything after all.

"I'd love to." I was a terrible dancer, but I'd worry about that later. "When?"

"Um, that's the thing ... The first one is tonight. I know it's awful short notice."

"That's all right." I had a vague memory of Aneta talking about not accepting last-minute dates, but I figured those nitpicky rules didn't apply to wallflowers like me.

His voice brightened. "Wonderful. I'll pick you up at seven."

The Hawthorne Club was the premier social organization of Western Electric employees. We laughed and skidded our way around the wooden dance floor. By the last dance of the evening, we weren't doing too badly.

The last song was *Let Me Call You Sweetheart*. As he held me close and murmured the romantic lyrics, I knew.

I was falling for him. Suddenly all those corny moon-and-June song lyrics started making sense. And if I wasn't mistaken, he felt the same way about me.

But between my fluctuating work schedule at the hospital and his shifts at the factory, we had a hard time actually seeing each other, although we spoke frequently on the telephone. We managed to make it to one more dance class at the Hawthorne Club, at which we practiced the tango amid gales of laughter, but that was pretty much the extent of our great romance.

On a hot July Sunday about a week after the tango class, I was sweeping the porch when Aneta's friends, Lil and Marguerite, pulled up to the curb in Lil's roadster.

"Clara, we're all going out to the flying field to watch the aeroplanes," Lil called from behind the wheel. "Come with us! It'll be fun."

"Thank you, but no," I said, giving the top step a good swipe with the broom. "I have things to do." The truth was, I wanted to stay near the telephone, hoping Jaroslav would call. Behind me, the screen door slammed. "You always say no," Aneta muttered as she brushed past me. "It wouldn't kill you to have some fun for once." She glanced at me over her shoulder with a sly smile. "But that's all right. I'll just explain to Jaroslav that you couldn't make it because you had to do the *sweeping*."

"Jaroslav's going to be there?" I stilled the broom mid-sweep and stared after her. "Wait! Don't tell him that!"

"Then come with us," she urged.

I glanced down with dismay at my dusty apron. "I'm not dressed."

"It's a flying field, not a cotillion." She opened the passenger door of the roadster. "You have five minutes."

I was still pinning on my hat in the backseat when the roadster peeled away from the curb. Lil Drummond was the first girl in our neighborhood to learn how to drive an automobile, and she did it with a great deal of flourish.

"I heard Katherine Stinson will be flying today," she said as she took a corner a little too fast for my liking.

I grabbed the edge of the seat to steady myself. "Who's Katherine Stinson?"

Sitting shotgun, Marguerite shifted to face me. "Only the most famous lady aviator *ever*."

"Imagine that," I mused. "A lady aviator." I was still getting used to the idea of ladies driving automobiles, much less aeroplanes.

The Cicero Flying Field was a large flat grassy area about a mile and a half square, surrounded by fencing. Lil parked the roadster amid rows of other automobiles, then we entered the field. The July sun beat down on us, and a stiff breeze threatened to blow my brimmed hat clear off my head. As we picked our way across the uneven ground of the field, I was glad I had worn sturdy shoes, unlike Aneta, who teetered around in delicate pumps.

"We should have had the men drive with us," Marguerite muttered. "How are we ever going to find them in this crowd?"

I agreed with her. There looked to be a few thousand people milling over the grounds.

"Well, *they* wanted to go out to breakfast, and *you* wanted to finish dressing," Lil said, sounding miffed at missing out on pancakes.

Finding them appeared hopeless, but eventually Edward, Bill, and Lionel caught up with us. Contrary to what Aneta had said, Jaroslav was not with them. I felt a sharp sting of disappointment. Seeing him was the whole reason I'd bothered to come out, although I had to admit, the aeroplanes were capturing my interest.

When we passed a painted sign signifying the Lillie Aviation School, Lil gestured with excitement. "Katherine Stinson learned to fly right here, from Max Lillie himself." She had to shout to be heard over the noisy rumble of the engines.

"I'd like to learn to fly someday," Lionel said.

"Then why don't you?" Bill asked.

Lionel rubbed his index finger and thumb together. "Too rich for my blood."

"Well, I'd like to learn," Lil declared. "Maybe I will. Someday."

"Women should not be pilots," Bill drawled. "Only passengers."

"What kind of outmoded attitude is that?" Lil countered, hands on her hips. She stood firmly on the side of women's rights. The previous summer, she had even marched proudly in a parade with a suffragette banner slung across her body. Secretly I admired her for it, although I didn't think I could have ever done something so brave.

"Why isn't Jaroslav with you?" Aneta asked Edward, craning her neck as though he might be trailing behind them. "I told my sister he was coming."

"Aneta!" I didn't need her spreading my personal business among all her friends.

Edward shrugged. "He had something else to do first. He'll be along shortly."

Hearing Edward's words cheered me up.

"That's her," Lil squealed. "That's Katherine Stinson. Oh, isn't she simply darling?" She pointed to where a young woman no older than I, wearing a short skirt and a leather jacket, peered beneath a wing of her biplane alongside a remarkably tall, thin man wearing gray mechanic's overalls. In my ignorance I'd assumed that a lady aviator would be more masculine in appearance, so I was startled to see that Miss Stinson was very feminine, almost frail-looking. She stood a good foot shorter than the mechanic and had a slender build. Long dark-brown hair curled over her shoulders from beneath a checkered cap.

She climbed into the cockpit and revved the motor while the mechanic shouted instructions. The roar shot a thrill through my chest. Imagine flying an aeroplane! I could imagine no such thing, yet Miss Stinson looked so calm and confident.

Suddenly I became aware of Jaroslav at the edge of the crowd. He gave a broad smile and wave and jogged over to where we stood. "There you are!" I said.

"Sorry I'm late," he said, a little out of breath. "Have I missed anything?"

"Katherine Stinson is about to perform," I said. "Where have you been?"

"Church."

"Church?"

I didn't know why that should have surprised me, but it did. Perhaps because the topic hadn't come up earlier in our conversation. Perhaps because going to church was not a part of my life nor my family's routine. But I didn't have time to discuss it further, because Lil pointed and said, "Look, everyone! She's about to take off."

Miss Stinson gave the thumbs-up sign to her mechanic.

A voice boomed over a megaphone, "And now, ladies and gentlemen, the great aviatrix, Katherine Stinson, will attempt a maneuver never before executed by a woman."

The mechanic spun the wooden propeller. The motor grumbled, then roared. He signaled to Miss Stinson. The aeroplane rolled to the edge of the field—*taxied*, Lil called it—and the next thing we knew, with a great rush and rumble, she was in the air. We craned our necks to watch as her aeroplane ascended into the hot blue sky. She circled above the field a few times, then turned her plane entirely upside down. After a moment, she righted it again. The crowd gasped, then burst into applause and cheers. She did it again. And again. And each time, my insides flipped right along with her.

Beside me, Jaroslav whistled. "Ain't that something?"

"And that, ladies and gentlemen, is called a loop-de-loop." The megaphone voice wavered with excitement. "You've just seen it executed for the very first time by a lady aviatrix in the United States of America, and it happened right here at Cicero Field."

Miss Stinson made a perfect landing amid enthusiastic applause and excited murmurs. She waved at the crowd and drove—no, *taxied*—her plane over to where her mechanic stood waiting.

"Wasn't that something?" Jaroslav said to me, eyes shining. "That was really ... something." Apparently he was as much at a loss for words as I was.

"Marvelous," I breathed. "Imagine, turning yourself upside down like that, way up in the sky." I shivered deliciously.

The voice on the megaphone boomed. "And next up we have Taras Weiner in a Wright Model B equipped with a Hensel stabilizer ... "

"Can I buy you a soda? or maybe an ice cream?" Jaroslav shouted over the roar of engines.

"A lemonade would be perfect, if they have it." The hot sun and dry wind had made me especially thirsty.

"Let's go and see."

Together we walked to the refreshment stand. There was little shade to be found, but we wandered to the edge of the field nearest the parking lot, away from most of the hubbub.

"I'm sorry I was late," he said. "I didn't know you were coming."

"That's all right. I was a last-minute addition."

"The preacher is a windbag sometimes. I kept checking my watch." He chuckled. At the refreshment stand, he placed our drink orders, then handed me a paper cup filled with lemonade. I took a deep sip through the straw and relished the cold liquid sliding down my throat.

"How about you?" he asked. "Where do you go to church?"

I swallowed quickly. "I don't. Go to church, I mean."

He lifted an eyebrow. "You don't? Ever?" I shook my head.

A look I couldn't quite identify passed over his face. I hoped it wasn't disappointment.

"I've only ever gone inside church buildings for weddings and funerals."

He didn't say anything, and I felt some responsibility to fill in the silence. "You see, my parents are Freethinkers."

"Oh." He looked at me with a curious expression. "And how about you? Are you a Freethinker, too?"

"I-I suppose so." No one had ever asked me that question before, not in so many words. It was just assumed in my home that belief in mankind, nature, justice, and science was a surer bet than putting one's trust in some faraway God. "Lots of Bohemians think that way. Back in the old country, the state church oppressed people with an iron fist, so when they came to America ..."

"I understand what Freethinkers are." I still couldn't read the tone in Jaroslav's voice. I hoped he wasn't angry with me. Suddenly this seemed to me a very odd conversation to be having while standing at the edge of the Cicero Flying Field with biplanes droning overhead.

"Shall we go and watch the aviators?" I suggested in an overly bright tone, trying to sound lighthearted despite a throat thick with apprehension and worry that I'd somehow spoiled both his day and mine.

"Yes, let's do that." We finished our drinks and tossed the cups into the trash can. Then he grasped my elbow, and we'd started to look for the others when suddenly I heard Aneta's voice pierce high above the din.

"You did so! I saw you!"

I looked around and spotted Aneta and Edward standing together in a shadowed area behind the hangar. Aneta's back and shoulders were stiff with rage beneath the folds of her white eyelet afternoon dress. Edward stood before her, submissive, cowed, spreading his hands open in a helpless gesture.

"But, sweetheart, it was only—"

"Don't you 'sweetheart' me," my sister hissed, her voice edging on tears. "I saw you with my own two eyes."

"Aw, Aneta, baby, don't be like that," Edward said in a pleading tone.

I hurried toward the hangar, Jaroslav right behind me. "What's going on here?" Normally I wasn't one to barge in on people's private conversations, but this was different. This was my sister.

Aneta flung herself at me and buried her face in my shoulder, sobbing. I looked at Edward, perplexed. His naturally pale face was crimson, and not only from the sun.

"What happened?"

He drew himself up, shoved a hand through his thick red hair. "She's just ... I didn't ..." He was avoiding my gaze.

Jaroslav's eyes narrowed. "What'd you do, Ed?" He pulled a clean handkerchief from his pocket and thrust it into Aneta's hand.

Edward tried to make a joke of it. "Oh, you know how women are ..."

Aneta lifted her head from my damp shoulder. "I *saw* him! H-he was kissing M-M-Marguerite!" She started sobbing afresh. I patted her shoulder in a helpless gesture of comfort and glared at Edward.

"Is that true?"

He didn't answer.

Jaroslav turned to him, voice frosty. "I think you'd better leave us."

"But—"

"Clearly the young lady is distraught, Ed." He signaled with his thumb in a *get lost* gesture. "We'll talk later."

Edward shifted, uncertain. He stared at Aneta's trembling back for a moment and seemed about to say something. Then he pressed his lips together, turned, and strode back into the crowd.

I looked at Jaroslav over the head of my weeping sister, who was in no condition to return to her friends. "I think I'd better take her home."

"Yes, of course. I'll drive you."

"Thank you. That's kind of you."

Jaroslav's automobile turned out to be a ramshackle, rusted affair seemingly held together by wire, twine, and a great deal of hope. It shook our bones and rattled our teeth but got us home. Aneta sat between us, her sobs muted into sniffles. Miserably I realized that my revelation about not going to church had thrown cold water on the tiny spark of a promising courtship. Oh, well. Better he find out now rather than later. It wasn't as if I'd really expected him to fall in love with me.

At the curb in front of our house, he came around and opened the passenger door. I stepped out. Aneta lurched after me and brushed past us, running into the house.

I looked at him. "Well, thank you for the ride. I'm very grateful, and so is Aneta. I'm sorry for all the—I'm sorry things ended up on such a sour note today."

"That's all right," he said. "I'm always happy to rescue a damsel in distress." He glanced toward the house. "I hope she'll feel better soon. Edward's not a bad sort of fellow, but he's not worth a single one of those tears."

"She'll be fine," I assured him. "I'll be surprised if they haven't patched up their quarrel by dinnertime. And if not ..." I shrugged. "My sister has never lacked for suitors."

He reached into the glove compartment, pulled out a sheet of paper, and handed it to me. It was a flyer promoting the Western Electric company picnic to Michigan City.

"It's this Saturday," he said. "Would you like to go? I think I can still get tickets."

"I'd love to," I said. "I understand Aneta and her friends are going too. Won't it be fun?"

But when I raised the topic later that night with Aneta, she looked at me as if I were crazy. "I'm not going to that stupid picnic alone."

We were seated around the kitchen table, Aneta and Mama and me. Aneta's face was puffy and her eyes red-rimmed, and Mama's wore a look of concern.

"But you won't be alone," I said, confused. "All your friends are going."

"Yes, all my friends," she said gloomily. "And *Edward*. And *Marguerite*."

She buried her face in her arms and sobbed. Mama patted her shoulders and gave me a reproachful look. "Clara, leave your sister alone. Don't you see? She no want to see that boy. He no good."

"Aw, come on," I said. "There'll be hundreds of people at the picnic. Think of the fun you'll have. Don't let stupid Edward ruin your good time." It occurred to me that the shoe was now on the other foot, with me trying to cajole Aneta into doing something rather than the other way around.

She was adamant. "I'm not going. I even ripped up my ticket."

But as the week wore on, she appeared to undergo a change of heart. On Tuesday she received a note from Edward that seemed to make her feel differently about the whole situation. On Wednesday night I awakened close to midnight to find her perched on our windowsill, fully dressed, prepared to shimmy down the drainpipe into the yard and from there into Edward's jalopy, which sat idling around the corner.

"Are you crazy?" I said. "Papa will kill you if he finds out."

"He won't find out if you don't tell him," she whispered. "Besides, it's his fault. He's forbidden me to see Edward after last Sunday's little debacle. Sneaking out is the only way for us to be together."

I sat up in bed. "Can you blame him, the way you carried on?"

She waved her hand. "Oh, everyone makes such a big deal out of everything. Edward apologized and we talked it through and everything's fine now. But Papa refuses to see that. He says Edward is not a man of good character."

"Papa's right. If Edward had good character, he wouldn't be asking you to sneak out of the house at midnight behind your parents' backs."

"Don't be such an old fuddy-duddy. I'll be back before you know it."

"Aneta, don't go. I'm warning you."

Suddenly she pouted. "Oh, Clara," she said sadly, "I thought of all people, I could count on you."

Sassy Aneta I could easily say no to. Sad Aneta was another story. I felt my resolve cracking. I really didn't want to be involved in her shenanigans.

I sighed. "One hour," I said.

"An hour? What can a person do in an hour?"

Exactly. "If you're not back in one hour, I'm waking Papa."

Her eyes widened. "You wouldn't do that."

"Try it and see if I don't."

"But—"

"The clock's ticking."

"Oh, all right," she huffed. "One hour." And she was gone.

I had every intention of doing exactly as I'd warned her. But I didn't, because before the hour was up, I fell asleep, and when I awoke, it was to the rafter-shaking of my father reading her the riot act.

"What is the meaning of this?"

She'd been caught.

"You will not see the boy again," he fumed. "And furthermore, you will not leave this house, not for an entire month except to go to work."

I couldn't hear my sister's reply. I didn't need to. I knew she wouldn't be sneaking out to see Edward, or any other boy, for quite some time.

I felt sorry, and yet at the same time, I didn't. I could scarcely forgive myself for not stopping her from going. How would she ever learn not to defy our parents?

🌿 35 🌿

March 1945

L ater that week, as she got ready for work, Clara found herself thinking long and hard about "Operation Red Rose" devised by Rosalie and Debbie and their friends. So clever for the girls to think of such an effective form of mutual support in the face of bullying. Apparently they got a kick out of the secret-code angle of spreading the word that somebody needed help. And then for Laurie and her workplace friends to adapt the same system to the factory as "Operation Yellow Rose," when seeking help from those in authority proved futile. Brilliant.

And yet, as she rolled the idea around in her mind, Clara felt guilty.

She was responsible, she knew, for turning her back on other nurses in need, just as many of the older nurses had turned their backs on her years ago, when she was new to the profession. Nurse Kent as much as said so in her evaluation of Clara's performance when she'd said she was a technically proficient and highly skilled nurse, but lacked the leadership skills, the ability to get behind people and help them succeed. And she'd been right.

Now Clara realized things didn't have to be this way. Following Rosalie's lead, perhaps she could change it.

When she got to work, she received the day nurse's report, as usual. Did her rounds. Checked on the patients. Then, seeing all was as it should be, she called all the on-duty nurses together for a meeting and laid out the plan, which was met by a surprising level of enthusiasm. Now they just needed an opportunity to put it into practice.

Feeling satisfied that her proposal had been well received, Clara thought about her career as she completed her duties on the remainder of her shift. Maybe she wasn't head-nurse material, after all, she admitted to herself. But she wasn't too old to change, to implement a new idea here and there.

Above all, she was a true nurse, through and through. And a good one. She stuck to her duty, even when the going got rough. And, truth be told, it never again got as rough as it had on that dark day in 1915.

The following Tuesday, Clara found herself with an unexpected day off, having swapped shifts with another nurse. Eager to repay Laurie's hospitality, she invited mother and daughter to stay for dinner when Laurie got home from work.

"We'd love to," Laurie said, gratitude shining in her blue eyes. "I don't think there's much of anything in my icebox beyond some wilted lettuce and a hambone that's seen better days."

At the last minute, Clara decided to invite Jerry as well. But when she telephoned up to his apartment, he declined, reminding her of his weekly poker game.

"Oh, that's right. Well, next time, then."

Over pork chops, dumplings, and gravy, Rosalie entertained the two women with stories about the goings-on at her school.

"No more problems with Albert?" her mother asked.

Rosalie shook her head. "Nope. We're all friends now. He's teaching us girls how to play marbles."

"That's good to hear," Clara said.

After supper was over and the dishes done, she and Laurie lingered in the kitchen over coffee while Rosalie took her book into the front room to read in peace.

"I had a letter from Will this week," Laurie reported, beaming. "I was so happy to hear from him. I've practically burned through the paper with reading it over and over. He sounded well."

"That's wonderful news," Clara exclaimed. "I'm so glad."

"He wrote out the lyrics to *Stardust*." Laurie's face took on a dreamy expression. "That's our song, the first one we ever danced to. Reading them was so romantic, almost like hearing him sing them." She blinked and swallowed hard. "He has a beautiful singing voice."

"That is indeed romantic," Clara agreed. "Will sounds like a gallant soul."

"He is." Laurie paused. "What about Jaroslav?"

Clara stared at her. "What about him?"

"Was he romantic, like Will? If you don't mind talking about it, that is."

Clara felt uncertain. Did she mind? She wasn't sure. From anyone else the question would seem like prying, but Laurie's naturally inquisitive nature and honest interest in Clara's life didn't strike Clara as prying. Clearly the young woman was in a mood to talk about romance, and Jaroslav represented the sum total of experience Clara had to draw on in that department. Further, she felt as if she knew Laurie well enough that maybe, just maybe, she could open up a little. Thirty years was a long time to stay silent on a topic.

"Well, he didn't have a beautiful singing voice," she said finally. "That's for sure."

"Whatever happened between the two of you?" Laurie asked, her voice barely above a whisper.

Clara glanced through the open doorway toward the front room, where Rosalie looked to be thoroughly engrossed by her book.

"The short answer? The short answer is that my parents forbid me to see him."

Laurie's eyes grew large. "And the longer answer?"

Clara looked at her, weighing the options of telling and not telling. At last she sighed.

"If we're going to discuss the longer answer," she said, rising to her feet, "then I'll need to put on another pot of coffee."

36

July 24, 1915

Very early Saturday morning, the telephone rang. Mama and Papa had gone to visit Aunt Minnie for the weekend, so it was only Aneta and me in the house. I lay in bed for several minutes, half hoping my sister would get up and answer it, but her gentle snoring continued unabated.

Finally, the ringing stopped, only to start up again a minute later. I heaved myself out of bed and into the hallway.

"Is this Clara Janacek?" said a brisk, authoritative voice after I'd lifted the receiver.

"It is."

"This is Nurse Blair. You're needed to fill in on a shift. We're down two nurses due to illness."

"But it's my day off," I protested.

"I'm sorry, Nurse Janacek, but you're needed here." She paused. "Need I remind you that you're still on probation?"

She needn't.

"I'll be there as soon as I can." I returned the receiver to its hook on the wall.

With a heavy heart, I returned to the bedroom and began getting dressed. My movements woke my sister.

"What is it?" she grumbled, her voice groggy with sleep.

"I've been called in to work," I mumbled.

"Can't you turn them down?"

"No. My standing with Nurse Blair and Doctor Graham is precarious enough as it is."

"But what about the picnic?"

My heart sank. "I forgot all about the picnic." I flopped back on the bed and rested my wrist against my forehead. "I'll have to tell Jaroslav I can't go. And hope he'll understand."

She sat up, eyes sparkling. "I know. I'll go in your place."

I lifted my head and stared at her. "What? No. You're not supposed to leave the house, remember? Papa's orders."

"Oh, he didn't mean it. He only said that in anger."

"I'm pretty sure he did mean it."

"Please? All my friends are going, and Edward gave me a ticket, but I was so mad at him, I ripped it up. Pleeeease?"

"No," I said more forcefully. "Papa would forbid it."

"Papa doesn't need to know."

I sat up and faced her. "Aneta, I'm not going to lie for you. Not again."

She nestled back under the covers, but her eyes held mischief. "All right. But it would be such a shame if Jaroslav lost out on the cost of the ticket."

I exhaled. She was wearing me down. And she so badly wanted to go. "All right, then. But if there are consequences, *you* explain to Papa and Mama how you twisted my arm."

"Do you mean it?" she said, looking hopeful.

I threw my hands up. "You might as well go. I'll feel awful if the ticket gets wasted."

She giggled, threw back the covers, and started pawing through her dresses in the closet. "What do you think? The white dress or the green one? Will it be sunny out?" She ran to the window in her skivvies. "Oh, no. Looks like rain, Clara. Rain will ruin everything!"

"Don't fret, Aneta. Nothing will spoil your fun. Certainly not a little rain. Now come away from the window. You're practically indecent."

I roused myself from the bed, went to the telephone, and dialed the phone at Jaroslav's rooming house. It rang a long time, and when it was finally answered, a groggy voice informed me he'd already left.

I hurried and got dressed. Just before I was ready to leave, Jaroslav rang the doorbell.

I rushed downstairs and pulled open the door. "I'm so sorry, Jaroslav," I said. "I'm afraid I won't be able to go with you today. I've been called in to work at the hospital. I thought that perhaps you might use my ticket to escort Aneta."

Disappointment and concern flickered across his face. "That's terrible news. But I do understand. Of course I will be happy to take Aneta." He didn't look happy at all, which made me feel better and worse at the same time.

"I promise not to be any bother," Aneta said lightly as she floated down the stairs in her prettiest white lace dress, the enamel rose from Edward pinned to her collar. "I know plenty of people who are going. You won't even know I'm there."

He barely spared a glance for her, focusing on me. "If you're sure—"

"I'm sure." Disappointment made me feel a little nauseated, but I pasted on a brave smile.

"All right. You take care of yourself. Perhaps I can stop in and see you this evening."

"I'd like that," I assured him, although it would probably be very late when they returned, since the picnic was all the way in Michigan City. No matter. I would wait up.

To Aneta he said, "We'd better leave. We don't want to be late and miss the boat."

"I'll be ready in a moment. I just have to get my hat." She hurried back upstairs, but the quick errand turned into a ten-minute ordeal of fixing and fussing while I sat on the edge of the bed, watching her.

"Aneta, get going! He said you're already running late. Don't keep him waiting any longer."

"All right." She kissed me. "Are you sure—?"

"Go. Have a good time."

Finally, she dashed downstairs, and I heard the two of them hurry down the porch steps. Then I left the house myself, heading for the streetcar, resigned to my fate.

I arrived at the hospital and changed into my uniform in the locker room. Then I made my way up to Women's Medical. When I arrived there, a sense of dread permeated the floor.

"What's happened?"

Nadine Olson, who'd been in my class at the training institute, stood frozen at the desk. She looked at me wide-eyed, then rushed up and hugged me.

"Clara! Oh, thank goodness, you're here. We all thought you'd gone on the picnic."

"I was supposed to," I said irritably, trying to extricate myself from her grip, "but I got called in to fill in for somebody. Graham's been on the warpath, so I didn't think I could say no. What's happened?"

"Oh, Clara, it's terrible. Just terrible. We've just received a call." She released her grip on me and stepped back, wringing her hands. "There's been an accident on the river. Something happened to one of the boats."

My brain fogged. "Boats? What boats? What in the world are you talking about?"

"The boats for the Western Electric picnic," she said. "There's been an accident."

Panic thumped in my chest. "An accident? What kind of an accident? A fire? A collision? What?" Poor Nadine. It was all I could do not to shake her.

"I don't know. I don't know," she cried. She shook her head, distraught. "I don't know the details. I've only heard that something's happened to one of the boats." She grabbed my hand. "Oh, Clara, thank goodness you weren't on it after all. I was so frightened when I heard ..."

My mind spun, but my voice sounded oddly calm in my ears as I said to Nadine, "I was supposed to go on the picnic. But my sister—my sister is there. My sister might be on that boat."

Nadine's face blanched. "Oh, no," she breathed. "Maybe she wasn't on that one, the one that had the—whatever it was, the accident.

Maybe she was on one of the other boats. There were several chartered, you know."

I couldn't listen to another word. Just then Nurse Blair rushed past carrying her black medical bag. "Come along, Nurse Janacek," she said. "The Red Cross has called for help. We're going down there."

Flooded with a sense of dread, I followed her. Undergirding my worry was the knowledge that Mama and Papa weren't home and I was in charge. My sense of emergency kicked in, and with it, calm determination. *I mustn't panic,* I repeated to myself. Surely it wasn't as bad as all that. News like this was bound to get exaggerated as it passed from person to person, like the child's party game of whispering a message around a table until the message got completely garbled.

ॐ 37 ॐ

Nurse Blair and I caught a crowded trolley to downtown. The vehicle was filled with people chattering to one another, "Have you heard? Have you heard?" and supplying varying accounts of what might have happened down on the river, most of which made it clear that nobody had a clue what had actually taken place. Someone said, "I heard the whole boat turned over." But someone else said, "No, no, that can't be right. They probably haven't even left the dock yet."

The trolley inched its way to the Loop through traffic-clogged streets. As we neared our destination, my ears picked up a strange sound swelling above the ordinary downtown-Saturday bustle. I couldn't quite make out what it was. It was a fervent clamor the likes of which I'd never heard before, and it was coming from the direction of the river. Something definitely was amiss. The very air seemed charged with anxiety.

My knees buckled as the trolley shuddered to a stop.

"We'll get off here and walk," Nurse Blair said. "There's too much traffic for the streetcar to get any closer."

Adrenaline shot through my body as we clambered off the

conveyance. A mounted policeman, looking officious and severe on his muscular brown horse, blocked our progress.

"Where do you two think you're going?"

The horse whinnied and snorted.

"Please," Nurse Blair said, "we need to get to the waterfront."

"You and everybody else," the policeman grumbled. "There's been an accident on the river. Best steer clear."

"But—"

"Move along, please."

"We're nurses," Nurse Blair said, lifting her bag.

"Move along."

We waited until he was distracted by something else. Then we made a run for it—as much of a run as we could, given the heaving throng of humanity and my own rubbery legs. My mind looped on a single thought: *Find Aneta! Find Aneta!* Once I'd found my sister, safe and sound, everything would be all right.

When we reached the river, at first I couldn't tell quite what the matter was. I heard hollering. Men and women alike ran through the streets and sidewalks, pointing and clutching one another's arms. I lost track of the number of fire trucks and ambulances, both horse-drawn and the updated motorized versions, roaring toward the Clark Street Bridge, gongs clanging and sirens screeching. I sniffed the air for the telltale smoke that would indicate a fire. The stench of the river, automobile exhaust, animal dung, and all manner of sewage assaulted my nostrils, but no smoke. So, no fire. But *what*, then? The crowd became a morass, and we had no choice but to let the crush of bodies push us along.

At long last we broke through the crowd enough to catch a glimpse of the river at a distance. Tugboats churned through the water, engines chugging and horns blasting. Several long white ships, excursion steamers, floated at the wharf's edge. I squinted to make out the names of the boats. The *Theodore Roosevelt*. The *Petoskey*. The *Racine*. The *Maywood*. Where was the *Eastland*, the name that seemed to be on everybody's lips?

As we approached the wharf, the din swelled until it seemed to shake the very ground beneath our feet. Terrible shrieks rang out across the water, and I realized that my own voice had joined them.

In front of me in the river, settled on her side like the carcass of a great white whale, lay the mighty *Eastland*, half submerged. She had capsized, still tethered to the dock by her forward lines.

Nothing could have prepared me for what I saw. The putrid water around the capsized vessel roiled thick with people thrashing and flailing or clinging to life preservers, bits of wreckage, and each other. Stragglers in the water dragged others down, or were dragged down themselves, pulled under the foul surface of the river, or bobbing up and clutching at whatever drifted past, whether a piece of timber, a barrel, a chair, or another human being. Bystanders on the docks hollered and threw objects into the water—crates, ropes, anything they could find—while others stood paralyzed by fear and confusion. Before my eyes, a hurtled object landed on someone's head, injuring the very victim it was intended to help.

I couldn't stand to watch, nor could I force myself to look away. Frantic to find my sister and Jaroslav, desperate to know they were safe, I began to shove my way along the wharf, through the chaos of dazed onlookers and dripping, ashen-faced survivors, past ladies swooning and grown men openly weeping. But Nurse Blair grabbed my arm.

"We have a job to do, Nurse Janacek," she reminded me. "We need to find the Red Cross station and get our assignments."

I had not yet recognized any familiar faces, which could have been taken as a good sign or a bad one. Maybe my sister and Jaroslav weren't in the river. Maybe Nadine was right and they had taken a different boat, or weren't on a boat at all. Maybe Aneta's dawdling really had made them late, and they'd missed getting on board.

I took comfort in knowing Aneta to be a strong swimmer. I reminded myself that she'd learned to swim that one halcyon summer in Michigan, and to this day, her idea of paradise on a sweltering summer afternoon was to dive in and out of the powerful Lake Michigan waves at one of the swimming beaches. I had no idea, however, whether Jaroslav even knew how to swim. Surely he did, being young and strong, would have somehow gotten himself safely to the riverbank. I willed myself to calm down and catch my breath, to clear my head and think about what to do next. As Nurse Blair said, we had a job to do.

Metal clanged and sparks flew as rescue workers used welding torches, sledgehammers, axes, and crowbars to carve out holes in the thick steel plating of the hull, responding desperately to muffled screams and pounding from inside the vessel. It was then that I realized with horror that not all the passengers had been thrown into the water. Many more—possibly hundreds more—were still trapped inside the boat, as if in a prison. I shuddered. Suddenly the people who'd been dumped into the water, away from the boat, seemed like the lucky ones. At least they could breathe. At least they had a chance to make it to the wharf, one way or another.

Men steered rowboats through the melee, pulling as many victims as they could from the water. Other men kneeled and lowered ropes through the openings they had cut, or through portholes, which only worked for those who were very slim and unencumbered by voluminous clothing. One by one they pulled people out from the lower decks. Some of the rescued screamed or sobbed, others seemed livid with rage, still others stony with shock.

Lying on the hull were rows of limp bodies, wrapped in sodden summer finery. I told myself that they were probably just unconscious, not dead, but in my heart, I knew the truth. If they were merely unconscious, someone would be loading them onto stretchers. My eyes filled with tears, seeing how many of the victims were children, even babies.

It was a comfort—a cold, small comfort, but a comfort nonetheless —that I hadn't yet spotted Aneta's body among them. Where was she? Was she looking for me? I didn't know why she would be. If anything, she would think I was still at the hospital, working. I couldn't rest until I knew she was still alive.

My first instinct was to jump into the river and start pulling people out, but I wasn't a strong swimmer and didn't want to add to the burden of the rescuers, of which there were dozens—firemen, policemen, crew members, and ordinary bystanders, hauling people out of the water and dragging them onto the overturned hull of the boat. From there, those who could walk were escorted to safety, either onto the wharf or onto tugboats stationed alongside the wreck.

I was there to be of service in some way, but there were so many urgent needs that I didn't know where to start, and I sensed that even the experienced Nurse Blair didn't know, either. One thing I did know is that digging in to work would settle my mind about Aneta until we could be reunited. It felt virtually impossible to find her in the teeming hordes of people crowding the wharf, but I knew my sister was feisty enough not only to survive the ordeal, but to busy herself helping others find their way to help and home. For all I knew, she was already on her way to Cicero. Years from now, I consoled myself, she would be telling the story in a dramatic fashion to her children and grandchildren.

Or not.

I inhaled sharply. This was no time to give in to despair. Until I could learn the truth of what happened to Aneta and Jaroslav, I needed to get busy doing something, not standing on the dock like a lump of dough.

"This way, Clara," Nurse Blair said, apparently forgetting formal protocol. She pointed to the base of the Clark Street Bridge. "I see a group of Red Cross nurses over there. Looks like they're setting up an emergency station." We hustled over, and she sought out the apparent leader to offer our services.

"We're nurses," she said, "from Memorial Hospital."

The woman straightened, blew stray hair out of her eyes, and gave us a quick once-over. "Good. There are already too many people trying to help but just getting in the way. In your case, we need all the help we can get." We all exchanged names—hers was Helen something—then she looked at me and gestured toward a stack of boxes. "You can start by unpacking supplies, over there. Nurse Blair, please come with me."

As they hurried off, I busied myself unpacking cartons of bandages and splints. It felt good to keep my hands busy and my mind on something besides Aneta, but I ached to be doing something more concrete to help the steady stream of passengers, who ranged from the emotionally distraught but physically uninjured to those lying unconscious on stretchers.

Finally, I got my chance.

"Nurse Janacek, we need you over here," Nurse Blair called. "You know how to operate a pulmotor, don't you?" She opened a case and revealed a contraption inside, a brass pump with hoses and a mask.

I'd learned to operate the lung machine, used to resuscitate drowning victims, but only in theory. In my training course we'd learned how to place the mask over a practice dummy's mouth and operate the machine so it pumped air into the lungs with a loud wheezing, rattling sound. I'd never actually used it on a living person. But the expression on Nurse Blair's face told me this was no time to display my lack of self-confidence. She touched my shoulder in a rare display of encouragement, then hurried off to help another patient.

I looked at the patient on the stretcher next to me and recoiled in spite of my professional training. She was a young woman about my age. Her chilly blue skin and lack of visible breathing made her appear dead, but suddenly she coughed.

"Pulmotor," the doctor said. I set the machine at his side, then watched carefully as he fitted the mask over her mouth. He left me to do the pumping and rushed off to aid someone else. There must have been fifteen or twenty such machines clustered in the Clark Street Red Cross station. With that many pulmotors going at once, the racket was ear-splitting.

"We're grateful for your help," an exhausted nurse said to me at one point.

"I was supposed to go on the picnic, but then—" I stopped, too exhausted to go over the whole story. I cut it short. "The Red Cross put out a call for more nurses. My sister was going on the picnic," I said around the lump in my throat. "I-I haven't found her yet."

The nurse looked concerned. "Shouldn't you be looking for her?"

Yes! I screamed inwardly. Outwardly I kept pumping the pulmotor. Doing my duty. "I'm sure she's fine," I said. "She was running late and might not have even been on the *Eastland* at all. And even if she was, well, she's a strong swimmer."

The nurse shook her head. "Even the strong swimmers got bogged down in their heavy, waterlogged clothes. Let me take over here. You should try to find her."

But a fresh load of patients was delivered. There would be time enough to find my sister when the emergencies abated. I was certain, down to my toes, that Aneta was fine, that she was probably at work somewhere, helping other people, or at least on her way home. Even so, I scanned the crowd frequently, hoping to catch a glimpse of her.

Soon a routine of sorts was established in the makeshift medical station. Rescuers brought the victims to us, carried in their arms, on stretchers, or on foot if the victim could walk. Drownings, suffocations, and impact injuries were the three main problems. We nurses hurried to each unconscious victim, knelt down, and checked each neck for a pulse. If we found none, we called a doctor over to check. If he found no heartbeat or other indication of life, he would say, "Gone."

"Clara, fetch some more blankets," Nurse Blair commanded. "This patient has hypothermia. He's slurring his speech and stumbling."

I rushed to get some blankets from the supply boxes and wrapped them around the pale and shivering man. His body temperature was too low, his breathing labored, and his heart rate barely perceptible. Nurse Blair rubbed his wrists.

"Cold water is good for slowing brain damage but bad for hypothermia," I said, trying to absorb the medical facts being hurled at me. Only by concentrating on the facts could I keep my feelings from running away with me.

Nurse Cavanaugh glanced up at me. "This one's ready for transport."

"Transport!" I shouted, and two men came and lifted the hypothermic man's stretcher at each end. Up on the bridge, at the top of the stairs, rows of ambulances stood waiting to transport patients either to a hospital or to the morgue.

"This one's going to Iroquois. Do you have a name?" one of the men said.

I shook my head, and so did Nurse Blair. On a clipboard, I jotted down a brief description of the man and what he was wearing and noted that he'd been taken to Iroquois Hospital, in case relatives came looking for him. We were trying to keep the best records we could under the circumstances.

Black-robed clergymen and nuns hovered raven-like over the

injured and the dead, pausing here and there, holding people's hands, touching the tops of their heads, mumbling things.

"What good could they possibly do?" I muttered as I hooked yet another patient to a pulmotor.

The nurse beside me followed my gaze and said, "They pray for people and bring comfort and peace to their hearts."

"I don't see what earthly good that does when what they need is proper medical care."

"It's not *earthly* good they're thinking of," replied the nurse. I shrugged and turned to the next patient.

We worked without breaks for I don't know how long. At some point two policemen in dark blue jackets, rain mixed with perspiration on their exhausted faces, walked through the makeshift medical station, distributing coffee, soup, sandwiches, and water.

"You should eat something," one of them said as he offered me a sandwich.

I took it and ate quickly, not tasting the food, and followed it with a few gulps of tepid coffee, loathe to interrupt my work.

"It's important to take a break now and then," the officer said to me. "You'll be no good to anyone if you collapse."

"I can't stop," I explained. "My sister might have been on the *Eastland*. My sister and my—my friend," I added, realizing I had no adequate word for my relationship to Jaroslav. "Friend" seemed inadequate but "suitor" seemed presumptuous. "She is a strong swimmer, though, and they may not even have been on the boat. In any case, I'm certain they're both all right." I said this with more confidence than I felt.

As the day wore on, fewer and fewer bodies brought to our station showed signs of life. Where once there'd been a din of much shouting and screaming, now the crowds grew almost silent, ominously so, as if no one had any will left within them to talk.

As dusk fell, we held out very little hope that anyone found would still be alive. So far neither Aneta's nor Jaroslav's name had turned up on any roster. I clung to hope that they were still alive, but I also knew that, in spite of everyone's best efforts, information was sketchy, incomplete, and sometimes just plain wrong.

Suddenly I heard my name.

"Clara!"

I wheeled around to see Jaroslav's tall, lanky form waving his arm from some distance away.

My knees nearly melted with relief. My heart sang with joy. He was alive! If he was alive, so was Aneta. I ran to him and practically knocked him over with my embrace.

His wool jacket was soaked with filthy river water and rainwater. I didn't care. I clung to him, unable to speak.

"I've been looking all over for you," he murmured against my hair. "I tried to call you at the hospital, but the lines were jammed. When I finally got through, they said you were here."

"I'm so happy to see you," I said through tears. Finally I took a step back and I looked all around. "Where's Aneta?"

He shook his head.

For a moment, the hope I'd held onto all day felt suspended between us like a leaf lifted by the wind.

But beyond that invisible leaf, Jaroslav's expression blew it away. "I'm sorry, Clara. So sorry. We got separated and—" His voice thickened as the terrible words got caught in his throat. "I don't know where she is."

38

"Nurse! Pulmotor!" a doctor barked, sounding very far away. But I could only think about Jaroslav's words, trying to make sense of the news he was trying to tell me through the rushing sound in my head. I touched his elbow and guided him over to a relatively quiet corner near the steps leading up to the street.

"So you both were on the *Eastland*. But we don't know that she's dead, or even injured," I said slowly, clinging to the facts as he'd presented them. "We simply don't know where she is. For the time being. That's all." I looked up at him beseechingly, silently begging him to tell me we'd both wake up from this nightmare and Aneta would be all right.

He ran a hand through his wet, matted hair. "I'm sorry. That's all I know. I feel responsible ..."

This wasn't the time for laying blame. I fought to keep my voice steady, cool, logically working through what he'd told me. "Tell me how you got separated."

He drew a breath. "We were among the last few to board the boat. There were other boats, of course. I suggested we wait and board the *Roosevelt*, but Aneta insisted on getting on the *Eastland*. Apparently it was the star of the fleet. She'd been hearing about how big and impressive it was, and she wanted to be on the same boat as her friends."

"That sounds like Aneta," I murmured. "Go on."

"Well, it was jam-packed with families. Every seat seemed to be taken, so I steered us toward the railing so we'd at least have room to breathe. But five or ten minutes later she heard the dance orchestra start up on the deck below us. Then she spotted Edward and some of her other friends on the crowded stairwell. They were heading down to where the music was. She wanted to dance, but I was feeling claustrophobic and wanted to stay on the open deck where I could breathe. So she excused herself and disappeared into the crowd." He paused. "I should have gone with her."

I touched his arm. "You didn't know."

"We felt the boat list one way, and then the other," he recalled. "Some of the passengers were even joking about it, but it didn't feel funny to me. I hoped the whole journey wouldn't be like that. I was worried I'd get sick and disgrace myself." The look when he said that, the disgust on his face, made me want to comfort him. But I didn't move to do that. I just waited for the rest of the story. "My feet started sliding out from under me, and I clung to the railing." He swallowed. "We started tipping again. The water came closer and closer, and the boat rolled over. It just … rolled over. Like a toy in a bathtub."

I could imagine the scene, little though I wanted to. "Go on."

"I was thrown clear of the boat with hundreds of others thrown in after me. People, picnic baskets, parasols—everything, just hurling through the air and dumped in the water. Small children. Babies." He paused to gather his composure. "I'll never forget what I saw. People everywhere, flailing in the water. A few were swimming. Others were clinging to bits of debris, to baskets or boards or whatever they could grab. People on the shore were throwing things into the water for people to grab on to. Everyone was screaming. It was horrible, all that screaming."

"Then what happened?" I prodded.

"People around me were panicking, but I prayed, 'Lord, help us.' And suddenly I felt oddly clearheaded and knew what I had to do. I shucked off my jacket and shoes and reached out to rescue a little girl who was floating past. But a fellow grabbed my arm and yelled, "Help me!" He started pulling me and the little girl under the water. I fought him off, but in the struggle I lost hold of the little girl. I—I don't know what happened to her after that. To them."

"But you managed to get to safety," I said, eager to move the story forward.

"Eventually, yes. But first I dragged as many people as I could out of the water. We hoisted them up onto the hull or wherever we could so that the rescuers could take over. I managed maybe ten or twelve people before the cold and exhaustion threatened to knock me out, and I had to take a breather. I didn't feel like I could stop as long as there were people in the water." He gestured toward the river. By now most everyone had been pulled from the water, but men were still hard at work on the overturned hull.

"After a while, some of us formed a bucket brigade with the firemen. We lifted body after body from the hull, most of them limp, and handed them off to the fellows carrying the stretchers, who took them to the medical station. My limbs grew numb, and my hands and back ached."

He looked stricken. "I lost track of time. Those were precious hours I could have been looking for Aneta, but I wasn't."

"But that time wasn't wasted. Look at the lives you saved," I said with forced cheer. "And, we need to look at the positive side. None of those people you pulled from the water was Aneta, right?"

His face contorted. "That's what I'm telling you. I wasn't able to find her."

"That could be a *good* thing. Couldn't it? It means she probably got rescued by somebody else, or even made it to safety on her own. She's probably somewhere safe and sound right now, and didn't need you to rescue her."

I failed to convince him. "She was my responsibility." He shook his head, as if he couldn't believe it himself. "But she wanted to be with her friends. With Edward."

"Of course she did." I felt a tiny glimmer of hope ignite deep in my belly. "Well, we just have to find Edward, then, don't we?" I said briskly. "Or one of her other friends. Wherever they are, we're likely to find

Aneta." I glanced around the emergency station. "The good news is, she hasn't been brought here. That means she's not in need of medical attention. Edward hasn't been here, either, nor have any of their friends that I'd recognize. So maybe they're all together somewhere. Maybe they're even home by now."

"She would have let you know."

"She wouldn't have known to look for me," I said, feeling more hopeful by the second. "She has no idea I'm even here."

"Nurse!" a doctor bellowed. "I need you. Now!"

Right. I had a job to do.

"You go on," I told Jaroslav. "You keep looking for her, for Edward, for anybody. I'll stick with the rest of the Red Cross nurses, so you'll always know where you can find me. Now go!"

By early evening our caseload in the emergency station had dropped off considerably. Those pulled from the wreckage who needed medical attention had largely been cared for and sent either home, to the hospital, or to the morgue. A volunteer handed me a mug of coffee and a sandwich. I drank the coffee but only nibbled at the sandwich. The Western Electric Company had donated twenty telephones, and I tried to use one to call my sister and also my aunt's home in Wisconsin to inform my parents about what had happened. Unfortunately, the lines were still jammed and I couldn't get through.

Nurse Blair approached me, looking every bit as exhausted and depleted as I felt.

"Some of us are going over to the Reid-Murdoch building to assist with the—the mortuary duties," she said. "You're welcome to come with us or to stay here and help with the remaining patients. It's up to you."

I certainly didn't relish working in the makeshift morgue, helping to identify bodies and console the grieving next of kin, but I had determined to serve where I was needed. I told Nurse Blair as much.

"But my friend is still looking for my sister," I explained. "I think it might be prudent for me to stay here in case he—or she—comes looking for me."

"I'd forgotten about your sister." Nurse Blair rubbed her forehead. "I'm sorry she hasn't been found yet,"

"I'm not," I said. "Not really. I think every minute that she's not found is further evidence that she's alive and unharmed."

The older nurse smiled weakly and patted my shoulder. "That's the spirit." She paused. "Nurse Janacek, if I don't see you again until after this ordeal is over, I want you to know you've done well. I'm proud of you. I'll be giving a good report to Dr. Graham."

"Thank you."

I watched as she joined a group of nurses and together they climbed the steps leading from the wharf up to Clark Street, their shoulders sagging in weariness.

I went back to work. The remaining nurses and I continued helping the doctors, now by gaslight, tending the sick and injured. We lent what comfort we could to the shocked and grieving and tried to keep records of who'd been treated and released, who'd been sent to a hospital, and who'd been declared dead. The work helped distract me from worrying about my sister.

After I don't know how many hours, Jaroslav reappeared, his eyes even darker than normal against the pallor of his skin. Even before he showed me the water-soaked rose brooch in his hand, I knew.

My vision dimmed as though someone had dropped a dark veil over my head. The roar of the pulmotors, the shouting voices, the fiery hiss of the blowtorches all faded as if everything had suddenly moved very far away.

He pulled me toward him, wrapped his arms around me. I couldn't understand what was happening. He started uttering words. He was praying.

"God, protect her. God, look out for her. God, give her strength."

Why was he praying for Aneta? Why would he do that? Aneta was gone.

Then I realized he wasn't praying for Aneta.

He was praying for me.

39

neta's wake was held in our front room. Her coffin, surrounded by banks of oppressively perfumed flowers, rested on a bier placed before the unused fireplace. Beneath it sat a block of ice that melted continually into a metal pan. I thought the sound of it would drive me mad.

Drip.

Drip.

Drip.

Mourners came and went through the black-draped front door, their hushed condolences mingling with the quiet, ceaseless sobbing of my mother. For most of the guests, our house was just one more stop on a depressing circuit of visits. The final death toll stood at eight hundred and forty-four, including twenty-two entire families. Among the dead were Edward. And Marguerite. And Lil. And so many others. House after house after house, up and down the streets of Cicero and surrounding communities from which Western drew its workforce.

I listened to my mother's keening, but I could not bring myself to cry. For some reason, the tears would not come. I longed to throw myself into her arms and wail the way I did as a young child. But every time I reached for her, she pushed me away. The pain of her rejection stabbed like a scalpel. My father grew cold and distant, as if the sight of me reminded him of all he had lost. I could read his thoughts: If I'd followed through on his discipline of Aneta and refused to allow her to go to the picnic—indeed, not given her my ticket and sent her off with Jaroslav—she'd still be alive. I locked my tears inside as if, by sending my sister to her death, I'd relinquished my right to release them. Instead I busied myself with playing hostess to the scores of visitors.

Seated around the front room or delivering food to the kitchen, friends and neighbors shared scraps of information they'd gleaned from piecemeal accounts in the newspapers. It wasn't clear to anyone yet why the *Eastland* had capsized, but that didn't stop people from speculating.

"I heard all the passengers ran to one side of the ship to look at something," declared Mrs. Dvorak from next door. "That's why she toppled over."

"Nope." Mr. Peterka chimed in. "They added extra lifeboats, and that made her top-heavy." That explanation sounded plausible to me. Since the sinking of the *Titanic*, maritime safety regulations had been tightened. But still, wouldn't the owners make sure the boat could handle the additional weight?

"Didn't matter anyway," Mr. Peterka continued, shaking his head sadly. "Nobody could get to those lifeboats because there wasn't time to unchain them. What a waste."

"The ship was unstable to begin with," said another neighbor, a survivor. "I could feel it right off. I sensed that something wasn't right the minute we boarded. I'm no sailor, but it didn't feel right under my feet. I made my family get off."

While the cause was unclear, all accounts agreed on one thing: that the boat had listed first to one side, then the other, before it turned over completely. "Real smoothly, like an egg in the water," one witness recalled.

I shuddered, imagining the terror of Jaroslav and other upper-deck passengers as the boat turned, tossing them into the frigid black river. They were among the lucky ones, the first to manage to swim to the wharf or scramble onto the hull, or stay afloat by clinging to some piece of debris. Many of those caught on the lower decks—like Aneta, who'd gone downstairs to dance—were trapped by skidding furniture and equipment. At least one passenger, I learned to my horror, had been smashed by a sliding piano. Others were trampled by people trying to escape.

Aneta's body, however, hadn't looked crushed or injured or even bruised. The coroner said she likely drowned from water rushing in through the portholes. I tried not to dwell on the circumstances of her death, only hoping she'd died quickly with little suffering.

The one person Papa refused to let in the house was Jaroslav. Jaroslav, who'd saved so many lives, suffered dearly for the fact that he hadn't saved my sister. On the first day of the wake, he'd shown up at our house, hat in hand, ready to pay his respects, but Papa refused to let him step over the threshold.

"Killer!" he shouted. "You let my daughter die."

Jaroslav turned pale and swayed slightly, as if he were going to be sick. I leapt to my feet. "Papa, no!" Other mourners who were present spoke up in Jaroslav's defense, reinforcing the fact that, given the circumstances, nothing he could have done would have saved Aneta. But no amount of reasoning made the slightest difference to Papa's senseless hatred of the man I loved.

Two days later, as we stood around the casket at the cemetery, just one among scores of other funerals that day, while the overworked undertaker droned on in meaningless drivel about "the hereafter" and "a better place," I spotted Jaroslav standing at a respectful distance. He didn't dare come closer, lest my father explode in fury, but Papa, consumed as he was in his and Mama's grief, didn't see him. It soothed my heart to know Jaroslav had been there, and I vowed to speak to him as soon as I had a chance.

One evening about a week after the funeral, I approached the topic. I'd just finished cleaning up the dishes after yet another evening meal none of us had wanted to eat. Mama had gone back to bed, and I was about to leave for work, my first shift back after being granted funeral leave.

I had time to spare before I left, so I sought out Papa in the front room.

"You know, Papa," I said softly, screwing up my courage. "It really wasn't Jaroslav's fault that Aneta died. She'd taken it upon herself to go below deck, where Edward and her other friends were. She wanted to dance. It was her choice. Jaroslav couldn't control what she did or didn't do." *Nor could you,* I wanted to add, but didn't.

Surely Papa would see the truth in my statement, now that the initial shock had passed. It did no good to assign blame. But I'd miscalculated the depth of his rage.

"Don't you dare mention my daughter in the same breath as that man!" he exploded. "It's his fault that we lost Aneta. He was supposed to look out for her, to take care of her, and he didn't."

"It was an accident," I shouted, trembling in righteous indignation.

"Don't contradict me, Clara. And you." He thrust an accusing finger in my face. "You were wrong to let her leave the house in the first place."

"But—"

"Stay away from him. Do you understand?" His voice shook with anger. He pointed toward the front door. "The day you walk out of that door with Jaroslav will be the last day you'll ever set foot inside my house."

I raced out the door to the streetcar, then stared unseeing out the grimy window all the way to the hospital. Somehow I had to see Jaroslav, to explain that I didn't blame him, no matter what my father thought. But I didn't know how to arrange it. I would need to be cautious from then on when I talked to him, taking care that my parents didn't see us together.

It was Jaroslav who made the first move. Early the next morning, I found him waiting for me outside the hospital during the short interval between the end of my shift and the beginning of his. We found a bench in a quiet spot at the edge of the hospital grounds and sat together, holding hands. His handsome face was etched with regret.

"You're almost twenty-one. You earn your own living," he said when I explained the situation. "Maybe it's time to start making your own decisions."

"I can't go against my parents' wishes," I said, miserable. "Especially now that Aneta is gone. I can't cause them any further heartache."

He looked at the ground as if hoping to find the answer lying in the grass. Finally he spoke.

"I don't want you to have regrets for the rest of your life because you caused your family pain. And maybe he's right, your father. It was my fault that—"

"But it wasn't your fault. It was an accident." Maybe if I repeated the truth enough times, it would finally sink in.

"If I hadn't allowed her to leave my side. If I'd kept her from going below deck to dance."

"And I blame myself for allowing her to go on the trip in the first place. But Aneta wasn't the type to allow anyone to keep her from doing what she wanted to do," I said. "My father will eventually come around to see that. I'm sure of it."

But he never did.

🌿 40 🌿

March 1945

"So then what did you do?" Laurie's eager voice broke into Clara's reverie, begging for more of the story. Clara blinked and looked around, disoriented, stunned to find herself seated on the Lucas's nubby gray sofa in their sparsely furnished living room, gripping a cup of tea. How had she gotten there? Somehow during the telling of all that had transpired concerning the *Eastland* and family and first love, Rosalie had fallen asleep and been carried downstairs and put to bed. Apparently Clara had followed them down and been given a cup of tea and a listening ear. And all the while she'd kept talking, talking, talking. Things she hadn't told anyone, not a soul, in thirty years. Her face grew hot with the realization that she'd completely taken over the conversation, had barraged Laurie with her torrent of memories. What must her neighbor be thinking? She hoped Rosalie had slept through the most harrowing parts of it.

But Laurie seemed far from scandalized, far from bored. "Don't leave me hanging," she begged. "What did you do next? What happened with Jaroslav?"

Clara set her teacup on the end table and tried to remember where she'd left off.

Oh, yes.

For a brief moment she considered telling Laurie that she couldn't remember the rest of the story, because surely she'd crumple, would dissolve, if she tried to tell it. But it was too late for that. The only way around was through.

She drew a deep breath.

"Following Aneta's burial, my parents and I moved through our days in a haze, as if all the color and light had gone out of our world. Mama took to her bed and more or less remained there, basically giving up. At least it seemed that way as I took over the running of the household, cooking and cleaning and shopping around my shifts at the hospital. I'd care for my patients on the ward, then care for my parents at home, then do it all over again the next day.

"Papa returned to his job at the Western and put in a few more years before retiring to sit in the front room and stare out the window as if expecting Aneta to come skipping down the street at any moment. Lines of sorrow etched his face. How I wished I could turn back the clock to the moment when I'd given her permission to go on the picnic in my place. I wished I had given her a firm 'No,' something she heard too seldom in her short life. She would have raged, she would have cried and cajoled, but she'd have still been alive. If I'd followed Papa's rules, she'd still be with us."

"You know it wasn't your fault, don't you?" Laurie interjected. "You know that."

"My parents needed to blame someone. Now that they'd banished Jaroslav, they had only me, the disappointing daughter. I can't help but think that if I'd died and Aneta had lived, they'd have found it easier to cope."

"Don't say that," Laurie pleaded.

But deep down, Clara knew it was true.

"For a few weeks, I sneaked around to see him. Sometimes we met outside the hospital before or after my shift, or at a certain picnic table in the secluded woods of the forest preserve, or at a restaurant or movie theater located far enough from the neighborhood that we were unlikely to run into people we knew. But that last bit was practically impossible, as Jaroslav's old jalopy had finally given up the ghost. I lived in fear, constantly looking over my shoulder, worried that someone would see us together and tell my parents. It was impossible to relax and just enjoy each other's company. Jaroslav and I both knew we couldn't continue this way, but I loved him so. We talked endlessly about my situation whenever we were together. We struggled to find a solution but never did."

"Never?" Laurie whispered, her face mirroring the regret now wrapping its tentacles around Clara's heart.

"No. It was too difficult."

Her mind went back to the chilly autumn evening they'd sat side by side on 'their' picnic table, entangled in yet another fruitless discussion about the situation. How she'd thrown her arms around his neck. Told him how she kept hoping my father would relent and accept him.

How he'd said, "We both know that isn't going to happen" as he gently removed her arms from around his neck.

She told Laurie about his dark eyes, the way they glistened with unshed tears. How he slid his fingers under her chin, lifted her face to his, and kissed her tenderly. And how she knew, without his saying a word, that it was their last kiss. How he walked her home, and how she watched the back of his jacket as he disappeared down the moonlit street.

"And that was that," she concluded. She took a long swig of tea. Talking was thirsty work.

Laurie stared at Clara, mouth agape. "No! You let him go? Just like that?"

"He let me go, more like," Clara said. "But I didn't blame him. What choice did he have? I'm sure that if my parents had given in, Jaroslav would have bent over backward to win them over. But they could never forgive him for not saving Aneta's life. And I was all that they had left. How could I choose between him and them?" She paused. "And then there was the matter of faith. As in, he believed in God."

"And you don't?"

"I don't know. I don't *not* believe in God. But I couldn't ever seem to connect to Him personally, the way Jaroslav did. He turned to God with his troubles, but frankly, I had derived as little comfort from God as from my own father."

Laurie winced at that, but she didn't respond.

They were silent for a few moments. Then Laurie sighed.

"In a way, Will chose me over his mother," she said, her voice tinged with regret. "That hasn't turned out too well on her part. But I'm glad he chose me. I don't think I could live without him."

"I didn't think I could live without Jaroslav, either," Clara said. "But of course I could, and I have, for all these years." She reflected. "I was trapped, you see. Trapped between my feelings for him and my duty to my parents."

"That's so sad." Laurie stood and refilled Clara's teacup from a china pot. "Did you ever see him again?"

"Yes." Clara sipped her tea, felt the warm, comforting liquid slip down her throat. "After we parted ways, I heard nothing about him for a while. Then about a year later I learned through a mutual acquaintance, a fellow nurse at Memorial, that he'd enlisted in the Army Air Corps. And then America was drawn into the Great War, and off he went to fight overseas. After he returned, he courted and married that same nurse."

Laurie's eyes widened. "Wow, that must have been awkward. Maybe he had a thing for nurses."

Clara chuckled. "Maybe. But by then, I'd moved on. Any lingering romantic feelings I'd had for him were long gone. Or, if not exactly gone, then buried deep down where I couldn't reach them." She took a thoughtful pause, remembering. "The funny thing was, out of all the nurses I've worked with over the years, his Marianne was one of my favorites. I really liked her. She was the closest thing to a best friend I ever had."

"Was?"

"She died," Clara said. "A few years ago. Cancer."

"I'm sorry."

"Because of Marianne, Jaroslav and I eventually became good friends. I guess that proves I wasn't truly in love with him after all.

And I was so fond of Marianne." She stood. "I've taken enough of your time. I apologize for talking your ear off all evening."

"I wanted to hear it," Laurie said. "But Clara, that's all over now. You know that, right?"

"It's my job to keep the memories," Clara said simply.

"Keeping the memories doesn't mean wallowing in them."

Clara pondered Laurie's words as she went to work. Did she wallow? She didn't think of herself as the sort of person who wallowed.

41

When she arrived on the Women's Medical ward, there was no more time to worry about wallowing as Dr. Pratt's signature bellow ricocheted down the hallway.

"What is the meaning of this?" he screamed at poor Cindy Novak, his scowling gaze fixed on her red face. He stared at her for a long terrible minute of absolute silence. Then he started in again over some perceived shortcoming.

The gnawing self-doubts crept into Clara's mind, but she pushed them away. It was time to show support to a colleague. Time to put her team's plan into action.

Mustering her courage, she walked past the former Betty Paulson— now Betty Jenkins—and muttered, "Operation White Rose." Then she walked up behind the beleaguered Cindy Novak and wordlessly placed a hand on her shoulder. She stood there silently, looking directly at Dr. Pratt.

"What do you want?" he demanded.

Clara said nothing.

Before long, Clara's "Operation White Rose" message was passed from nurse to nurse. One by one they stopped what they were doing and joined Clara behind Cindy with their hands on her or another nurse's shoulders, gazing silently at Dr. Pratt.

The sputtering doctor backed off, muttering to himself. Finally, he spun and strode down the hallway.

When he was gone, the nurses broke formation and grinned at each other in grim relief.

Cindy looked like she was about to collapse.

"Good work, ladies," Clara said. "And now, I believe, there are doughnuts in the break room."

Later that afternoon, when Laurie came to pick up Rosalie, Clara invited her in and told her the story.

"It worked," she reported proudly. "Rosalie's 'Operation Red Rose' idea worked not just on the playground, but in your factory, and now at the hospital. Although, as far as we nurses are concerned, I felt it only right to call it 'Operation White Rose,'" she added modestly.

"That's absolutely brilliant," Laurie exclaimed. "But, you know, the original idea wasn't actually Rosalie's."

"Whose was it?"

"God's." Laurie grinned. "'If one member suffers, all suffer together; if one member is honored, all rejoice together.' First Corinthians chapter twelve, verse twenty-six. Of course, Paul was talking about the church," she clarified. "But the concept still applies to schoolmates or workmates. Even nurses."

"Well, I'll be." Clara shook her head. "I've only just started reading the Bible. I have so much to learn."

Laurie touched her hand. "You and me both. But the good thing is, you don't have to learn it all at once. I'll help you. And so will Jerry."

A deep sense of gratitude washed through Clara. "It's still hard to wrap my head around the idea that God even wants me. If you and Rosalie had given up on me—"

"You are His," Laurie said. "If it hadn't been us, He would have used somebody else to reach you."

"I understand that," Clara said, holding Laurie's hand. "But I'm awfully glad He used you and Rosalie."

"We didn't do much at all," Laurie said. "Just prayed."

An unfamiliar impulse rose up in Clara's chest. She blurted, "Would you pray with me?"

How many times had Jerry said those exact words, and Clara had cringed? But now, she wanted to pray for her friends. Yes, that's what the nurses were—her friends.

Mutely Laurie nodded. Clara closed her eyes.

"Dear Lord, please bless my nurses. Help them to adjust to their circumstances and to stand up to abuse when it's warranted. Life is too lonely to go it alone. Let us be a family, Lord, on the Women's Medical ward at Memorial Hospital."

As Laurie squeezed her hand, Clara marveled that she'd performed a second courageous act within twenty-four hours. First she and her nurses had stood up together against the fearsome Doctor Pratt. And now she, Clara Janacek, had prayed. Out loud. For the very first time.

42

April 1945

When Laurie stepped off the streetcar in front of Western Electric, ready to begin her shift, she was startled to see two police cruisers parked outside the main entrance. In the locker room she approached a group of women gathered together, deep in conversation.

"I saw two squad cars outside," Laurie said. "Do you know what's going on?"

"We don't know any of the details," one of the women said, "but we heard something big is happening up in switchboard assembly."

Switchboard assembly? That was Laurie's department. Her blood pumped harder, and she quickened her pace.

When she reached the factory floor, it appeared no one was working. Instead, workers huddled in little whispering clumps, much like the women in the locker room. Heads swiveled in her direction.

Laurie had no time to ask questions before Ted Palmer's voice shouted to her.

"Lucas! In here, now."

Not again. But this time was even worse, with everyone watching. She felt sick as she crossed the floor, feeling all eyes on her. What if she'd really screwed up this time? What if she screwed up so badly that the police—she couldn't even finish the thought.

Two men in business suits stood with Ted Palmer in his glassed-in office. Were they plainclothes policemen? Crazy thoughts swirled in her head. Was she going to be arrested? Hauled off like a common criminal in front of everyone for some mistake she didn't even know she'd made? How would she get word to Rosalie? Who would care for her daughter? Cold sweat dampened her palms and poured down her back in rivulets.

"This is Mrs. Laurie Lucas," Ted Palmer told the men. He said their names, too, but her racing brain didn't retain the information. At any rate, she didn't need to know their names. They'd all have plenty of time to get better acquainted while they hauled her off to jail.

"Please sit down, Mrs. Lucas," one of the men said.

Shaky-legged, she did as she was told. "What's going on?" she asked, her voice quivering.

"In short," Mr. Palmer announced gravely, "Carl Bowman was found tampering with parts last night. He's been arrested on suspicion of espionage."

"Espionage!" She couldn't believe what she was hearing. Oafish Carl Bowman, with the IQ of a gnat? It wasn't possible.

"Turns out his real name is Karl Baumann." The detective spelled out the name for her. "He's a German national."

Much as Laurie disliked Carl, she felt her fear enflame into indignation. "He's not German," she countered. "He's as American as you and I." She couldn't believe she was speaking out in defense of her nemesis. She resented the man intensely. But a German spy? She couldn't believe him capable of such things.

"He was born in Germany, to German parents. That makes him German," Mr. Palmer said.

"This is America," Laurie said. "You can't suspect a man of spying simply because he has a German name."

"Mrs. Lucas," Ted Palmer interjected in a warning tone.

"With all due respect, ma'am, yes, we can," one of the policemen said. "But the real issue here is not his name but the fact that he was caught tampering with parts and equipment. And those parts and equipment happened to be yours. So we will need to take a statement from you."

"I see." Laurie was glad she was sitting, as relief melted every muscle. She'd been vindicated. He had been tampering with equipment, after all, and he'd gotten caught.

Mr. Palmer led them all to a private conference room, where Laurie could speak freely, away from the prying eyes of the other employees. She told the detectives everything she knew about Carl Bowman: the pranks he'd pulled, the rude remarks he'd made, his suggestive language, the fact that he'd displayed an obvious dislike of her from her first few weeks on the job. She left no detail out.

"He's an odious man," she concluded. "I've long wished he would leave me alone. I believe he tampered with my work to get me in trouble. But I *don't* believe he's a spy. I don't believe he'd be capable of it."

Finally one of the men asked Laurie, "Would you be willing to testify in court, if necessary?"

"I would."

The men stood. "As this is an ongoing investigation, please do not discuss it with anyone."

Laurie agreed.

After the men had gone, Ted Palmer turned to her.

"Mrs. Lucas, I owe you an apology," he said. "I accused you of doing sub-par work. now I am convinced it must have been Carl Bowman who tampered with your parts, trying to make you look bad. You've always done excellent work. I should have been more suspicious, asked more questions, when a bad batch turned up from your station."

"Thanks, Mr. Palmer," Laurie said. "I'm glad he was caught, and I'm glad he won't be able to do this to anybody else."

"Still, I need to ask your forgiveness."

"You have it," she assured him. And she meant it. Anything to put the whole mess behind her.

Before she returned to her work station and the questions of her coworkers—none of which she'd be allowed to answer—she sat in the ladies' locker room a while, trying to catch her breath and think through what had happened. Then she bowed her head and prayed for Carl Bowman.

And she meant that, too.

❧ 43 ❧

May 1945

V E DAY - TODAY!
The *Chicago Daily News* headline announced the end of
the war in Europe. All over the city, church bells rang and
people poured into the streets, whistling and cheering. Germany had
surrendered unconditionally to Allied armed forces.

Laurie, Clara, and Jerry had stayed huddled in front of the radio in
Clara's apartment for the larger part of the day, absorbing every scrap
of news. Rosalie had gathered with other neighborhood children to
wave flags and sing patriotic songs.

But war still raged in the Pacific. Laurie didn't want to put a
damper on the others' joyful elation, but an insistent pressure built in
her chest as she thought of her husband. Was he rejoicing, too? Did
she dare hope that a victory over the Nazis would bring about a swift
ending to the conflict with Japan? Would her beloved Will be coming
home soon? She understood all too well that there were no guarantees.
And where was "home" anyway? Would he be content to stay here in
Cicero, with the people Laurie had come to love as family? Or would

he expect them to return to the strained atmosphere of his mother's home in Pine Bluff, Arkansas?

Desperate for some concrete task to do, as well as a few moments alone to collect her feelings, she stood. "I think this calls for a celebration," she said heartily. "I believe I have a bottle of sparkling cider and some cheese and crackers downstairs. I'll go fetch them."

"I'd help you, but I'm busy," Clara joked. She was "busy" with not disturbing Rosalie, who had fallen asleep across the sofa with her head in Clara's lap.

"I'll give you a hand," Jerry said.

"Thanks, but I don't think I need any help," Laurie said quickly. Being ever the gentleman, he rose to his feet anyway and trailed her out the back door and down to her apartment.

In her kitchen, she told him where to find the cider and cookies while she rummaged through a cabinet for some glasses. She didn't feel much like talking, but he did enough for the both of them.

"Sure was fun to see your Rosalie so excited about the news," he remarked. "Plum wore herself out, riding her bike around the block with the other kids and blowing them whistles. I didn't know how much a kid her age would understand about the war. Not like it's happening in her backyard, after all. Although I suppose they learn about these things in school."

"She understands more than you might expect," Laurie said. "We talk about it pretty regularly, with her father stationed way off in —" Her voice thickened, cutting off her words. She busied herself with rinsing her best goblets, which had grown dusty with disuse.

Jerry placed a fatherly hand on her shoulder. "Say, Laurie, I'm sorry. Here we are, getting all caught up in the celebration, while your Will is still over there fighting."

She brushed a tear away with the back of her hand, impatient with herself and her emotions.

"We're right to celebrate," she said firmly. "It's an occasion worth celebrating."

"But it doesn't make it any easier for you to be without him. Especially raising a sweet little girl without her father."

Laurie drew in a deep breath. "Yes, well, we manage." She turned and looked at him through her tears. "And we owe a great debt to you and Clara. You've stepped in as substitute grandparents for Rosalie, and we couldn't be more grateful."

"Aw," he said, his face reddening. He picked up a dishcloth and dried a goblet. "I had a daughter once," he said softly. "She passed away the day she was born."

"Oh, I'm sorry. I had no idea."

"It was back in '20. She would be, what, twenty-five years old now, had she lived? Same age as my wife when I married her." He squinted. "Hard for me to imagine."

Laurie handed him another goblet to dry. "Why, she'd be practically my age. I'm twenty-nine."

He said nothing, but she saw his eyes glisten.

She swallowed. "I miss Will so much. If only I could see him. I'm so afraid he's going to die, and I don't know what I would ever do without him. I love him so much." With that, the dam burst. She began crying as if she would never stop.

Jerry searched the pockets of his vest for a handkerchief but didn't find one. "Wait here," he told her and went into the bathroom. When he returned with a handful of tissues, her sobs had subsided. Gratefully, she dabbed at her face. He guided her over to the table, and they both sat.

"I-I beg your pardon," she said, embarrassed. "This happens every so often. 'Turn off the waterworks,' my mother-in-law would tell me."

He reached across the table and took her hands in his. "It hurts very much to lose someone you love."

Tears started afresh. He scraped his chair across the linoleum, close to hers, and she buried her face in his shoulder and wept.

She was vaguely aware of Clara entering the apartment, of her calling out brightly, "What's taking you two so long?"

"We'll be along in a minute," Jerry reassured her. But by the time Laurie had stopped crying and washed her face and they returned to Clara's front room with cider and crackers, the radio had been turned off. Rosalie slept soundly on the sofa, covered with a blanket. And Clara's bedroom door was firmly closed.

❧ 44 ☙

Seeing Jerry and Laurie locked in an embrace had unsettled Clara. Not shocked her, exactly, because she'd always known he had warm feelings for Laurie. But the sight of them sitting with their arms around each other knocked her off balance.

Open expressions of deep emotion always made Clara uncomfortable. Where others seemed to be touched by such sentimentality, Clara instinctively shrank back. Her lack of emotionality, she reasoned, was part of what made her a good nurse. Thirty years of carrying out her duties in the presence of hundreds of worried spouses, distraught friends, and grieving family members without getting sucked into the vortex of sentimentality made her effective at her job. But when it came to herself, she didn't know what to do with emotions, how to handle them.

At that moment, standing in Laurie's kitchen, very much aware of being the third wheel, Clara hesitated to interrupt their intimate moment. Silently, she turned and went back upstairs to her own apartment. She pulled an extra blanket from her closet and tucked it around Rosalie, leaving the child snoring gently on the couch. Then she lay on her own bed, fully dressed, and stared into the darkness, taking stock of the situation.

She was astounded to discover that she was jealous. She had no right to be. But she was.

First of all, there was nothing inappropriate going on between Jerry and Laurie. That much she knew. They were both too upright to indulge in any kind of morally questionable behavior.

But that didn't preclude their developing a deep and abiding friendship, the kind Clara had never been able to form. She and Jerry were good friends, to be sure, and shared a long history together. But he'd had his wife, his true love, and could feed on those memories during the lonely times. Clara had no such memories and doubted she had the emotional capacity anymore—if indeed she'd ever had it at all—to offer a man like him that kind of love and devotion. Determined to avoid personal entanglements, she'd kept her distance from people, Jerry included.

The funny thing was, she never felt lonely. Or perhaps it was just that loneliness had become such a part of her that she no longer recognized it as such.

And then there were Laurie and sweet Rosalie. Clara had grown to care deeply for them, more than she'd ever cared for anyone. But they were only in her world temporarily. Just for a season. VE Day was a reminder that the war couldn't go on forever. When it ended and Will Lucas came home, he would swoop through Cicero like a cyclone and whisk Laurie and Rosalie straight out of Clara's life.

The smartest thing to do, she realized, would be to close herself off, to lock up her heart so she would never risk losing it. Even if it meant living alone forever.

Better to live alone than to have your heart ripped into little pieces.

A misty fragment of memory, a rose-twined porch overlooking a sun-drenched lake, pushed its way into her consciousness. Maybe it was time to dust off that old dream about the lake cottage, She might not be ready to retire yet, but a few weeks of vacation might be just the thing she needed to put distance between herself and her neighbors. To disengage her heart from messy entanglements.

She got up and changed into her nightgown. On her way to the bathroom through the dim apartment, she saw that, at some point, someone had come and taken Rosalie to bed, leaving the blanket neatly folded on the sofa. When she returned to her room, she pulled the photograph of the Bluebird's Nest from the mirror frame and placed it on the dresser, face down, where she'd see the phone number of the Michigan real-estate company first thing in the morning.

🌺 45 🌺

The next morning, Clara made the call. She was elated to learn that, not only was the real-estate company named on the back of the photograph still in business, but the cottage at the address Clara read to the agent was still standing. Even more amazingly coincidental was the fact that it was currently unoccupied and available for rent. Clara couldn't believe the good news. "Thank you, Lord," she whispered.

She gripped the telephone cord. "How much is the rent?" She braced herself to hear a number far above anything she could afford. But to her amazement, the agent, a Mr. Cowley, named a figure that fell well within her budget.

"Why is it so reasonably priced?" she asked, suddenly suspicious. In her experience, things that sounded too good to be true usually were.

Mr. Cowley coughed delicately. "It hasn't been lived in for quite a while," he admitted. "It may need some sprucing up."

"What kind of 'sprucing up'?"

By the end of the conversation, Clara had agreed to rent the cottage for one month starting May fifteenth, only a week away. She'd negotiated an even lower rent in exchange for doing the necessary cleaning and repairs. And after her vacation, if she loved the place—if it was everything her misty memories thought it would be—she'd have the option to buy it as her very own retirement cottage.

That evening, she went to the hospital early, before her shift started, to meet with Nurse Kent. She needed to request her four weeks of vacation, which might take some fancy talking. She knew the time was owed to her, having accumulated over the years as she'd declined vacations in favor of working. But Nurse Kent might not be enthusiastic over her taking the time all at once and on such short notice.

Ah, well, she thought. The worst the superintendent could do was fire her, leaving her with even more time to spend at the cottage. Which, funnily enough, didn't sound like a terrible consequence at all.

To her relief, Nurse Kent heard her out.

"It sounds like an adventure," she said after Clara finished her spiel. "And it sounds as if you've got a good plan in place for covering your duties while you're gone. I agree with you that Nurse Paulson—I mean, Jenkins—will do an excellent job acting as charge nurse in your stead. In fact, I'm glad you came to see me today. I've been meaning to talk to you about something."

A sense of foreboding writhed through Clara's stomach. What could be the trouble now?

"Joy Kolar will be leaving us," Nurse Kent explained. "She has accepted a position with the tuberculosis hospital in Hinsdale."

"Oh. I'm sorry to hear that," Clara said, mildly surprised that her regret was genuine. She had come to appreciate Joy and her sunshiny attitude. Already she missed their daily chats over the shift-change report.

"While we don't want to rush, we're naturally eager to fill the head nurse position," the superintendent told her. "We know how highly qualified you are, and I've noticed some real effort on your part to get along with the other nurses and show strong leadership."

Operation White Rose, Clara thought. Over the weeks since the incident, Dr. Pratt had given them no more trouble—well, not as much as usual—and there had been a marked difference in the way nurses pulled together and supported one another, not only when one of them was under attack, but at other times as well.

As for the job offer, she should have been ecstatic. The head-nurse position. Wasn't this what she had longed for? The promotion she had coveted for months. Years, even.

Yet, oddly, now that it was practically within her grasp, she wasn't sure she wanted it. And if she no longer wanted it, what *did* she want?

She cleared her throat. "May I have a few days to think about it?"

"Yes, of course. Just don't take too long. We want to make a decision promptly." Nurse Kent regarded her steadily. "Clara, I hope you know how valued you are here. I understand that you're planning to retire in just a few short years. We need all of your skills and experience to stick around here after you've gone. This will be your legacy. As head nurse you'll pass all of that knowledge to the next crop of nurses coming in."

Then she tilted her head and resumed her normally brusque manner of speaking. "I must say, I'm surprised, Nurse Janacek. I thought you'd eagerly grasp this opportunity, based on our earlier conversation."

So had Clara. Nurse Kent was saying all the right things, telling her exactly the words she'd longed to hear for so long.

But as she went about her rounds that evening, she felt weighed down and listless. What was wrong with her? She should be over the moon with excitement. Her career was in nursing. She lived for it. She even, by some accounts, excelled at it. So what was the problem?

Sleep eluded her the next day. She dozed fitfully, feeling flighty and indecisive. Finally she got up, did her household chores, and worked on the flower beds, but her mind was far away. In the late afternoon, she felt distracted during her time with Rosalie. Thankfully the girl, deeply immersed in the pages of *Little Women*, didn't seem to notice. When Laurie came to pick up her daughter, Clara sat them both down and outlined her plan.

"It's only for a few weeks," she explained "I'm sure Mrs. Jedlicky will be happy to have you back in her care for a month."

"But I want to stay with *you*," Rosalie protested.

"Now, sugar, you know you were only to stay with Miss Clara on a temporary basis while Mrs. Jedlicky recovered from her accident,"

Laurie interjected. "She's gone beyond the call of duty to keep looking after you all this time."

"It's been my pleasure," Clara insisted quickly. "And I do hope we can return to our usual arrangement when I return from vacation."

"By then school will have let out for the summer. Rosalie will need all-day care," Laurie said, her blue eyes meeting Clara's. "Perhaps it's for the best that she return to Mrs. Jedlicky permanently."

Disappointment zinged through Clara's heart, but she nodded. After they left, she felt gloomy. Her excitement over spending a few weeks in Michigan had been diluted over the question of who would care for Rosalie. But even if Clara stayed in Cicero, Rosalie would have to go back to Mrs. Jedlicky's during the summer break from school. Laurie was right. Clara couldn't care for Rosalie every day from morning till night; she needed to get her sleep.

She practically wore down the carpet with her pacing. By the time she left for work, she felt exhausted. The night seemed endless as she wrestled about whether she was making the right decision.

❧ 46 ❧

May 1945
Southwestern Michigan

Clara stared anxiously through the grimy window as the bus heaved into the Benton Harbor depot. The rental agent, Mr. Crowley, had promised to meet her at the station and drive her the twenty-some miles to Sister Lakes, a gesture which struck her as beyond the call of duty, but he'd insisted. She had no idea what Mr. Crowley looked like, but as she surveyed the platform, one man stood apart from the crowd, wearing a suit and tie and fiddling with the end of his mustache. Pegging him as Mr. Crowley, she caught his eye and offered a tentative wave. He waved back; her guess was correct.

Once they'd gotten underway in his sedan, the talkative agent pointed out various things to see as they passed.

"Over there, that's the Pearl Grange Fruit Exchange." He gestured to a long gray building on the right. "Southwest Michigan grows some of the best fruit in the whole country."

Clara didn't doubt it, seeing acres and acres of fruit trees. She began to relax as the clear blue sky and fresh country air soothed her travel-frazzled nerves. As they passed quaint farmhouses and sweet-looking cottages, she began to daydream that Bluebird's Nest would be similar to them.

It wasn't. In fact, it was quite the eyesore, this ramshackle dwelling with its peeling paint and sagging excuse for a porch. But the man hadn't promised anything different. And she still preferred this, the exact cottage of her childhood memory, to a better-maintained rental, even if there were one available which, Mr. Crowley had assured her, there wasn't.

Clara accepted the keys to the Bluebird's Nest from Mr. Crowley and arranged with him to have the lawn mowed and the gutters cleaned. After he'd gone, she stood on the porch, looking out over the water and thinking she was experiencing a little taste of what heaven must be like.

True, the cottage was more or less in shambles. Mr. Crowley had understated things when he said the cottage hadn't been lived in for a while. From the sagging porch to the peeling paint to the gutters filled with rotting leaves and who knew what else, Clara had her work cut out for her.

Fortunately, she didn't mind. Working hard would keep her mind off of other things, like how much she already missed sweet Rosalie. The little town was just as she remembered it from 1906, smelling of clean, fresh lake water and lilac-scented breezes. To be sure, more cottages had been erected over the years. More private piers had been inserted along the shore. More rowboats plied the water, and Clara was certain there would be many more motorboats, too, once the war was officially over and gasoline was no longer rationed. But at its core, the little lakeside town matched the essence of her dream.

After a rest, she walked to the small general store in town and stocked up on the necessities, including cleaning supplies, a first-aid kit, candles, matches, and simple fare for the pantry—boxes of crackers, cans of tuna. She hoped there wouldn't be any major storms or power outages during her month-long stay, but one never knew. It was always wise to be prepared. She recalled, from her family's visit four decades earlier, a doozy of an electrical storm that had crackled and thundered, waking them all in the middle of the night.

Her purchases put away, she went into the sparsely furnished bedroom, changed out of her traveling clothes into the shabby house-dress she'd brought along for this purpose, tied on an apron, and set to work.

For one full week she swept and dusted and scrubbed and polished until every last cobweb, mold spore, and dust bunny had been banished from the premises. She gave the pump in the kitchen a good priming until fresh, clear water poured forth into the porcelain sink, which she then scoured to a fare-thee-well.

On that first night, only after the bedroom had been cleaned and aired could she lay herself down on the freshly laundered sheets she'd brought from home—just to be on the safe side—and sleep soundly, rocked into dreamland by the music of the gentle waves lapping at the sandy shore and her own bone-weary exhaustion. The next few nights weren't quite as successful. She supposed her body was having trouble adjusting to sleeping at night and being awake during the day. She also found herself oddly missing the sounds of Cicero: the honking of auto-mobiles, the clanging of streetcars, the banging of screen doors, even the lilt of Laurie's voice, crooning along with Bing. When she couldn't sleep in the wee hours, she took to switching on the bedside lamp and reading her Bible. The ancient words of Scripture, almost Shake-spearean in their rhythm, calmed her spirit.

When the interior of the cottage had been scoured to her exacting standards, she set to work sprucing up the exterior. She swept the front porch and walkways until her arms ached and scrubbed bird droppings from the windowsills. She hosed off screens and outdoor chairs and wiped down the windows. The very worst job, the scrubbing and whitewashing of the outhouse, she left for last.

In the shadowy tool shed she found a few rusted gardening imple-ments with which she attacked the weed-infested flower bed and neglected hedges. She thrilled to find a wild rose bush growing at the side of the cottage and took it to be a sign of good things to come. *A blessing*, Laurie would call it. She tested the word on her tongue. *Blessing*. Life was full of them, if you knew where to look and you thanked the One who gave them to you.

At the end of her first exhausting week of wrestling Bluebird's Nest into a decent place to live, Clara felt ready to begin the remaining weeks of her real vacation. As the evening shadows fell, she sat in her rocker in the living area and surveyed her work with satisfaction. The cottage looked almost exactly the way she'd pictured it in her memory. Clean, shining, glowing in lamplight, starched curtains fluttering in the breeze from the open windows. The only thing missing were her parents, relaxed and smiling, and her sister.

She smiled at the memory of Aneta, then eight years old, skipping through the cottage in her navy-blue swimming costume with its short-sleeved, wide-collared blouse and bloomers to the knee. Clara had worn a matching ensemble, except hers had been red.

She gazed around herself. Yes, every inch of the cottage was exactly the way she wanted it, from the clear glass mason jar filled with wild-flowers on the table to the pan of bread dough rising in the pantry. As was her new practice, she picked up her Bible and read a few lines, thinking about what they meant. Some passages were clear as the morning; others she couldn't make heads nor tails of. But she read on nonetheless. Then, as Rosalie had shown her, she bowed her head and uttered a few simple sentences of gratitude for her blessings and care for the folks back home.

Looking up from her reading, she was filled with the soul-deep satisfaction and profound joy at realizing God had made her dream come true. Here she was, at her cottage on the lake. And not just any cottage, but the same exact cottage that had been the focus of her dream all these years. True, she'd only rented it for four weeks—this time. But if things worked out, if she finished out her career at Memorial and collected her pension and continued to save money, she could live here all year long in blissful solitude. Never having to take care of anyone except herself. Never having to answer to anyone. Never having to accommodate anyone else's needs and preferences and opinions. Never being disappointed or having her heart broken.

And suddenly, from far beneath the deep joy and satisfaction, another sensation rumbled, threatening to burst through on the surface. It was a familiar feeling, one she'd felt often throughout her life but rarely let herself name or acknowledge.

Clara Janacek was lonely.

❧ 47 ❧

Laurie trudged home from the factory, tired and thirsty, regretting her decision to walk instead of taking the street-car. The few coins she saved weren't worth the extra effort. She was looking forward to putting her feet up and sipping a cold lemonade and not fixing any dinner, unless and until she felt good and hungry. Her evening was her own. Rosalie was away on an overnight camping trip to the Indiana Dunes State Park with the Hendriksons. Laurie had been invited to go, too, but she had begged off, not being the camping type. It would be a wonderful experience for Rosalie who, now that school was out and Clara on vacation, had to spend long summer days cooped up at Mrs. Jedlicky's.

Clara had written with a generous invitation for Laurie and Rosalie to come and stay with her in Michigan for a week or two, assuring Laurie that there was plenty of room in the cottage for all of them. But this opportunity, too, Laurie had had to decline. She had at least another month to go at the factory before she'd qualify for vacation time. She'd send Rosalie, but she didn't know how she'd manage to get her there, refusing to pack her off all alone on a bus.

She stopped in the front hall to pick up her mail. She thumbed through the small stack and saw with annoyance that, once again, she'd received no letter from Will. She was in no mood to find, mixed in among the bills and sales circulars, another envelope addressed to the previous occupant of her apartment, the elderly gentleman with the long Czech name. Surely by now he could have updated his address at all the places from which he expected to receive mail. She toyed with the idea of throwing the letter away or pretending she never saw it, then felt ashamed at the impulse.

In her exhausted state, the last thing she felt like doing was calling on Jerry Stevenson, who could be prone to chattiness, but her conscience wouldn't let her ignore the letter. She climbed the stairs to his top-floor apartment and knocked on the door. He opened it wearing a T-shirt and suspenders over his work pants, clearly not expecting company.

"Sorry to bother you, Jerry, but here's another misaddressed letter for your former tenant. It was in my mailbox." She handed over the letter, feeling a bit snippy, as if Jerry could have prevented it if he'd wanted to. She handed him the envelope and turned to go back down the stairs.

"You mean Mr. Havlicek?" Jerry said, his forehead creased. "He died."

Laurie turned back. "Who died?"

"Mr. Havlicek."

"Who's Mr. Havlicek?"

"The old man who used to live in your place. He moved in with his daughter. Last I heard, he'd passed away. Back around Christmastime, I think."

"If that fellow's Mr. Havlicek, then who's this?" She pointed at the envelope in his hand.

Jerry peered at it for the first time. "Not wearing my spectacles, but ... Oh. Jaroslav Stepnicka." He looked at Laurie. "That's me."

"That's you?" Laurie squinted in confusion. "But you're Jerry Stevenson."

He shrugged. "I Americanized it when I started selling real estate. People seemed more comfortable doing business with a guy whose name they could pronounce." He waved the envelope. "Thanks for bringing this by. Sorry it got into the wrong mailbox."

"That's a coincidence," Laurie remarked, turning to go downstairs. "Jaroslav must be a common name in Czech."

"Pretty common. Why?"

"Because Clara was telling me about a Jaroslav that she knew, back when ... Wait." She turned back. Before her eyes, Jerry's face turned pale. She stared openmouthed as all the pieces clicked and clacked together in her mind, like a kaleidoscope. "You're Jaroslav? *Clara's* Jaroslav?"

His face turned from pale gray to pink. "I don't know that I'd say ..." He looked at Laurie. "Did *she* say that? *Her* Jaroslav? She told you about ... about us?"

Her mind racing, Laurie backpedaled, fearing she'd broken Clara's confidence. "She didn't say anything. She was just talking about some fellow she used to know named Jaroslav."

Jerry looked at her for a moment as if weighing his options. Then he stepped back and opened the door wider.

"Then I suppose you'd better come inside. We should have a talk."

❦

NEARLY TWO HOURS HAD PASSED BY THE TIME JERRY FINISHED HIS story.

"So that was that. After both her parents had died, Clara moved in our building and was a very dear friend to both of us. When Marianne became so ill, Clara helped me take care of her, as she had her own parents. I consider her my dearest friend."

"Did you ever want more than friendship?" Laurie asked.

"No," he admitted. "Not as long as Marianne was alive. She was a wonderful wife, and I loved her very much. And we both loved Clara, as a good friend." He paused. "Since Marianne's been gone, though, I have often thought that Clara and I should be together permanently, to spend our twilight years together. To rekindle what we lost so many years ago. She won't have it, though. And, too, our differing views on God—my faith, her lack of faith—has always been, and will always be, a stumbling block between us."

"I think you'd be surprised." Laurie told him about her and Clara's conversations about faith, about her interest in reading the Bible.

Jerry's bushy eyebrows lifted, and his dark eyes shone. "You don't say." He'd started to ask more questions when the doorbell rang.

"Who could that be at this hour?" He started to get up, but Laurie beat him to it.

"I'll get it. You stay put. Better yet, you have any crackers and cheese? I'm starving."

"I'll do better than that. How does ham on rye sound?"

"Perfect!"

She hurried down two flights of stairs to the foyer, her mind bubbling over ,with questions she wanted to ask Jerry. She flung open the heavy front door to see a young man standing on the top step. Behind him, leaning against the railing, was a bicycle.

"Mrs. Lucas live here?"

"I'm Mrs. Lucas."

He thrust a bright yellow envelope in her direction.

"Western Union."

She ripped it open. And all thoughts about Jerry's revelation fled her mind as her heart shattered on the hexagon-tiled floor.

❧ 48 ❧

June 1945
Sister Lakes, Michigan

Clara loved her life in Michigan. She loved puttering around her scrubbed and painted cottage. She loved sitting on her little porch with a good book and a tall iced tea. She loved watching the boats on the water. She loved donning her bathing suit— modest, yet so much more comfortable than those bulky woolen ones of yesteryear—and taking a dip in the cool lake. She loved playing pinochle with her neighbors, Jean and Howard Brown, a friendly couple about her own age. And yet she missed home. She missed Jerry and Laurie and sweet Rosalie. Now that she had her dream cottage, she was having second thoughts about wanting to live in it all the time, all year round. She might have to revise her vision of retirement life a wee bit.

On Sundays, Clara attended a little church in the village with the Browns. The people she met there were friendly and alleviated some of the isolation of the cottage. They were also her source of news, since she hadn't yet equipped the cottage with a radio and hadn't thought to bring hers from home.

"They say it's just a matter of weeks until it's over in Japan, too," Mr. Dennis, owner of the local burger joint, had said.

Clara hoped and prayed that was true, for Will Lucas's sake. And his family's.

One day she was thrilled to receive a letter addressed in pencil with Rosalie's careful schoolgirl cursive. Her joy turned to dismay, however, when she opened it and read "we both miss you" and "Mama cries a lot."

Alarmed, Clara hurried over to the Browns and used their telephone to call Jerry.

"It's good that you called," he said. "Laurie got a telegram."

Clara clutched the phone. "Oh, no," she breathed.

"Will's alive," Jerry clarified quickly, "but he's wounded."

"Wounded," Clara repeated. *Not dead.* Relief rushed through her. "How badly?"

"She doesn't know. Badly enough that they're transporting him to a military hospital in D. C. Laurie's getting ready to travel there to be with him."

"Who's going to take care of Rosalie?"

"Since school let out, she's been going to Mrs. Jedlicky's. As for the rest of the time, she can stay with me."

"Nonsense," Clara said, suddenly energized. "I'm coming home."

Hope tinged Jerry's voice. "I could come get you with the car."

"What car?"

"A used car I bought. It's a jalopy, but it runs good." He paused. "What can I say? I missed you."

"Oh, for Pete's sake. You missed me, so you bought a car?"

"Something like that. So you want I should come get you?"

"And waste all that gasoline? No, that's not necessary. I'll close up the cottage immediately and catch the bus tomorrow. Or tonight, if I can."

She packed hastily. Mr. Brown drove her to the bus station in Benton Harbor, where she managed to catch the last bus out. It pulled away from the depot with a hiss of air brakes and a cloud of diesel fumes, jammed to capacity.

After a few miles had rolled past, her seatmate asked, "Where are you headed?"

"Home," she said decisively. "Home to my family."

It felt glorious to be needed.

Clara napped fitfully as the bus rode through the night. Very early the next morning, weary and disheveled, she hailed a cab for the trip from the Chicago Greyhound station to Cicero. After paying the cabbie, she let herself into her flat and dropped her suitcase on the floor. She didn't bother unpacking before rushing upstairs and knocking on Jerry's door. There was no answer. A quick trip to the basement apartment showed that it, too, was empty.

Puzzling over where Jerry and the Lucases could be, she returned to her own kitchen and reflexively lit the burner and filled the tea kettle. Then she sat at the kitchen table and sipped her tea, wondering where they could have gone. She heard steps coming up the back porch. She flung open the kitchen door, and in walked Jerry and Rosalie.

"You came!" Rosalie flung herself at Clara and sobbed. Clara patted her back and stroked her hair. Over her head she gave Jerry a questioning look.

"We just got back from driving Laurie to the bus station," he explained. "In my new-old car."

After Clara unpacked, they spent the day together, working in the victory garden and tending to the front flower beds, which had gotten a bit out of control during Clara's absence. It seemed to help Rosalie's worry and sadness to stay busy. Clara wasn't very good at emotions, but she could keep the child's hands and mind occupied, at least.

That evening after supper the three of them played a board game, then Clara got Rosalie settled down in bed.

"I'll be sleeping right next door, in your mama's room," she assured the child. "I'll be very quiet when I come to bed, so I won't wake you."

"Will you listen to my prayers?"

"Would you like that?"

"Yes."

"All right then."

Clara seated herself on the edge of the bed. She had listened to Rosalie pray before. Had heard her earnest petitions for Mama and Granny Josephine and Auntie Melba. For her friends Debbie and Ruthie and Susan. For Miss Clara and Mister Jerry. For Daddy's safe return from the war. Now, she added that he'd get better in the hospital. The knowledge of what Will Lucas might be facing made Clara's heart hitch.

Clara had heard it all before. The difference was that this time, she prayed too.

When she stepped outside to return to her own apartment, she saw Jerry had gone out to the backyard and was sitting on the picnic table. She slid a cardigan over her shoulders and joined him. Together they sat and watched as the moon rose and the first twinkling stars pierced the purple twilight.

"How's our girl?" he asked presently.

"She'll be asleep soon," Clara said. "She's had an exhausting day."

"So have you."

"I'm not tired."

After a moment, he said, "And our other girl? I'm a little worried about Laurie. She's been in quite a state since getting that telegram."

"She'll be fine," Clara said. "She'll be back with her man soon. And she's strong."

She tightened her cardigan against the soft evening breeze.

He put an arm around her shoulders. "Chilly?"

"Not really." But she didn't move away.

He asked her about Michigan, and she told him all she'd done.

"Is it everything you dreamed of?" he asked.

"Almost."

"What was it lacking?"

"Rosalie. Laurie." Clara cast him a sidelong glance. "Do you like Laurie?"

"Laurie? Of course I like her. What's not to like? She's such a sweetheart. Such a good mother to Rosalie."

"But do you—I mean..." Heavens, this was awkward. "Do you have feelings for her?"

Jerry's bushy eyebrows rose. "What? You mean romantic-like?" He burst into laughter. "My goodness, she's young enough to be my daughter."

Clara stiffened. "She's an attractive woman."

"For a woman half my age. And let's not forget, she's happily married." He looked at Clara with curiosity. "What put that idea into your head?"

"I don't know, really," Clara mumbled. The idea did seem rather preposterous, now that she'd spoken it out loud. While she'd never suspected he'd do anything improper, well ... feelings were feelings. A person couldn't always control who they found attractive. It reassured her to know that his feelings toward Laurie were of the fatherly sort, nothing else.

"And as for Laurie," Jerry continued, "she's never so much as hinted at such a thing, not to me, nor said anything the least bit inappropriate."

"No," Clara said. "She wouldn't. She's a perfect lady."

"You're a goose." He chuckled softly.

She ducked her head, sheepish. "She's just so young and pretty and —and full of life. She's fun. She reminds me so much of Aneta. The young men were always buzzing around my sister. They didn't give me the time of day. I guess I just assumed you were buzzing."

"I assure you, no buzzing has taken place." Jerry tightened his grasp around her shoulders.

"I was afraid. I've always been afraid."

"I know."

"I never earned the right."

"The right to what?"

She sighed, wanting to let the truth out but afraid of what would happen if she did. Finally, she surrendered to it. "To happiness. To you."

A moment passed while they watched the clear star-studded sky. Into the darkness, he said, "Tell me again who you missed while you were in Michigan."

"Rosalie. Laurie." She swallowed past the sudden lump in her throat. "You."

They were silent again. She laid her head on his chest and listened to his heart beat under his rough jacket. She remembered the strength of his arms around her, the feel of his kiss. After so many years of friendship at arm's length, it felt wonderful to let herself love again.

"Look here, Clara Janacek," he said finally, his voice husky. "I don't like living here without you. Either you stay here with me, or I go there with you. Them's your choices."

A tear formed at the corner of her eye. She drew in a deep, steadying breath. "We've wasted so much time."

Jerry took her hand in his free one. "No such thing as wasted time. The Good Book tells us that the Lord restores the years that the locusts have eaten."

She didn't know what he was talking about, but she figured he did. She made a mental note to look it up later in the Bible she'd only begun to read, and hadn't yet made much sense of. And she didn't question his words because she so wanted it to be true. "It's not too late? Truly?"

Gently he took her chin in his hand and turned her to face him.

"Clara Janacek, I aim to grow old with you."

He disengaged his arm, slid off the picnic table, and held out his hand.

When she stood, he pulled her close. She breathed in the comforting, familiar aromas of cotton, bay rum, and a faint whiff of machine oil. Gently he slid his fingers down the side of her face, then lifted her chin. Leaning down, he tenderly kissed her. The decades melted away, and she was twenty again, the joy of being near him the only sensation of which she was aware.

He broke the kiss, tightened his embrace, and began to sway. Laying his cheek against her hair, he hummed the lilting melody of *Let Me Call You Sweetheart*, and they waltzed together under the stars.

🏵 49 🏵

June 1945
Bethesda, Maryland

In the streaming sunlight of a Maryland morning, Laurie stood in front of Bethesda Naval Hospital and sweated through her blouse, feeling thoroughly intimidated. The hospital's tall, awe-inspiring white tower arrowed toward the sky, surrounded by numerous smaller buildings and expansive, manicured grounds. The entire complex looked to be surrounded by high fences topped with razor wire, and Laurie had no idea where to go next.

She'd arrived at Washington, D.C.'s Union Station the evening before, following a two-day trip on a hot, crowded train. There was not a hotel room to be had anywhere in the city. Thankfully, her pastor back in Cicero had made a connection with a Bethesda church, which in turn found a family who graciously agreed to accommodate Laurie in a spare bedroom in their red-brick Colonial, just a short cab ride from the hospital.

Now, knees quaking, her great desire to see her husband laced with fear of what she might find, she had half a mind to get right back into that cab and head to the station. But no, she told herself sternly. She was here for Will, and she would persevere at finding him.

Dismayed at seeing access to the hospital so restricted, she at last located one of the openings in the fence and approached. A tall, grim-faced Marine clad head to toe in camouflage and what looked to be a full array of weaponry stepped forward from a guard tower and barked, "What's your business?"

After seemingly endless checking of Laurie's credentials, she was at last granted admission. A different Marine escorted her into the lobby of the gleaming white tower, where a Navy nurse took over and led the way to a bank of elevators.

"No visitors in the wards," the nurse said crisply. She deposited Laurie in a sunny window-lined visiting area with a view of Bethesda and a smell of antiseptic. "Wait here."

Alone in the room, Laurie prayed. After a time, a white-coated doctor came and sat with her and spoke in low tones, describing Will's injuries. A shattered leg, the doctor said, but at least he didn't lose it entirely. However, he would need the aid of crutches and then a cane for a long while, maybe forever. A head wound, mostly superficial. Nothing that wouldn't heal in time. Through the rushing in her head, Laurie clung to that phrase. *Nothing that wouldn't heal in time.*

The doctor left, and Laurie sat, trembling. She prayed, and prayed some more. Anxiously she scanned each face that passed. Where was Will? And what would he look like? Would he even look the same? Laurie steeled herself, knowing she might be shocked or even horrified at what she saw but determined not to let Will read anything in her expression other than love, joy, and gratitude that he was alive.

At last a nurse wheeled in a chair, and in the chair slouched a thin, pale man. A bandage that had been wrapped around his head obscured some of his features. Her heart quivered with joy and fear. But when he looked at Laurie and grinned that familiar, lopsided grin, she was flooded with relief and wonder. Her prayers had prevailed. Everyone and everything melted away as she shot to her feet and ran to him.

$\maltese$ 50 $\maltese$

C lara stood in the doorway of her cottage and surveyed the scene before her with a little flutter of joy in her chest. The day could not have been more perfect for a wedding, fresh and fair, with only a few fluffy white clouds gracing the summer-blue sky. Wooden folding chairs, borrowed from the local church, had been set up in a couple of neat rows on the soft green lawn. In front of the chairs stood a white lattice arch that the church youth group had entwined with roses and pink silk ribbons, now fluttering in the refreshing breeze off the lake. Guests, few in number but lively in enthusiasm, had begun to arrive. If Clara were going to make her move, she had to make it now.

She grabbed her shears from a bucket on the porch, stepped lightly down the front steps of the cottage and danced across the lawn to the rosebush, serendipitously located in the opposite direction from where people were gathering. She moved carefully so as to avoid soiling her ivory silk dress, recently acquired under Laurie and Rosalie's expert guidance from DeMar's Dress Shop on Cermak Road. Mr. DeMar explained that the dress, while never worn, was not brand-new, but had been manufactured before the war, before silk became impossible to obtain.

"But it's a classic style and suits you perfectly," Laurie had assured Clara, fingering the rich fabric. "It's as if it were simply waiting here for you to come along."

Indeed, wearing such a luxurious garment made Clara feel practically regal. All it needed was a small pop of color. Now she looked over the rose bush, snipped off the prettiest bloom, and trimmed the stem. *A rose for remembrance.* She wished her sister could be at her wedding. Her parents, too, if their being present meant they'd forgiven Jaroslav and accepted him into the family. But Aneta for sure. If Aneta knew Clara was finally marrying Jaroslav, she would approve. Clara was sure of it. *You see, Aneta, I did finally catch a husband, after all,* she thought, smiling to herself. *Or he caught me. Or, perhaps neither,* she corrected. *Perhaps we caught each other. Finally. The Lord made sure of that.*

From the porch, a male voice broke into her reverie. "Watch you don't prick yourself on them thorns."

She wheeled around. "Jerry Stevenson, you *know* you're not supposed to see the bride before the ceremony. It's bad luck." As he approached her, grinning, she made a sweeping motion with her hand as though batting away a fly. "Go on. Shoo."

He reached out and drew her into his arms. "I don't believe in luck." His voice was hoarse with emotion. "Only in the goodness of God to finally bring us together after all these years." He gazed into her eyes, then ran his work-roughened knuckles gently down the side of her face as if marveling at her beauty. And seeing his expression in that moment, she truly believed she was beautiful.

"Happy?" he asked.

"The happiest." She stood on tiptoe and lightly kissed his mouth, breathing in the spicy scents of bay rum and Brylcreem. Then she stepped back, held out the rose, and pulled a pearl-headed straight pin from the collar of her dress. "Here. If you're going to go breaking all the rules, then you might as well make yourself useful. Help me pin this bloom to my shoulder. And mind you be careful with that pin. It will never do to walk down the aisle with a bloodstain on my bodice."

As Jerry fumbled with the blossom, Rosalie appeared from inside the cottage looking fresh and sweet in a peach-and-white gingham dress with a circlet of flowers on her head and a white wicker basket in her hand. She spotted them, hurried over to where they stood, set her basket on the lawn, and took the rose and pin from Jerry's fumbling hands.

"Let me do that, Grandpa Jerry." Her voice was teasing yet urgent. She nodded in the direction of the rose-covered arch. "Pastor Wilson says it's time. You're supposed to go on up to the front. They're waiting for you."

"Yes, ma'am." Jerry handed off the task, gave Rosalie a brief bow, and winked at Clara "See you on the other side."

Rosalie finished pinning the rose to Clara's bodice.

"There you go, Grandma Clara," she whispered. "You look delicious, like a cream puff."

"Thank you, sweet girl." Clara gave her a kiss on the cheek. She didn't think she'd ever received a nicer compliment in her whole life.

She also didn't know when "Miss Clara" had become "Grandma Clara." But, once again, she liked it.

Rosalie picked up her basket. "Evelyn and Debbie are here," she reported, "and some of your nurse friends. They all rode together in someone's car. Although I don't know how they all fit."

"Did they?" Clara's heart was touched, grateful that anyone would make the three-hour trip from Chicago just to see her get married. *Her nurse friends.* The phrase had a reassuring ring to it.

From behind the rows of folding chairs, matron-of-honor Laurie signaled to Rosalie, and the girl clasped Clara's hand and guided her into position at one end of the makeshift aisle. At the other end, behind the rosy bower, stood Pastor Wilson of the local church, along with Jerry and, leaning on his cane, Laurie's husband, Will, who was serving as the best man.

As Pastor Wilson's youngest grandchild sawed away at the Wedding March on his violin, Rosalie glided up the grassy aisle, scattering rose petals as she went. A few steps behind her walked Laurie, resplendent in a chic, pale coral shift. Clara waited until Laurie was halfway down the aisle, then took a hesitant first step, the heels of her unaccustomed high heels threatening to sink into the lawn. It wouldn't do to take a tumble in front of all these watching eyes.

Just then Jerry caught her gaze and gave her a wink. And suddenly nothing mattered anymore except getting married to that exasperating, maddening, loveable man. Clara fairly floated down the aisle, barely aware of anyone or anything else besides the sensation of Jerry's strong, hardworking hand folding around hers.

After the ceremony, as the jubilant Mr. and Mrs. Stevenson greeted their guests, Clara's heart overflowed with gratitude for everything everyone had done on her behalf. Laurie and Rosalie had made sure she was decently and appropriately clad for the occasion. The church ladies had thrown her a bridal shower. So had the nurses at Memorial, on her last day of work before leaving to become Mrs. Stevenson, complete with a fabulous chocolate whipped cream cake from Dressel's. Whoever would have believed that cranky old Clara Janacek would be surrounded with such kind friends?

But she wouldn't be leaving Memorial forever. In a few weeks, as summer waned, she and Jerry would close up the cottage for the winter and drive back to Cicero, where they'd take up residence in Jerry's upstairs flat. Clara would return to Women's Medical. She loved her job, and she was good at it. And after all, there was still a war on. Experienced nurses remained in short supply. However, before leaving for Michigan, she'd asked to be moved to the day shift, and the new head nurse, a former pediatrics nurse whom Clara respected very much, had readily granted her request.

The Lucas family would take over Clara's former flat. Still recovering from his injuries, Will needed a home with as few stairs as possible while, to her amazement, stairs no longer presented a problem for Clara's knees. It was as if falling in love all over again had somehow peeled back the years, put a spring in her step and lightness in her soul.

While everyone feasted on punch and cake, Clara and Jerry stole a moment and strolled together down to the lake. The waves lapped lazily on the sand. Arm in arm, they walked out to the end of the pier and watched the late-afternoon sunlight glitter on the water.

"I have a surprise," he said.

"A gift?" She frowned. "I thought we agreed not to exchange gifts."

"It's not just for you. It's for me too. For all of us." He reached into his jacket pocket, pulled out a sheet of paper, and handed it to her. She unfolded it and skimmed the formally worded paragraphs. Her forehead puckered.

"A deed?"

"Yes, indeed. In-deed." He chuckled at his own joke. "We're now the proud owners of Bluebird's Nest. Now we can come here every summer, and bring Laurie and Will and Rosalie, and build our own happy memories. Would you like that?"

"Would I!" Still clutching the paper, Clara threw her arms around his neck. "It will be marvelous. You can teach Rosalie to swim, and go fishing with Will. Already the fresh air and sunshine have done him a world of good. His color is so much better than it was when he first returned. And Laurie can help me build a rock garden, and—"

Jerry held her at arm's length, laughing. "Hold on there, *milàčku*. One thing at a time." His expression sobered. "If we spend our summers here, we might not be able to visit the river. At least not every year. Will you be sorry?"

"Sorry?" She thought for a moment. "No, I don't think so. I no longer need to go to the river. That was my parents' way of mourning, but it needn't be mine. I'll always remember Aneta. She'll always be in my heart, no matter where I am. And I think if she had a say in the matter, she'd want me to be here. With you."

Slowly she unpinned the rose from the bodice of her dress and tossed it into the water. They watched as it bobbed on the sparkling waves, glistening brilliant in the sunshine, before it disappeared from view. Then they turned and walked back, hand in hand, into the laughing circle of their family.

THE END

Dedicated to the memory of all who perished in the capsizing of the *Eastland*, and all who have mourned them.

AUTHOR'S NOTE

Readers of historical fiction often like to know which parts of a novel are fictional and which took place in real life. *The Rose Keeper* is a work of fiction, with invented characters, settings, and details.

While all of the characters are fictional, the town where they live—Cicero, Illinois—is a real place, a brawny factory town bordering Chicago to the west. Originally called Hawthorne, Cicero became widely known during the twentieth century as the home of the massive Western Electric Company and many other manufacturing facilities. Regrettably, over decades the town has also made headlines for a few less savory reasons, including Al Capone's gangster activity in the 1930s, race riots in the 1950s, and governmental corruption in the 1990s. Nonetheless, the vast majority of Ciceronians, then and now, have been upstanding citizens working hard to make an honest living and provide for their families—including several members of my own family. Throughout its history, Cicero has been populated by immigrants and descendants of immigrants representing a vibrant mix of nationalities, a legacy that continues to this day.

The Western Electric Company was real, but all of Laurie's experiences there, including all of her coworkers, are fictional. For most of the twentieth century, the Western Electric Company was Cicero's primary employer. It was the chief manufacturer of telephone equipment for the Bell Telephone System (later AT&T) and other consumer goods, such as electric fans and refrigerators. The sprawling Cicero plant, called the "Hawthorne Works," was considered a state-of-the-art facility when it opened in 1905. At its peak, it employed 45,000 workers. It closed in 1984 with the dismantling of the Bell System. Today the property is the site of a shopping center, with only the tower remaining from the original structure.

In 1925, Elton Mayo of Harvard University conducted well-known industrial studies at the Hawthorne Works. One lasting outcome of those studies was "the Hawthorne effect," in which individuals adjust their behavior when they're aware of being watched. Many artifacts and documents pertaining to the Western Electric Company can be viewed at the Hawthorne Museum operated by Morton College in Cicero, Illinois.

Most other Cicero and Chicago businesses mentioned in the story, like the National and Grocerland stores, DeMar's Dress Shop, and the Illinois Training School for Nurses, really did exist. Others, like the Berghoff Restaurant, Orchestra Hall (now Symphony Center), and Bohemian National Cemetery, still do. The Seneca Restaurant was a popular spot on Cermak Road for many years; however, I took liberties in placing it in 1944, as I wasn't able to determine exactly what year it was established.

Memorial Hospital, while entirely fictional, was very loosely based on MacNeal Hospital in Berwyn, Illinois (my birthplace). The real MacNeal Hospital was built in 1919, later than the relevant events of this story.

I wish I could report that the *Eastland* storyline was fictional, but it was all too real. Cicero was especially hard-hit by the *Eastland* capsizing, a tragedy affecting hundreds of local families. Excellent sources of detailed information about this event include The Eastland Disaster Society and the Chicago Genealogical Society, as well as the following books:

Eastland: Legacy of the Titanic by George W. Hilton

The Sinking of the Eastland: America's Forgotten Tragedy by Jay Bonansinga

Capsized: The Forgotten Story of the SS Eastland Disaster by Patricia Sutton

Ashes Under the Water: The SS Eastland and the Shipwreck that Shook America by Michael McCarthy

WITH DEEPEST THANKS TO:

My father, Donald Lamont, for sharing a rich lode of stories about growing up in Cicero

My husband, Thomas Leo, for his unflagging support and enthusiasm for yet another story that's too often left me glassy-eyed and lost in thought at the dinner table

Editor Robin Patchen, who wields the magic pen that makes every story better

Book designer Hannah Linder for her keen design eye, and Chelsea Lamont, Linda Nelson, and Diedre Osman for their careful proofreading

Jeffrey Lamont, M.D., and Sandy Keller, R.N., for their valuable consultations on medical procedures and helpful insights into the nursing profession

The Hawthorne Museum at Morton College, The Eastland Disaster Society, and The Chicago Genealogical Society for research assistance, information, and photographs to help make the story as accurate and vivid as possible

The members of the "Cicero and Berwyn Memory Lane" group on Facebook, for generously sharing information, stories, and memories of their hometown

ALSO BY JENNIFER LAMONT LEO

Thank you for reading! If you enjoyed *The Rose Keeper*, let other readers know by leaving a review, and check out Jennifer's other novels:

- **Moondrop Miracle** (Windy City Hearts #1):
- **You're the Cream in My Coffee** (Roaring Twenties #1)
- **Ain't Misbehavin'** (Roaring Twenties #2)
- **Songbird and Other Stories**
- "The Violinist," a novella in **The Highlanders: A Smitten Historical Romance Collection**

Be the first to hear when the next book's coming out! Sign up for Jennifer's newsletter at **https://jenniferlamontleo.com/**

Jennifer also hosts the podcast **A Sparkling Vintage Life**, celebrating the grace and charm of an earlier era. Give it a listen, or subscribe wherever you get your podcasts.

Made in the USA
Middletown, DE
26 June 2021